PRAISE FOR
INTO THE BLUE
PENE HENSON

"[STARRED REVIEW] The plausibility of the miscommunications and the realism of the young men's relationship and personalities are exceptional. Readers eager for more diversity in romance will appreciate the nuanced portrayals of the leads."

—*Publishers Weekly*

"*Into the Blue* is the debut novel by Pene Henson, and it is stunning... Pene Henson is an author to put on your watch list, because if her first novel is this good, imagine what we can look forward to."

—USA Today's HEA blog

"FOUR STARS: Henson's debut is a thoughtful, poignant story of love in its many forms, as well as a love story to Hawaii and surfing. It is a deeply satisfying novel, and a perfect bit of escapist reading. ... Fans are sure to be swept away into this lush setting and the sensual romance."

—*RT Book Reviews*

Storm Season

Storm Season

Pene Henson

My darling Robbie, who always turns out the light.

"There is a great deal of unmapped country within us"
—George Eliot

THE STEREO'S UP LOUD; THE band's a local indie outfit with tight guitars and an even tighter rhythm section. Lien flings the stained glass doors of her bedroom open to the narrow balcony and the nighttime noise and pace of the street directly below. The buzz of traffic filters through from Oxford Street. A bark of laughter sounds from the next house.

Sydney's full of tiny neighborhoods, interlinked islands of personality and culture. This one, Darlinghurst on the city side of the Eastern Suburbs, has been Lien's home since she graduated from college. She knows its best qualities: the crooked Victorian terraced houses, the quirky shop-fronts and narrow tree-lined streets, the local cats who hold post on every corner. She loves the crowds and the dark bars packed with aging hipsters and hopeful writers and twenty-something white boys working out who they are over a schooner of craft beer. Sure, the rent's high for the small house, and the neighborhood is ethnically homogeneous after Hong Kong and Singapore, but it's

Sydney's epicenter of artistry and music. Lien likes calling this area her home; she likes what that says about her. This is where she belongs.

"Right," she says aloud to the empty room. She doesn't often talk to herself, but there's packing to do.

The room is lit by a frosted-glass ceiling lamp, which looks as though it came with the house, and strings of rainbow fairy lights that Lien looped over the window frames and along the picture rail when she first moved in. The lights turn the walls rose-gold and pretty. They don't quite make up for the mess she's making.

Her bed's covered with clothing, layer upon layer of it, all absolutely and inarguably indispensable for this camping trip. A belted all-in-one shorts-suit in olive green half covers a pale lemon crocheted cardigan she found in a garage sale on the Northern Beaches. She's piled up an old army shirt with rolled sleeves, a short pleated skirt, high-rise 1930s shorts, and men's khaki plus fours that button tidily at her knees. Lien might not want to go camping, not really, not one tiny bit, but her fashion aesthetic for the trip is entirely on point. It's olive green on muted neutrals, lemon and lavender on white, vintage safari meets "this summer is too fucking hot to wear anything much." Every piece is exactly right. The trouble is there are a whole lot of pieces.

Lien flops onto her bed on top of them. She sighs aloud. She has to accept the truth. There's no way she can fit all these clothes into her rucksack, and it's been made very clear that she can't take more than one bag. The car's already going to be tight with four of them in it along with their camping gear. And they do probably need the tent and the bedding and the food more than Lien needs a third cute T-shirt with an old-style caravan on it or the amazing utility suit she got a deal on through eBay last week.

Beau's flawless golden-brown hair appears around her door before the rest of him steps into the room. The rainbow lights pick up his cheekbones and the perfectly landscaped stubble on his jawline.

"Beer?" he asks, offering one to Lien. Both beer bottles are already open.

"God, yes." She sighs. "You're a prince among housemates."

She takes the cold bottle and follows Beau to the balcony. Sitting on it, they're mostly hidden behind the mottled trunk and shivering silver leaves of the gum tree that grows out of the sidewalk at the front of their house. Similar trees are set in front of every second house in the row. They lean over the narrow street.

Lien and Beau perch on wrought iron chairs placed either side of a tiny wrought iron table. Lien looks up. The weather's weird. The clouds are wild as they tumble across the dark sky. They reflect the city lights and shift between gray and orange. The air is heavy with humidity and something more, something charged. But the beer is crisp and refreshing, exactly what Lien likes. She looks down at the heads of passing pedestrians and admires a head of turquoise and purple mermaid hair. A shining pageboy walks past. Lien's pretty sure she could get away with that haircut.

She takes a mouthful of beer and scrunches her face to consider Beau.

"So, I'm packing."

He raises an eyebrow. "I'd noticed."

"It is *not* going well. There's so much stuff I need." She frowns. "And Nic says it's ridiculous to take a vintage safari suit camping."

"Nic's not wrong."

"Beau." Lien huffs air through her nose. "I don't know why I assumed my best friend would understand."

"Even though your girlfriend doesn't?" He tips back in his chair and sucks on his beer.

Lien fixes him with a glare.

"Li, it's a safari suit."

"It's vintage Hermès."

"And you want to take it camping?"

She plants her beer on the table and counts on her fingers. "Number one: I battled peak hour on William Street in torrential rain to purchase that safari suit. Annie called me the second it arrived at Clothes Were the Days. It would've been gone if I'd waited until morning. Number two: I have never overlooked an opportunity for fashion, even when that opportunity involves a camping trip in the middle of summer. In any case, this trip's work for me. Once we're at the festival, it's my job to look the part." She can't expect up-and-coming indie bands and critically acclaimed musicians to take her seriously in just any old dusty shorts and flannel shirt. She takes a breath and remembers to add, "Number three: Nic is not my girlfriend."

"Hmm. That's not what she says."

Lien would rather keep arguing about the safari suit than talk about her relationship with Nic. But she has to ask, though she's already resigned herself to Beau's answer. "Yeah?"

"Nic chatted to some of the guys that night last week when you were home on a deadline."

"Oh." Lien thinks back and shudders. "*Oyster*'s summer fashion issue." She stayed home to finish it for more days and nights than she likes to recollect.

He nods. "So unless she's seeing some other former pro-soccer-playing fashion-and-music journalist she met at the Australian Institute of Sport, then you two are girlfriends, in Nic's head at least." He peers at her. "Um, congratulations?"

"Damn." Lien gusts out a sigh. She likes Nic, likes her enthusiasm and self-confidence and her truly exceptional abs. She likes dating someone who's not one of their usual crowd. But the two of them have only been together for a couple of months. Lien's not one to leap into being anybody's girlfriend.

Beau shrugs. "What can you do, babe? It's not your fault you're irresistible."

Lien rolls her eyes. "Shut up. It's not like that. You know it." She guesses that she should start thinking more seriously about this girlfriend thing. Nic's great. She's sweet and gorgeous. Only it's so soon.

Lien and Beau fall into the friendly, noisy silence that's possible between people who know one another well and are surrounded by the ceaseless clamor of a busy city. An ambulance wails as it races toward the hospital. Someone walks by talking into their phone. "Yeah. I'll be home next week, Dad. Promise... No, it's not that I don't want to come."

"So, I've resigned myself to this trip," says Beau after a time.

Lien gawks at him. "You've resigned yourself to—? What the—?"

"The way I see it, we live in this huge, beautiful country. Somewhere out there are sweeping plains and red deserts and giant monolithic rocks and a whole endless outback, but all I ever see is this one tree." He pats the branch jutting past him. "And the tiny sliver of sky above the city. You and I could do with some space and quiet campfire conversation. Some hiking and nature and stuff. We'll get to know our land. It'll be good for us."

Lien narrows her eyes. "Unbelievable. You *made* me come with you... you're *forcing* me to camp somewhere in the middle of nowhere just so you can invite my girl Annie along. And now, *now* you tell me you've resigned yourself to it." She raises her voice. "You made me come *camping* with you, Beau."

Beau has the grace to blush to his ears. "I know. I know, Li. It was kind of a spur of the moment thing. The others were going and Annie— Well, she came out with us that night and I idiotically watched her be adorable and somehow I danced and laughed and talked with everyone who wasn't her, again. I need a change. Camping sounded romantic: a new place, strange night noises, starlight." He takes a breath. "If I'm going to ask her out, I'll need to do something out of the ordinary. Fuck, Li, I've had a crush on her for about a hundred years."

It's only maybe two years really. But his eyes are pleading. They're gold and brown in the streetlight. Lien touches the back of his hand. She's known him since she was nineteen and he was twenty-one.

"Sorry," she says, though she has nothing to apologize for. But all his immaculate suits and bravado don't mean he's worked out how to talk to a boy or girl he finds cute, especially when they're out at a noisy club and everyone's around. Camping in the middle of nowhere will, at least, be different. "You're right. This plan sounds good. We'll get out there, do something a bit new. Mix things up and see what happens. Annie's a darling. And you're my favorite boy in the whole world. It's not a problem." She takes a sip of beer. "Camping will be… fun."

Beau's shout of laughter echoes against the terraces across the road. "I know you, Lien Hong. You don't need to lie to me." He's quiet for a second. "I really appreciate you coming. It'd be hard without you. I mean, I don't have any idea what she thinks about me."

"Annie thinks you're incredible." Her best friends might not know one another super well but they're her favorites for good reasons. There's no way they don't admire one another. "You're hot, funny, smart, sweet. A gentleman. A thinker. How could she think anything else?"

Beau shrugs his shoulders and looks out over the street. "Of course she does. I don't know what I was thinking."

"You want to know if she'd date a trans guy?" Lien asks. Beau meets her eyes. "I mean, I've never brought it up with her, but I'm sure." She thinks. "I can ask if you want."

"Nah. It's not like I care whether she'd date just any old trans guy."

"You care whether she'd date you."

"Yeah." Beau toys with the label on his beer.

Lien tries to be stern. "Seriously. She'd have to be flattered. You're amazing. Gorgeous. You're pretty much annoyingly perfect."

"She's really smart."

"So are you. I'm not friends with stupid people."

"She's on her way up in the world. She has career plans. She's studying to be a lawyer of all things."

"So what? You don't care about that shit. You have ambitions. And talent. And creativity. Annie's told me she'd never date a lawyer anyway. They talk too much."

Beau nods as he takes this in. He smiles, swallows the last of his drink, and stands. "Right then. Well, thanks for that pep talk, lovely. I'd better get back to work."

"Anytime. Wait. Back to work? I'm sure you're already packed. If I know you, you packed last month."

Beau twinkles at her. "Hardly. Accurate weather reports aren't available that far in advance." She's pretty sure he's teasing. "I packed last weekend. And amazingly, I managed to avoid taking a safari suit. Vintage Hermès or otherwise."

"You'd look good in one," Lien says, considering him with her head to one side. His long torso is well-defined. The boy works out.

Beau holds up a hand. "Nope. Definitely not. No way."

"Fine, fine. But you, my dear, are distressingly unimaginative. You're stuck in a fashion rut."

"You call it a rut; I call it classic elegance," Beau says. He smooths his shirt at his waist. "Just 'cause I don't buy any old vintage knickerbockers that catch my eye and figure they'll look great with whatever argyle crop top I found at the charity shop. You're a magpie, Lien." She opens her mouth, but he keeps talking. "Anyway, let's not argue when I'm clearly right." He grins as she glares. "Tonight I'm working on getting all our playlists and some new music merged into one mega-list. It's essential road trip prep. You'll thank me tomorrow when we're halfway there, and no one's arguing about the tunes."

He goes inside but sticks his head back through the open door. "Oh yeah, by the way, they're predicting rain up there for the week."

Lien groans.

Beau shrugs. "I know. I'm sorry. I'm holding out hope. Meteorology is an arcane art, and the weather people are often just plain wrong."

He disappears through the door. A siren sounds up on Oxford Street. There's a hum of activity from the bars on the square. The noise calls to her. It's not late. The night won't quiet down for a while. Lien swallows the last of her beer and pushes back her chair. This is a holiday. She doesn't need to rush with her packing. Later there'll be time to decide what shoes are right for outback camping and whether she needs the pith helmet Annie found in the back of the vintage shop where she works.

"Beau!" she calls. She steps inside. "Do you want to go up to Gigi's? Xian Lo is deejaying there, and I want to check her out."

"No can do. Playlist, remember?" Beau says from his room. "And you're supposed to be packing."

"I'll pack later. These are our last few hours in civilization, Beau Michaels." Lien leans against the door frame of his room. He's cross-legged at his computer. "The night is young. We're young too. All that other stuff can wait till we get back."

He hesitates. "I'm not that young."

"We'll get home early," she says.

His hands are on the keyboard, but his eyes are on her. She beams at him and bounces on her toes.

IT'S ONLY A FEW MINUTES' walk to the bars of Oxford Street and Taylor Square. People are queuing outside Gigi's: about thirty people in line on a Thursday night.

Lien slows down. "I guess—"

"The club puts you on the list at the door for a reason," says Beau, taking her arm. "Come on. Might as well make use of it." He steers her toward the front of the queue.

Lien flushes as she passes all the people. But she offers the bouncer a confident nod. "Hi," she says.

"Hi." He's new. He tilts his head, waiting.

"I'm Lien. Lien Hong. I'm on the list."

"Just a mo." The bouncer's called Winston according to his nametag. He's bulky but not as huge and beaming as Jimi, who's usually on the door here on Thursdays.

"Jimi off tonight?" Lien asks.

"Yeah, he's back home for a week. Something's up with his dad." Winston runs a slow finger down the page on the clipboard. "You said your name's Leanne?"

"Lien," she says. About five hundred people glare at her from the front of the line. She reads the list upside down. "There." She points out her name. She's not sure what worried her. Her name's always on the door here and at a bunch of other places. The bars and venues count on her to report on who's wearing what, who's getting cozy with whom, what clubs are big, and what DJs are making waves. She writes up all that for the social news columns. She's paid by the word, and she helps the venues seem legit.

The bouncer lifts his head, taking her in. "Sure. Go right on in. Sorry about that." He pushes open the blue and black painted door.

"Thanks. No worries at all."

The guy turns to Beau and opens his mouth to speak again. Lien takes Beau's hand and tugs him into the club behind her. "He's with me." As she goes in she mouths, "Sorry," to the women at the front of the line.

The tiny ground floor bar is full; the room upstairs is throbbing. It's still early in the evening, but some half-famous out-of-town DJ is on the table, so everyone's here. He's not bad. Lien and Beau stand side by side and let the music swell through the soles in their feet and buzz in their bones.

"Pretty good," Lien mouths at Beau, and he tips his head and nods in reply. Someone waves to Lien across the room. She waves back.

On their way up the stairs, they pass a couple of people they know. The back bar is through an arch on the third floor. Some of their crowd will be holding court in there.

"Li!" says Athena, patting the stool beside her. "Come! Sit! We thought you guys had already left the city."

"Nope. We get going tomorrow." She makes sure Beau doesn't catch her grimace. "Time for one last drink in the big smoke." She's not being a princess about this. Or whatever, maybe she is being a princess, but

9

she's fine with that. She's the cool type of princess who knows what she likes and is still up for anything.

A warm body steps up behind her. "Babe! You were gonna stay in and pack for the trip," Nic says. Lien turns in her arms. Nic isn't accusing; her face is open and smiling. With her dyed-blonde ringletty curls and dimpled cheeks, she is refreshingly sweet.

"I had a last minute change of heart. This sounded like more fun." Lien turns her body and reaches up to Nic as the music throbs around them. Nic smiles into the kiss; her body bends easily into Lien.

Between just one more drink, just one more, twist my arm, and conversation with Beau and their friends, and flitting back and forth to grind against Nic on the dance floor, it's long past midnight before Lien thinks about going home. She's sweaty and easy in her head.

"Coming?" she says to Nic as she and Beau leave. Nic nods happily and allows herself to be dragged back to Lien's place.

LIEN OPENS HER EYES TO sunlight filtered through the leaves outside her room. She can tell by the traffic noise that it's not early. Nic's beside her; her breathing is softly nasal. Lien tries not to find it irritating. She stretches from her head to her toes. These are good sheets: Egyptian cotton, one-eighty count and pale bamboo green. She's going to miss them for the next couple of weeks, and the ceiling fan, and the bathroom right outside the bedroom door.

As daylight spreads out and warms the room, Nic opens her eyes and blinks. She looks childish in the morning, puffy-lipped and full-cheeked and drowsy, though she's definitely not a child. She reaches a hand between Lien's legs and traces her thumb up Lien's inner thigh to the crease at its top. Her hand is warm from the night before, and Lien's thighs are sweat-slick. Lien shivers and lifts her hips to rub herself lazily against Nic's palm.

"Oh, shit," Nic mutters. She pushes her lower lip out in a pout. "You have got to stop that."

Lien laughs. "You started it."

Nic groans. She runs her hand over Lien's neat strip of pubic hair, then gives it a pat before rolling away. "I need to get home and change. I can't turn up at work like this."

As she's currently naked, Lien tends to agree. Nic wriggles into her skinny jeans with some difficulty. She tosses her bra in her bag and throws on the ripped T-shirt she was wearing last night. Her small breasts move comfortably against the cotton.

"I'll come downstairs and let you out," Lien says. She swallows a yawn.

"No, baby girl. Stay there. I can handle the door. I want to remember you like this."

Nic plants her knees on the bed, lowers her body over Lien's, and presses her against the mattress for a lingering kiss. Lien squirms with pleasure.

"Two weeks, baby." Nic sighs. "God. It'll feel like forever."

Open-mouthed and sleepy, Lien kisses back.

Nic sits up and pulls her curls into a crooked ponytail. Her cheeks are flushed and freckled. She swallows. She opens her mouth to speak. When she meets Lien's eyes her gaze is soft with something more than casual desire. Lien's seen that gaze before. It's the look that comes before someone shares all the romantic thoughts that are in their heart.

Lien moves, lifts her head, and glances at the clock. It's definitely not the time for sweeping declarations. She speaks before Nic can say what's on her mind. "Oh damn, you need to race, Nic. It's almost eight."

Nic blinks. "Oh, fuck. Okay." She hesitates.

"Sorry for keeping you. You distracted me last night," says Lien. She smiles to hide her guilt. "Thanks for coming over."

"Of course. Anytime." Nic bends for a kiss. "I'm so glad you found me last night. Wish I could come camping with you. I'm bummed that I have to work this week."

"Me too." Lien runs her eyes over Nic's delicious body and sweet face. Athletic and hot with it, she's younger than Lien. She's good in bed, both energetic and appreciative. She's fun. She enjoys an adventure a lot more than Lien does. Camping might be better with Nic along to share a tent and protect Lien from giant spiders and crocodiles.

"I'll miss you," says Nic for the third time.

Lien kisses her. "Go," she says. She flops back onto the bed as Nic closes her bedroom door. Nic's footsteps creak down the stairs.

Lien closes her eyes. They're leaving this morning. She doesn't have time for guilt. She grabs her laptop from beside the bed and shoots off two short pieces about the club last night to two different publications. She posts a couple of pics on Instagram. She checks how her tweets from last night are going. The clothes from her bed are in a massive pile on a chair in the corner. She tossed them there last night as a problem for "future Lien." Only trouble is, "future Lien" has turned into "present Lien," and "present Lien" is not as happy about this development as "past Lien" hoped. She gets up and grabs all of the clothes. She rolls and folds and squeezes them into a larger bag than the rucksack she was planning to use. She's going to spend this trip dusty and stupidly hot. She might as well bring enough excellent outfits.

"Done," she says.

She passes Beau on her way into the bathroom.

"Two weeks without a well-lit mirror." He shakes his head. "God, Li. What was I thinking?"

She rubs her eyes. "You look great. You always do."

"I've spent an hour in there. I'd better look okay. At least I'll start the trip perfect." He kisses her cheek.

It's not that Beau's vain, not really; no more than Lien is. But he watches people, he reads magazines, he's interested in fashion and aesthetics. Anyway, it took a long time and a lot of work for Beau to like what he saw in the mirror. It's important for him to maintain some control of that.

"Anyway," Lien says, "there'll be mirrors. We're not leaving civilization altogether. Are we?"

He frowns and wrinkles his nose.

"Oh, crumbs. I'll pack a hand mirror," she says. She has one her mother sent from Dubai that might have floated up from undersea Atlantis.

Lien checks that the balcony doors are locked. Beau pokes his head into the room as she sits to power down her laptop. She takes a peek at her notifications. "I can't believe how many people are interested in whether queer farmer chic is about to be big in Sydney."

"And yet you posted about it. Hey, have you packed the bug repellant or should I keep hunting for it?"

"I've got it. Sorry."

They're not quite ready when Megan turns up in her car with a sleepy looking Annie in the front seat. Lien's packed. Well, she's mostly packed. She runs back in for a more sensible pair of boots and some dry shampoo. She collects her pith helmet too. That's definitely everything. Beau lopes upstairs to grab an extra razor. Megan climbs out of the car and rubs a hand through her thick, short hair.

"We're ready," Lien says.

Megan rolls her eyes at them as she helps with the bags. Megan is broad and muscular. She stands like she owns the space around her. Her blue eyes are watchful. Half of her words are obscenities. On first meeting, Lien was daunted. But it turns out Megan's a loyal friend and a sweetheart with a real taste for local music.

It's still technically morning when they pull away from Lien and Beau's terrace. The four of them are squeezed into Megan's VW hatchback with food and clothes and the mostly borrowed camping gear. Megan drives, her body taking up the width of the seat, her hands blunt and capable on the wheel. She's a good driver. Annie's in the front with her. Her lipstick is perfect as ever, and she looks too adorable for camping with her black-and-white polka-dot skirt tucked up between her curvy legs. She rests her bare feet on the dashboard in a strip of sun. Lien's never known her to camp. They'll have to look out for one another.

"I like the Bettie Page," Lien says. Annie's black hair has a new bangs.

"I'm going for Anna May Wong," Annie says. "Chinese-American and classic."

"It suits you," says Beau.

Lien and Beau sit in the back with a pile of bedding squished between them. Beau's knees are close to the back of Annie's seat, but Lien's small, so she's comfortable.

Lien looks out the rear window at their house. It sits close to the street, lined up with all the other two-story terrace houses. The outside is painted a traditional muted cream that's seen better days. It's home.

"You'll make it back," Beau says. "Unless the dingoes get you."

"Shut up," Lien says. Beau's right. Nothing much will change, but it's important to say goodbye.

2

As the car crosses the Sydney Harbour Bridge, the wind is up. The water far below is white-capped and mobile. Above them the clouds twist into dark gray alien shapes. Lien closes her window so the wind doesn't whistle.

They turn north onto the freeway, staying inland. The road opens up.

"Bloody hell. Finally. It takes way too long to get out of the city," Megan says. She drums on the steering wheel.

"We're on our way now," Annie says.

"Off into the wild," Beau adds. Annie turns from the front to give him a blinking smile that turns into a yawn.

Lien sits back in her seat. She leans her head on the bedding between her and Beau. The road flies by.

It gets hotter as they go farther north. Lien presses her fingertips against the window. The glass is warm to the touch.

Outside, the yellow and green fields have turned to muted greenish gray bush broken up by farmland. It's windy and overcast. Above them, the shifting sky is layer after layer of dark gray on pale gray. Now and then blue bursts through, only to be hidden again as the clouds shift. Lien sighs. Despite the clouds, it's pretty out here. Lone trees on hilltop fields look romantic as they bend and sway with the wind. But she's not easy with this place. The air is hot, and the sky is huge. She can imagine being alone here. This is not her kind of prettiness.

Lien braids her hair in two plaits and secures them with hair ties from her pocket. She checks how she looks on her phone camera. The layers fall about her face, and the plaits show off her undercut: practical and cute.

"Nice," says Beau with a lift of his chin.

Lien slides her phone under her thigh. "Next in vogue: queer campfire chic."

They eat a late lunch at a roadside sandwich place. The bread's fresh, even if Beau and Annie's vegetarian options are pretty much green salad between bread slices. It's been a long drive, but they squish themselves into the car with refilled water bottles and snacks to go farther north.

The AC's running wearily. Beau's road trip mix seems to have more of Annie's music than is strictly fair, but he's right, its variety is a godsend. The current pop tune is sweet and catchy with a mournful undertone. Lien likes music that's a bit rougher, but she gets the appeal.

"I know this one," Annie says as the song switches over. She hums along. Megan sings too; her voice is rich and strong. Lien glances at Beau as he joins in. She can't help but add some backseat dance moves.

"That's what this road trip needed," Megan says as the song fades out. "A bit of a sing-along to torture the kangaroos out there. Got anything else we know?"

They spend an hour singing and fighting over the next song to sing. Sometimes it's hip-hop. Beau and Lien manage the rap, while Annie beat-boxes pretty well, and Megan sings a counter-melody. Sometimes it's an 80s power ballad, with all of them wailing through the chorus at full voice.

"You know, I think between us all we've gone through every musical genre," Annie says as they finish a song. "Hilltop Hoods is hip-hop, and we've had pop, R&B, rock, soul, and whatever that noisy track from Li's playlist was."

"Alt-punk," says Beau.

"It's a new local band. They're awesome," Lien adds. "I'm going to get them to come in when I guest host on FBi radio in a few weeks."

"I think Beau snuck in some trance, too, earlier in the trip," Annie says.

Lien groans. "For a change."

"I'm not complaining. I liked it," Annie says.

Lien steals a glance at Beau. He opens his mouth, then closes it.

"I didn't hear any reggae," offers Megan, glancing away from the road. "Or classical. Or theater music, thank god."

"I like theater music," Annie says.

"Of course you do. You like everything," says Lien.

Annie shrugs. "Anyway, you catch my drift." She turns, looking for support from the back seat. She has a little frown on her face as she tries to make herself understood. Beau's cheeks flush under his tan. The whole thing makes sense. Annie's curvy pretty; Beau's always liked curvy and cute in any gender. Annie is full of bright enthusiasms and sweetness. She's a complete darling, even to Lien, and Lien's known Annie since third grade and the Mandarin Chinese classes they took together after school.

"I think some of this music counts as country," Lien offers when Beau continues to say nothing.

"Plus I caught some J-pop in there," Annie says. "And your indie folk, Li-Li, and rock, and Beau's dance club stuff."

"Okay, okay," says Megan. "I yield. We've covered everything."

"Except death metal," says Beau.

Annie turns. She's pouting, but her eyes laugh under her bangs. "Don't tell me you're switching sides on me," she says.

"No, no. Definitely not. Never."

The car is quiet. The sound system switches to a new track, a jangly Brit pop guitar with a swoony bass line.

"Turn it up," Lien says to Annie. "This is a good one." Annie turns to the front.

"Nice," Beau says across the bedding, and, as the bass slides in, he and Lien grin in quick accord. They don't always share musical taste, but they agree on the essentials, and good bass lines are an essential.

"I'm gonna go out on a limb and call this one indie pop," says Lien.

"It's my new favorite," says Annie from the front. That's about the fifth time Annie's said that this trip. Beau presses his lips together, but his eyes crinkle at the corners. Lien's heart twists with something close to jealousy. It's not because she wants Beau to look at her that way. Their connection has never been about that. He's gorgeous and smart, but he's her best friend, her ally and confidant. He gets her. Lien doesn't dream of heart eyes from him, but for a second she'd like to feel that way about someone else.

The mountains of the Border Ranges appear through the windscreen ahead, rising from the plains, rich green shrouded in low clouds. A love song, a cover of a Cheap Trick track, is playing.

Lien blinks away the power of it. Beau blushes. "Well, that's romantic," Lien says. She doesn't mean to tease, but Beau can hardly complain. He's teased her for as long as she's known him.

Annie sighs. "It is. It's a nice reminder." She talks toward the windscreen. "Sometimes I'm amazed that anyone can love anyone else."

It's not a question, but Lien opens her mouth to answer. "Annie! Don't say that! You're the most optimistic person I know. If you're getting cynical then what hope do any of us have?"

Annie turns. She grimaces as she says, "I'm still optimistic. But we're studying family law this semester. It's a mess. You forget love and that stuff can ever be good."

Lien pats her arm. "Megan's the expert on love. You and Kamila have made it a year now?" The road winds into the bush. Rows of eucalypts line up on either side of the car and meet above it. The world seems secretive.

"Yeah. Just over a year." Megan's nod is certain. She's not a talker, but they all wait and she goes on. "With Kam—I don't know—we met and things fell into place. All the things I'd avoided: long mornings in bed and knowing one another's schedule and nights alone over dinner and sharing everything. It wasn't so terrifying anymore."

"You found the right person," Annie says.

"So Li. Is it that way with Nic?" Beau asks.

She glares at him. He knows the answer. "Some of us are happy having fun. Anyway, I don't think everyone gets that kind of magic. Not like that."

Megan shakes her head. "I don't mean something magic. Not like everything's perfect. Not like she's a soulmate or anything. But—she's good. I prefer this imperfect life to any life I can imagine that doesn't include her." They travel on for a way. "It's not magic; we're just happy."

Lien shrugs. "I'm happy, too. Nic's happy. I saw to that last night." She half laughs.

Megan ignores her as she goes on. "I think some of it's about being okay trusting another person. We fuck up. It's inevitable. But it's okay, because she's there beside me. And I don't mind that most nights she falls asleep before me and I have to turn out her light and lie there and listen to her breathing."

Lien turns away and looks out the window. She's not hunting for that kind of thing. Definitely not.

THEY'RE THE LAST TO ARRIVE at the campsite. Lien climbs out of the car and stretches her legs.

She supposes the area is beautiful, though the site itself is just grass set among gum trees and ferns and huge sandstone boulders.

Everywhere she looks is thick foliage and sky. The rainforest slopes up from the site to the rushing clouds on one side. The other side opens out into a valley. Through the trees is a steep canyon, orange and creamy sandstone. Lien can hear the creek that twists through it. It's running fast. A lone gray-green cabin is set into the hill beyond the canyon, shadowed high up near the ridge, looking out over everything.

"Look." She points to the cabin. "I think it's deserted."

"Creepy," says Annie with a shudder.

Lien helps Beau and Annie unload their tent. Two tents, Raf and Matty's and Megan and Kam's, have been set up in the campsite. Beau drops theirs on a flat grassed area. He sighs, looking the other tents over.

"It's like they're taunting us," he says. "All those taut guide ropes and neatly pegged tarpaulins."

It is disheartening. Raf and Matty's tent even has an annex with a purple princess inflatable couch. Megan's is an ordinary tent-shaped green tent but it's perfectly set up, all clean lines and consistency, with a mat lined up with the door flap. Megan's sharing it with her girlfriend Kam who, it seems, knows a thing or two about tents. Kam's also wearing a hands-free headlamp thing that is not even a tiny bit fashionable but works on her. Everything works on Kam, who's tall and boyish and Indian and doesn't care what people think.

Lien rubs Beau's shoulder. The three of them clear the ground of rocks, then Lien opens the drawstring storage bag and removes the tent and the little sacks of pegs and ropes. She drops them on the ground and folds the storage bag.

"Don't think about it. We can do this," she urges. They practiced once in a backyard; no wind, soft ground, the owner's input. But she doesn't want the others to help, not really.

Above them, the sun is filtered, streaking as gold fingers through heavy cloud. The light'll be gone soon; the sun will sink behind the tallest of the hills. "Okay," Lien says. "We'd better get on with it. I'm guessing tents and ropes and stuff are harder to work with after dark."

By the time Beau, Lien, and Annie have set up their tent the ground is dark. The hills nearby are black, and the clouds are gray in the blacker sky above. It's not raining yet, but it doesn't seem hopeful.

Everyone's sitting in the clear space between the tents. Beau unfolds a striped rug and stretches out his long legs. He's relaxed his usual uniform of tight jeans and is wearing a pair of pin-striped shorts with a pink T-shirt. Lien sits beside him, cross-legged on the hard ground. She sighs and shifts her weight to see if she can get comfortable. Beau pets her thigh. Raf hands her a beer.

"You'll get used to it," he says.

"I'm fine." She doesn't want sympathy. She wants to be somewhere with a little less silence and space and a whole lot more lounge chairs.

Raf smiles at her. His dark eyes twinkle above the facial hair he seems to have grown in the three days since she last saw him.

"You are a hairy man," Lien says.

"That I am," Raf says. "Want to see my hairy belly?"

"Raf, you'll frighten the children," says his boyfriend, though everyone knows they adore one another. Where Raf's short and stocky, Matty's slim and pretty. His fair hair is starting to thin, but no one would ever tell him that. He's grown it long and streaked it with platinum in protest.

Despite the threatening rain, it's bushfire season, so there'll be no campfire. Someone's cleared a space near the electric barbecue Raf and Matty brought. It's too warm to huddle around it.

They eat vegetables that have been crisped on the barbecue and lamb kebabs or tofu. It's not complicated food, not what Lien's used to from the restaurants near their place, and there's a leaf in it, but it tastes pretty good with a beer.

"Where's your girlfriend?" Matty asks Lien.

Lien rolls her eyes. "She's honestly not my girlfriend." No one responds. "If you mean Nic, I invited her. But she was working." She did invite Nic, but she wasn't particularly encouraging. Nic isn't herself with Lien's friends. Maybe they find her difficult. Her focus is physical stuff: sports and yoga and how to take your body to new levels of excellence. And Lien and her friends, they've all known one another for a long time and they understand the same world: music and fashion, all the best venues and DJs and promoters.

"Any insider tips on the bands at Rivers Fest?" Kam asks.

"Of course. Yeah." Lien runs over some of the bands she's excited about. "And I'm following Stickler about for a day. They're going to be big. They play the Saturday night."

The barbecue's turned off, and the night is cooling. Despite the heat of the day, the air is crisp. Lien rummages through her bag inside the tent. She pulls on a little cardigan. It's lemon yellow and pretty. It'll get dirty out here. It was probably a silly choice. But it's so cute, and she's warm now so she can't bring herself to mind.

"They're predicting a nasty storm tonight. Seems like it's coming in already," says Kam as Lien settles down beside Beau. Lien nods. The air's heavy and electric. The wind's unpredictable. Up above, the clouds are taking more defined shapes and dashing to cover the moon.

"Hope everyone's got the tents up properly," says Megan. She stands to check on the guides and pegs. Kam stretches her legs and goes to deliberate with her.

The consensus is that the tents should all hold together, even Beau, Annie, and Lien's, but it might be a tough night. Between them, they put the barbecue and other equipment in the cars. Raf lets down the couch. The pink and purple princesses collapse as the couch deflates.

It's only just after ten. At this time they're usually heading out for the night, but Lien's tired. Annie's playing cards with Matty. Lien doesn't join them. She's not sure she'll sleep here.

The storm hasn't broken.

Beau kneels to open the flaps of their tent. Lien pauses. Beau transitioned five years back. He's confident of himself and he's lived with Lien for three years, but he likes to keep some level of privacy. The tent doesn't offer a lot of that once they're all inside.

"I'm going to take some pictures," says Lien, "before the storm breaks. I won't be too long." She doesn't want to bump into anything dangerous, but she would like to get some photos to put up on Instagram. "No one online will believe I was here otherwise. There was lots of chat about whether I'd even come. Bastards." She pauses then asks, "Are there dingoes out there?"

Beau meets her gaze blandly. "Um, no. There aren't any dingoes. Watch out for the drop bears though."

Lien narrows her eyes. "Drop bears?"

"Carnivorous koalas, honey. They can smell an outback tourist. One of them might take a nibble on you."

"As if," says Lien. She hesitates. "There's no such thing as carnivorous koalas." She glances at him and is reassured by his amusement. "I'm done listening to you, Beau, you're as much a city kid as I am."

"Fine." His grin is bright in the moonlight. "But us city kids managed to pitch a tent, so I'm proud of us. I'll get dressed and see you in a minute or two. Thanks." He kneels as he zips up the tent door.

Lien steps away from the tent. The bush spreads out around her, tree after tree to the end of the world. Without her friends' conversation to distract her it's foreign: wide and overwhelming. The wind eddies above. Occasionally a noise sounds from the trees, the call of some unfamiliar animal, maybe a bird or frog or giant insect or platypus. Lien stands still, turns back to the tent, hesitates. She doesn't need to take photos now. That can wait.

In the torchlight, Beau's silhouette pulls his shirt over his head.

Lien takes a breath, steels herself. He needs his privacy. She heads into the dark. It's rough underfoot, the tangled ferns are treacherous, and her lace-up Volleys are white and not exactly snake-bite proof. She bought them because they were cute. She walks carefully and lets her eyes adjust to the dark. She's not happy alone with too much time to think, but she has to admit this place is beautiful. She reaches the edge of the campground and tries to get a photo of the outlook. They're up pretty high, everything sweeping away from the site. Behind her are the tents, canvas flapping in the wind, flashlights, a shout of muffled laughter, murmurs. But ahead it's loneliness and blackness, clouds scudding by fast and the lights from that single cabin, high on the nearby slope, flickering in and out as the great trees move.

The isolation fills her lungs. The sky is the size of the whole world. Silence courses over her. She wants to hold onto the space—how huge and tiny she is at once. But she also wants to share it. She has a responsibility to share it. After all, she has followers. She needs to tell them all about her newfound spirit of adventure.

She turns the flash off on her phone and sets it up for night photography. The photos are disappointing. Every one turns the scene into a wash of gray. It's hard to trap vastness on a 5.5 inch screen. She can't capture the layers of black ground and crowds of trees, the sky and the moving clouds and wind and scattered stars. They're impressive in real life but on her phone they seem muted and tiny. Like nothing.

She clambers through tangled brush and heads down the slope toward the canyon. The hills are a dark line against the sky. There don't seem to be any wild animals, and it's possible that snakes sleep at night. She hopes so. She breathes a little deeper and easier, getting herself accustomed to the lack of noise. This isn't like Sydney. Here you can stand with two feet on the earth and connect with the sky. She walks on. The trees close in around her. The darkness is more complete as she gets farther from the campsite. The ground begins to drop away more steeply. She's careful. A mistake could turn into a headlong plunge into the canyon. She holds on to a sapling and leans out over a little gully with her phone out. The creek burbles below, winding its tight path between the boulders.

As she leans forward, her shoes slip on the dirt and leaves beneath her; the sapling bends and pulls out of the ground. She scrabbles for footing and reaches for a plant, which slices her palm and doesn't hold. For a moment she hangs in the air, then she tumbles down the gully, almost vertically toward the creek, head over feet. An avalanche of dirt and leaves and gumnuts rains down behind her. The wind's knocked out of her at the first blow. Her knee cracks hard against the ground. She crashes down. A log bangs against her thighs. She's stopped by a boulder, and spills half into the creek. Her phone falls out of her hands, thumps on a rock, and lands with a disheartening splash.

She lies still. She's an idiot. An idiot with her ass half in a creek, gazing at the towering black trees and sky and wearing a vintage safari suit with cute shoes. Her knee hurts. And her wrist. And her hand. And her butt. She releases a shaky, shaky breath. Her head spins.

Down here, the world seems lonely and darker. She'd better find her way back. She pushes herself to her hands and knees on the boulder. A white pain lances her right knee.

She whimpers and rolls to take the weight off her knee. Her eyes prick with tears. Her knee has been a problem since she trashed it eight years ago in top division soccer. But it's never done anything like this. Of course, she usually doesn't throw herself down rocky cliff slopes in the middle of the night.

She takes a breath and calls out. The campsite is a good distance away, up the slope and through the trees. She pushes herself upright again to try to crawl out on one knee. The rock is slippery and treacherous. She moves forward a few grueling meters, slips, and lands on her hip.

She inhales through her teeth and calls more loudly. "Hello! Beau? Annie?"

Her words are caught up in the swirl of wind. They echo at her from the gully banks. She slides toward the slope she plummeted down, holds onto a tree, drags herself up onto to her good foot, but she can't put any weight on her other leg and she can hardly hop up the ravine.

"Hey! Hi! Help!" she cries. It's no use. The wind whips around her. They'll realize she's gone soon, but she's got no idea how long it'll be until someone can find her. Why would they think she'd wandered down here? "HELP!" She calls more loudly, but the wind steals her voice and sweeps it away.

The dark surrounds her, burying her. The creek water is cool. The trees swirl above her head. Lien doesn't want to cry, but her knee hurts, and she's covered in mud and caught at the bottom of a cliff without her phone. She's frightened she'll fall farther. A bird or bat wheels above her near the treetops. Animals chitter off to her right. Something's going to eat her, and no one will know. She gives in to the tears.

She takes a steadying breath. And another. "Okay," she says aloud.

She peers upward into the dark. There are trees and thick, exposed roots up the cliff. She needs to drag herself up there. If she goes slowly, maybe she'll be okay. As she reaches for the nearest root, the noise of the wind breaks. Through that tiny silence she hears a footstep. It's unexpectedly close. It couldn't be someone from the campsite; it's on the wrong side of her, unless the fall flipped her admittedly dubious sense of direction. Another tread sounds. Human. Probably. Lien's heart pauses; her hand slips a bit. Her nerves are at the ready.

"Hello?" she says. Her throat is tight as she swallows. A silhouette looms out of the dark. Lien looks up, up, up farther to see a head. "Hello?" Her voice shakes.

"Hello," comes a low voice. The woman leans over the precipice from the shadows. "Ranger service."

Standing up there in the dark with the wind and the sky behind her, the ranger is superhero-tall, broad-shouldered, and solid. Lien's so grateful she could cry. "Oh, fuck. Thank fuck." Lien takes a breath. "Shit. Sorry, language." She squints at the woman through the dark. "I'm genuinely so glad to see you."

"I'll bet you are." The superhero's voice is kind but faintly amused.

Lien goes on. "I'm so sorry to bother you. I fell and. It's my knee. Can you—Is there any way you could—? I can't get out." Lien tries to get a handle on her voice but it shakes. She blinks. She has to assume the woman really is a park ranger and not someone who likes to pretend to be a ranger, there in the dark, waiting for someone to fall down a cliff like an idiot. That does seem unlikely. The superhero takes in Lien and her precarious position. She doesn't say anything. She might be the brooding type. She leans out farther to examine the slope.

Lien can't help herself. "Be careful not to fall. It's slippery."

"Thanks. I'll be fine." The woman's tone is dry. "Okay. Right. How bad is that knee? Can you climb out?"

"I *have* tried that." Lien's voice has an edge to it. What does the woman think she was doing here? Sitting on her ass crying about her safari suit? That's only partly true.

"How about with a rope to support you? I'll help drag you up, do what I can to lift you from up here."

"Okay?" Lien figures she can try it.

"We'll need a little more conviction than that."

"Yeah. Yep. I can do it." Lien injects certainty into her voice.

"Good on you." The superhero doesn't sound as super-impressed as Lien deserves. She disappears.

The only sound is the wind. Lien listens. She's certain she didn't dream up her park ranger; she'd have made her friendlier, for one thing, but the silence is not reassuring. Has the woman left her?

"Here it comes."

The ranger's voice comes from up the slope. Lien sighs with relief. A rope slithers part way down, catches. The ranger shakes it from above, and it slithers the rest of the way. It hangs near enough for Lien to reach at a stretch.

"Loop it around your waist."

Lien does as she's told, tying it as best she can. The rope goes taut and tightens around her middle. Lien makes the slow climb up. The rope partly supports her weight. When her feet slip and scrabble on the rocks, the rope holds.

The ranger grabs Lien's hand as she reaches the top. Lien clambers over the lip and lies on the ground, letting her thrumming heart slow down. She smells earth and eucalyptus. Beau will be impressed by how much she's bonding with the land.

"Thank you," she says. She drags herself onto one knee and then pulls herself up on a tree. She stands on her good foot. "Thank you."

"Just doing my job," says the ranger.

"Can—how will I get back to the campsite? I'm staying at the Upper Creek." Lien wants to get out of here. Maybe she can convince Beau and Annie that they should all go home or at least find a cheap hotel in town.

"Yeah, I know. I heard you guys come in earlier. The campsite's across there." The ranger lifts her chin to point to the other side of the gully. And she's right, of course. Lien hadn't thought about it but in climbing back up from the creek, she's on the other side of the running water.

"Can I get back?"

The ranger turns her head. "You want to climb back down there?"

Lien looks with her. The ground drops away sharply to the water.

"Is there a way around?" Lien asks.

As if in answer, the rain starts: a deluge that pours over Lien's hair and soaks her clothes in seconds. The storm's come.

The ranger steps away from the creek. "I'll get you up to my cabin. It's dry. Come on."

Lien should ask the ranger for ID or something. Her parents taught her not to follow a stranger. But it's raining and dark. Anyway, the woman might have left her ID at home. It's not as if she'd often need to identify herself to some city kid who's got herself fucking lost in the bush. Lien takes a breath. *This is okay. This woman's already rescued me once.*

When she puts weight on the bad leg she stumbles a little and half falls, muffling a cry. The ranger comes back down the slope. "Okay." She reaches out a hand to help Lien clamber to her feet. Her palm's large; her grip is firm, even in the soaking rain. Her hand is everything you'd expect a ranger's hand to be. "Lean on me."

3

In vain Claudie wipes rain from her eyes. The storm's turned into a significant weather event, a bigger one than Claudie expected. It's heavy. The thunder shakes in her ribs; the rain and the lightning intertwine and slash the sky.

Claudie counts their steps in her head. She breathes in time as they walk. She avoids thinking about the way the rain pours from her hair. It runs over her forehead and down her face. *Left and right and in and out. Left and right and in and out.* With the girl beside her and needing her help, every step is difficult.

The hill face has turned into a fast-moving torrent, all mud and running water between the rocks and ferns and gum trees. The rain is drenching. It seeps in at Claudie's collar and over her breasts and back. The cabin inches closer.

Thunder crashes, echoes against the clouds and the far escarpment. The girl startles and loses her footing. Claudie slips. She grabs at a branch as they both almost tumble over in the mud. The branch holds. Claudie's heart hammers.

She's briefly, brightly furious. She steadies herself as the storm rages. She breathes. *In. Out.* Don't show your nerves.

They clamber on. Claudie supports the girl's weight with her arm wrapped around her back. Though the rain and lashing wind drown most sound, it's clear the girl's breathing is labored. Her lungs seize when her bad leg takes any weight. She doesn't complain, though.

The walk home is only five hundred feet, but it seems much farther. They're moving uphill, and the rain ruins any visibility and runs in rivers around their feet so it's hard to avoid the roughest of the ground. Claudie's boots can handle the water, but the girl's shoes are a waste of time and slip uselessly on the slopes. Time slows to a soaking wet and frustrating crawl. More than once, the girl's feet slip, and Claudie plants her boots in the mud to keep them both from going ass over elbow.

As they move on, the girl stumbles again and grabs onto Claudie. Her feet slide. Her fingers dig into Claudie's forearm.

"Are those the only shoes you have?" Claudie asks through her teeth.

"They're the only ones I have with me right now," the girl flashes back. "I didn't know I'd need my mountain climbing gear and water skis tonight. I didn't plan on any of this."

Claudie doesn't answer. The girl's response was fair. Though, really, why anyone would ever bother with impractical shoes is a mystery.

Lightning streaks across the sky; its silver and white brilliance highlights the girl's wet face and black braided hair. The girl's miserable. She's shivering. She's under-dressed. She's clearly inexperienced and out of her depth. She's also beautiful.

"Come on," Claudie says.

The cabin's a welcome sight, emerging from the bush with its lights shining golden through the rain. It's still slow going, but they have a goal: the cabin is a beacon of hope and safety and welcome and a good chance of one day being dry again.

"Not far now. We'll need to get up the stairs," she tells the girl over the rain. She ignores the girl's suppressed groan. They'll handle it.

They take it one step at a time with the girl in front so Claudie can catch her if she falls. The wind swirls around them, and the wet gum trees lash against one another above them. The rain is almost sideways. The girl keeps going. Claudie follows. She laughs in relief as they finally reach the deck.

Claudie fumbles at the handle and staggers through. Lien follows. Inside, Claudie closes the door behind them. It seals to shut out the storm. They're safe. They can rest. Claudie's heart steadies.

The two of them stand awkwardly close to one another; Claudie still supports the girl. Water drips from their clothes and pools on the wooden floor.

Claudie lets the girl get her balance, then steps away to shake off the intimacy. There's something intense in providing help, in holding another human upright and hearing their breathing. It brings a sense of camaraderie. But it's not real. It's built on a tiny shard of knowledge of one another that comes with battling a shared enemy, even if that enemy is heavy rain and a knee injury meeting a five-hundred-foot slope.

Claudie opens the wardrobe space to find dry towels and tosses one to the girl. The girl catches it. She stands near the edge of the room with most of her weight on one foot. After drying her face, she squeezes out her braids into the towel. She dries her dripping legs and pats at her clothes. She must be exhausted—her eyes are shadows—but she has excellent balance. Her legs are muscular. The girl manages to make being dripping wet, scruffy haired, and wrapped in a towel almost like an art work, as if this were how she intended to look. Claudie can't tell if this confidence is conscious or if it's built into the way this girl moves. She moves as though she knows her skin and knows that people will watch her. She moves as though people will like what they see. That's a safe assumption.

Claudie turns away. "You don't need to stand there all night," she says over her shoulder. "There are chairs." It's ungracious, but she's suddenly awkward. After all, she rescued the girl. She doesn't need to be nice to her too.

"Thank you." The girl glances around the main room, past the two mismatched lounge chairs in the corner between the big windows, the small sofa on the side wall, and the upholstered dining chairs at the dining table toward the back wall. "I don't want to get everything wet."

Claudie pushes a kitchen stool out from under the bench.

"Thanks." The girl perches on it and stretches out her bad leg. She gives a hopeful twist of a smile. "Hey, so, I'm genuinely sorry about this. I really am." Even spent and in pain, she's polite and sweet with her earnest brown eyes and sodden black hair. She takes a barely-there breath. Her hands move as she speaks. "I should tell you my name. Lien. Lien Hong. And god, thank you so much for rescuing me. Honestly. We're up from Sydney, for the music festival you know. Or maybe you don't—well." She shakes it off. "That's not important. But thank you. I'm not great in the dark by myself." She blinks. "God. Sorry, I don't even know your name. I don't usually run on like this."

"It's the adrenaline," says Claudie. "Don't worry about it." Talking like this, the girl's less art and more just lost.

"Oh. Yes. I guess—um. Sorry."

"How bad's the injury?"

Lien frowns at her knee as though it's annoying her. "It'll be better tomorrow. I don't need to tell you the whole story. My knee—it's not a new problem, but I can live with it. It's just impractical right now, which is—ugh. So I appreciate your help. Really." She talks fast and soft as though someone's pressed a switch, and she can't help saying everything that pops up in her head. It's hard to get a read on Lien. Her voice has a smile in it, her hands are mobile, but her eyes flicker to Claudie and about the room, tired and cautious.

"Claudia," Claudie offers when Lien leaves a gap between words.

Lien blinks at her, puzzled. "Oh. Your name. Sorry, I should have let you get a word in."

"No problem." Claudie can't help but smile. "Hi."

Lien swallows visibly. Claudie's throat is tight. She's not accustomed to having her solitude invaded.

Both of them speak at once.

"So you live in a ranger cabin. I never thought—"

"You're lucky I saw you out there."

Claudie's not usually up so late, but her boss and friend Shelley at the ranger headquarters warned her about this storm. And, with the wind circling the cabin and battering the windows, Claudie had been on edge, hovering in the main room with an eye on the shifting dark of the sky and the landscape. The light of Lien's phone moving through the bush caught her eye. She watched, wondering what kind of idiot was walking around the bush so late at night with a storm threatening. Then she saw the phone's light sputter as it bounced down the slope and blinked out to black.

Lien nods. "So lucky. Thank you so much."

They fall quiet. Lien's eyes are bright through her straight wet lashes. She's very lovely, quick-eyed and fine-boned with a wide mouth. Lien's gaze swings away. She pulls the towel close around her ridiculous outfit. She's unnaturally pale with pain or cold.

"You need some clothes," Claudie says. "Dry ones." She doesn't add her thoughts about wearing pale yellow and tiny little shorts, nothing even faintly practical, while camping. What the fuck was the kid thinking?

Claudie goes to grab some clean clothes from the bedroom.

"Oh, no," she hears. When she turns, Lien has a hand up to cover her mouth. "Oh, god! Um. Shit. I need to let Beau know I'm okay. He's back at the campground. I told him I'd only be a few minutes getting a photo for Snapchat. With the rain and—He'll be worried sick. You don't have a phone do you? I dropped mine when I fell." Her brow is furrowed.

Claudie's not sure how this city girl thinks she communicates with the rest of the world. By pigeon? Smoke signal? Tapping out messages on an ancient telegraph machine and hoping someone out there answers? "I have a phone." She grabs it from the kitchen bench and hands it to Lien.

Lien exhales on a laugh. "Of course you do. I didn't want to presume. Thank you." She bites her lip as she punches in a number.

Lien's face and shoulders sag when someone picks up. "Beau, it's me," she starts. "No, no stop. I'm okay. I'm okay." There are tears in her eyes when she hears this guy Beau's voice.

She's a little dramatic, this Lien. It's not as though she's been gone for days. Claudie roughly towel dries her own hair and tries not to listen in as Lien talks.

"I am such an idiot," Lien says. "I'm so sorry."

The rain hasn't relented; it's coming in angled sheets of water, like waves, lashing rhythmically against the roof and the western window and whipping at the tree tops.

"Okay, babe. I love you too," Lien finishes. She hands back Claudie's phone. "Thank you." Her hair is drying so Claudie can see the pale bird's-egg-blue streaks in its straight, black shininess.

"Your boyfriend?" Claudie asks.

"Oh! Gosh! No. My housemate. My best friend. He must have been so fucking scared." Lien runs a hand over her face. "I wish I'd called him sooner."

"You were getting out of danger. I wouldn't have let you make a phone call while we were in the storm."

Lien tries to stand and winces.

"I have ice," Claudie says. "I'll get that and something for the pain."

"Thank you."

"But first these." Claudie hands over a T-shirt and some yoga pants. They'll be too big, but Lien's clothes are unwearable as they are, soaked with mud and rain.

"Thank you." Lien nods. "I'll just I'll uh—change."

Claudie blushes. "Go ahead. Or you can go into the bedroom." The world smells like rain, wet earth and wet wood, and that electric scent of lightning.

"Oh. No, I'm fine," Lien stammers. Claudie turns away and walks to the freezer for ice.

Lien moves about behind her, sucks in a sharp breath. "Okay," she says. "I'm done."

Claudie turns around. In Claudie's over-large clothing Lien seems even younger than before. Her dark brown eyes are smudgy and worried in her pale face.

Claudie offers her a hand into one of the comfortable chairs in the corner. The chairs seem to clash even more than usual, one wooden-legged with flame orange upholstery, the other low-profiled and gray-blue. Lien frowns as she settles down in the flame orange one. She fusses over her knee and wraps the ice in a cloth. With a murmured thanks, she accepts the striped blanket Claudie offers.

"How about some tea?" Claudie says.

"Oh. Thank you. I'll, um, can I help?"

Claudie quirks an eyebrow at her. "It's just tea, kiddo. I can handle it." Claudie steps past the wood-topped bench that divides the main room from the kitchen area. The kitchen and the main room are side by side. They look out to the deck and over the valley.

The kettle takes its time to boil. Claudie faces away from Lien. Steam rises to condense on the windows, pale against the black of the storm outside. Lien's presence fills the room. Claudie's so ill accustomed to having people in her space that she's aware of every breath Lien takes.

Tea ready, Claudie hands Lien a mug and lowers herself into the gray-blue chair facing her. The springs of the chair squeak and sink.

Lien holds the mug in two hands and takes a sip. Her shoulders relax. "So. What's a park ranger's job entail?" she asks. "Aside from rescuing idiot campers." She crinkles up her nose. "Sorry about that."

"It's all floods and fires and picking up trash people leave behind."

"All in one day?"

Claudie shrugs. "Sometimes."

Lien fixes her with a sincere look. "I'm not messing with you. I'm interested to hear more."

It's late. Claudie's accustomed to outback hours, and, even though she's sure Lien's not, the girl is injured and has had a long night.

"We can talk tomorrow," Claudie says. "We'll have plenty of time for it then." She blinks. Her eyes are heavy.

"Oh, no." Lien winces. "Sorry. I'm keeping you up."

"It's fine."

"It's not fine."

"It's *fine.*"

The cabin has one bedroom opening from the main room, and one bed. Claudie didn't ask for a visitor but she's not about to let an injured girl sleep in the chair. Lien's eyes look bruised with exhaustion.

"There's a bed in the other room," says Claudie. "You take it. I'll sleep out here."

"No way," Lien says. "No. Hey, you rescued me. I am not taking your bed, too."

"Yep. You are." Claudie's not about to be argued with. "It's my house and my choice. The better you sleep, the sooner you'll be better."

"And the sooner I'll leave you alone. But surely there's something else." Lien scans the room. "There must be somewhere for you—"

Claudie tips her head. "What—Are you hoping to spot a secret bed? An extra room?"

Lien blushes. "Hush."

"Because I've lived here three years. I think I know my own place."

Claudie helps Lien to her feet. Lien's hand is cool on her arm. They shuffle through the narrow doorway from the living room. Lien uses the bathroom while Claudie checks that everything's set up in the tiny bedroom.

Claudie's bedroom is small. The bed and a bedside table are squeezed between the walls. It's draped in mosquito netting that Claudie bought in town and hung from the ceiling that first furiously hot and miserable summer. Claudie turns on the little lamp. She's protected here in a swathe of fabric and the circle of clear lamplight—safe, at least from the few mosquitoes and moths that find their way inside despite Claudie's best efforts to seal the house, attracted by the one lone light out in the bush.

Claudie draws back the netting as Lien joins her. Lien sits. She gingerly turns her body to move farther up on the bed.

"It's a double bed," says Lien from the far side. "We can both fit."

Lien lifts her weight on her arms to slide her butt back and angles herself to slip between the sheets. It's been a long time since Claudie shared a house, let alone a bed. Her stomach twists.

"I don't think so," Claudie says.

Lien doesn't argue; she nods. "Thank you."

CLAUDIE FORGOT TO COLLECT HER pajamas. She could take off her bra and jeans and sleep in her T-shirt but with someone here in the next room, she's wary. She sighs and stretches out as much as she can in the gray-blue chair. From here she has a view of the bush and the rain. She finds the dark vastness reassuring. She doesn't bother to pull the curtains closed; she wants to keep an eye on the storm. She also wants to be up early to check on the roof. She keeps watch as the wind and rain batter the walls.

This cabin's her place now. It's been in the National Parks and Wildlife Service for decades. It's on the hilltop with unimpeded views into the valley. It's made of wood and fibro cement sheets old enough that they've discolored. The cabin's edges have roughened to match the hillside. The place has grown into the landscape around it.

The main room's windows are large, taking up the whole of two sides of the cabin. They're designed for keeping a lookout for bush fires or other trouble.

Claudie's become pretty good at the upkeep for this place. She fixes slamming doors and dripping taps. The second summer, she climbed into the roof space to put insulation into the cavity, then crawled under the floors and insulated them too. She spent her down hours for a couple of weeks overhauling the rainwater tank that's nestled beside the cabin. It's a big enough tank, but she doesn't use much water. They're predicting more rain and it's already been a hot, wet spring, but she grew up through years of Australian drought. Even when she traveled overseas, when she lived in the US for a year, she was economical with water.

Usually, if she was up this late, she'd hear the last of the night's cicadas, a chitter from passing bats, and the young frogs chirruping to one another down by the creek. But it's too wet for that. Instead the wind sweeps through the wet trees, lashing them over and over like monster waves against shifting sand. The rain pounds on the sloped roof.

There are no lights here, no city bustle and chatter. Only a few people, Shelley and a couple of others, even know where she is. She tries not to imagine what her old friends are doing, what new bands they're listening to, how their projects are going. She hasn't thought about her former life for ages, but Lien brings all of the past rushing back. This is the life Claudie chose and this is the life she would choose again, over and over. It's the life she loves. She has a few friends, a job, the view, her music. She needs nothing more.

She looks out at the familiar darkness and listens to the rain. She evens out her breathing. After weeks of everything dragging, the night has raced by, and it's late. But it's hard to stay still. She's wide awake. There's a stranger in the cabin, a stranger sleeping in Claudie's bed.

Even Claudie can be lonely out here, far from anyone she knows. She hasn't felt lonely tonight.

The rain continues on and on. It pours over the house and the trees and the great wide world. It closes them in.

4

LIEN OPENS HER EYES TO pale gray light through the draped mosquito netting. The netting is exotic, as if the bed is on safari in the 1920s. It's too bad her pith helmet's stranded at the campsite, and any passing lions or giraffes remain silent.

Lien shifts. The bed's fine, and she slept well, but her knee throbs. She doesn't want to think about that. She can't even distract herself with social media. She'd love to work out the perfect tweet about this.

She stands and treads gingerly to the window. The glass is spattered with drops. The half-light is filtered through them. The storm hasn't eased and the wind is still up.

Shifting her weight, she tests her knee as she watches the rain. This is the same injury that derailed all of her plans eight years ago. The pain flings her brain back to those days when everything she'd ever dreamed for her future was over forever. But then all her dreams were focused on soccer. Knees don't matter so much now. A bit of a limp is not going to keep her from music reviews, interviews with bands, fashion watching, and articles about the festival lineup and the crowd and new Australian music at Rivers Fest.

Wind and rain batters the tin roof. The chair in the other room squeaks. The sound is just audible over the noise of the storm.

Right. Claudia.

The night before is a haze of stupid decisions and rain. And a superhero park ranger. This morning is going to be better. Lien limps into the main room on bare feet, careful to make no noise. The early morning light is delicate, hazy green and gray. It creeps across the walls and over the wooden floorboards.

The main room takes up the whole width of the cabin. Outside the windows, a few trees stand near the cabin and shoot straight from the earth to the sky. Beyond them the valley drops away and the view is a canopy of treetop after treetop, stretching green over the nearby mountains as far as Lien can see. The seclusion seems boundless.

Musical instruments hang on the white walls: a couple of acoustic guitars, one of which has seen better days, a twelve string, a bass, an autoharp.

Lien's superhero park ranger is stretched out in the blue-gray chair. In the fear and shock of the night before, Lien didn't take Claudia in except as Wonder Woman with glorious shoulders. Now, with Claudia safely asleep, Lien can't help but look her over. She's older than Lien, somewhere in her thirties. Her face is angular, with prominent cheekbones, a wide mouth, and dark hair and eyelashes. Her hair is roughly layered, like a cut that's growing out from something that was cool on Joan Jett in the 70s. Somehow, though, it perfectly frames Claudia's face. Even asleep, she seems comfortable in her solid, long-limbed body. She was comfortable moving, too, even when she was supporting Lien. Her shoulders take up most of the width of the chair. She has slim hips and a broad back and muscular thighs. She's not fashionable, but she seems confident, with that accidental gorgeousness Lien sometimes envies.

Her perfectly fitted jeans look old enough to have molded to her thighs. Lien wishes she'd thought to ensure Claudia had a chance to get into her pajamas or whatever she sleeps in.

Even asleep Claudia's imposing, impressive, though maybe that's hero worship talking. It's hard to see past that.

Claudia stirs. Lien freezes when she blinks awake. Her eyes quickly fix on Lien. They're dark clear gray, reflecting the sky and the rain.

"Hi," says Claudia.

Lien glances away. Claudia's distracting. Maybe she can't tell that Lien was staring, cataloging Claudia's striking features. This whole thing is awkward.

"Hi," Lien says. She tries a tiny smile.

If she had Beau or Annie here, she could laugh about last night, laugh about her shoes and the rivers of rain running down her hair and into her underwear. Instead she's faced with this serious woman dressed in a boys' T-shirt and jeans, with the outdoors etched into her face.

Lien gestures to the instruments hanging on the wall. "You play?"

Claudia glances at them. "Yep."

"All of them?"

"They're not decorative," says Claudia. She yawns.

The subject is shut down. Lien's accustomed to constant conversation. She's used to being a person strangers want around, a person everyone listens to when they want to know what music's good or what club to check out or whether or not their outfit is the cool kind of retro 80s.

Lien's pretty sure Claudia doesn't give a shit about whether she's the cool kind of retro.

Claudia unfolds herself from the chair and stretches. Her arms and shoulders are clearly defined against her faded T-shirt. She turns to meet Lien's gaze. Thunder rumbles far off.

Lien can at least smooth things over, make her rescuer like her. She was raised for all sorts of unusual social situations. No one taught her

41

the specific etiquette for being rescued by an attractive park ranger and trapped in a cabin, but that's okay. Lien's good at improvising.

"Did you sleep well?" Lien asks.

Claudia raises an eyebrow. Lien shrinks under that scrutiny.

"I slept fine," Claudia says. Behind her, lightning streaks across the horizon. Thunder rumbles through the walls. Claudia glances out the window and back.

Lien keeps talking. "Oh. Good. I was pretty scared. I don't think I've ever been anywhere this silent. I'm sorry you had to sleep out here. So, can I make you some breakfast or, um, tea or something?"

Claudia eyes her. She smiles—a bright flash. "Why don't I get the breakfast? Seeing as you have no idea where everything is. And should probably rest that leg."

Lien blushes. She can't seem to stop talking. Everything she says is off-target. "Okay. Let me know if I can help."

"Will do."

Claudia walks to the wide windows. Her feet are bare. She's silhouetted, like a tall statue in the light. She ties her hair in a loose ponytail. Her shirt stretches across her back. Thunder rolls in, much closer now. Lightning cracks through the sky.

"I don't see you getting out of here today," Claudia says without turning back to Lien.

Oh. "But. There's a road right? I saw it. My friends have cars. I could get one of them to come collect me."

Claudie turns. "I'd drive you the long way round myself but the road's gonna be washed out even if the causeway held. Which I doubt it did." She holds her hand up to stop Lien interrupting. "And don't think about walking. You won't make it down to the creek and back up that canyon to the campsite, especially on that knee. It's steep, and the rain hasn't let up. It'll still be like walking in a river. Look. I'll check in with the emergency services but I think you're stuck here with me for now."

Lien doesn't mean to sigh aloud.

Claudia's glance is sharp. "Unless the rescue chopper comes in to get you, there aren't any options. I'd rather the rescue guys spent their time on real emergencies."

Lien nods. But inside she's still arguing. *This is a real emergency.* Lien's not used to sitting still with no Internet and no one to sympathize with her about the lack of Internet. She's not comfortable with silence and alone time. More than that, she's not comfortable imposing on Claudia, who clearly prefers her own company to Lien's. Lien might find Claudia charming: reserved and brilliant and unmistakably hot, but it's hard to imagine talking with Claudia about fashion or club music, whether studded cuffs are coming back for queer kids, whether indie music is a real genre.

Lien steps forward to stand beside Claudia. The sky's dark gray; the bush is by turns silvery and lush green, striped by tree trunks. Lien can't see much beauty to it, but she stays still and catches something there, behind the storm and rain and the swishing wet leaves of the eucalypts, something in the great span of the place.

"So," Claudia says. "I guess we'd better get used to this. If we're going to spend a day or two together."

"Really. A day or two?"

"It's a tropical storm, Lien. They knock out towns. There's a good chance you'll be here more than two days." Claudia's tone is back to sharp.

Lien hurries to make it better. "Sorry, that's—It's not that I don't want to be here. Honestly. I just don't want to impose. I'm sorry."

"I know you are," says Claudia, more gently. "Okay. First things first. You have got to stop apologizing."

Lien can accept that. She nods. "Okay then. Right." She needs to work with the reality of her current situation. "So if we're stuck here, is there anything we can do? Anything you need to work on in the house? Like, painting or—" She trails off as it's clear the place doesn't need paint. "What about...?" She hesitates, realizing anything she says will seem rude. "I don't want to be a burden; I want to help out."

Claudie's mouth crooks into a smile. "I take it you don't like silence." Lien's stomach clenches. "I'm sure I can find something. But for now, you should get off your leg. You need to put that up. Ice it again. No point in suffering and making it worse."

Lien capitulates. She's in pain and she needs to get better. Claudia switches on the light in the kitchen, grabs a tea towel, and reaches into the freezer. She hands Lien a tea towel full of ice.

"Here. I'll make us some toast while you sit," says Claudia.

Lien sits in the chair and settles the ice around her knee. In the narrow kitchen, Claudia opens a cupboard for the bread. Everything Claudia does is efficient; every motion works in the space. She presses down the lever on the side of the toaster.

The lights sputter. They drop out. The fridge sighs into silence.

"Damn," says Claudia. She kicks the fridge. She frowns and kicks it again. Lien smiles into her lap. The fridge does nothing. Lightning splits the sky at the horizon. Thunder rolls in. "Damn," Claudia says again.

CLAUDIE STEPS OUT THE FRONT door and dodges the rain to stand under the wide eaves of the cabin. She opens the mains box and checks the switch. She flicks it up once, twice. It's no use. The generator has a breaker that activates if it's standing in water. Either that's in effect or the connection between the panels and the generator has blown. Either way, the power's gone. And the rain is not about to stop, so Claudie can't access the generator. Not today.

Perfect.

The rain sweeps in under the eaves and spatters her face.

Back inside it's even quieter than usual. The fridge's background hum has gone. She can't turn on music or use the tiny TV.

"I'm checking in with the boss," she says to Lien. That's another annoyance of having a visitor, the need to explain herself.

Shelley answers first ring. "Mate! Good. You haven't been washed down the mountain. It looks chancy out there."

Claudie pictures Shelley running a hand through her dark cropped hair the way she does when she's worried, her light brown eyes scrutinizing the storm.

"I'm okay. You've got some campers at the upper Iron Pot site, though. Might need to get them out."

"Already taken care of. They tell me you've got one with you."

"Yep."

"Don't you go breaking her. My mob takes the welcome to country seriously." Shelley's from the Bundjalung Nation and has more right to the land than the National Parks and Wildlife Service she works for.

"Course not. Falling down the gorge did a number on her knee though. She can't walk out. We're stuck until the road's passable."

"Nasty. Well, the weather bureau reckons this'll keep up for at least two days. I hope you've got some board games up there."

"Yeah, not exactly."

Shelley laughs. "You'll cope."

"No doubt. Thanks, boss."

Rain drums on the roof. Ordinarily Claudie would find the steady noise comforting. But now she's caged, trapped indoors with everything colored by Lien's presence. It's not the girl's fault. She's uncomfortably easy to look at in a too-big T-shirt; her legs are well-defined in Claudie's running shorts. But she's no trouble. It's just strange having anyone else take up room and watch Claudie move. Lien's presence prickles up and down Claudie's spine.

And now they have to sit together with no lights and no distractions and wait for the growing dark, when everything will be even more awkward.

"Hey," Claudie says. "I have a bunch of old music magazines. *Vibe Mag* and *Mojo* and *Clash* and stuff in a box somewhere."

Lien's eyes brighten. "Cool."

Claudie is warmed by her enthusiasm. "Shall I drag them out?" She knows the answer.

"Mm-hmm. Yes, please." Lien nods. She's quick to add, "If it's not too much trouble."

Claudie pulls the box from the bottom of a cupboard. "Sit closer to the window. You'll have enough light there until later this afternoon." They pull Lien's chair over the floor, and she sits back down. Claudie grabs a crate for Lien to use as a footrest. Lien shoots her a grateful glance.

Lien bends over the box and flips through the magazines. She's so excited she's almost vibrating. She pulls out a magazine. "Oh. I've never seen this cover. I thought I'd seen all of the early 2000s."

"You're into music?" Claudie asks.

"Yeah. Um, it's sort of what I do. Music journalism." She goes back to the box. As she searches, she talks to herself. She hums over the options, then selects one. She stretches her bare leg to rest on the crate, wraps herself in the over-large olive green hoodie that she seems to have appropriated, and smiles up with a magazine in her lap. "Want to join me?"

Claudie wasn't planning to, but it's raining, the road's a mess, and she has nothing much to do. Anyway, there's something inviting about the idea of sitting with this girl and poring over articles from a time she left behind.

"I won't tell anyone you wasted time on something superficial like magazines." Lien twinkles at her.

"Hah. Thank you, but that is not a problem," says Claudie. "You do realize they're my magazines, yeah?"

Still, it's an unusual indulgence on Claudie's part, to sit and read in daylight and in company. She expects Lien to chatter. It's almost a disappointment that they read in silence, companionably turning a page now and then. She hands over a particularly good issue of *Clash*. Lien passes her a magazine open to an article about women as the saving grace of new country music. It's pleasant, thoughtful but low key, easy in a way Claudie wouldn't have expected.

Mid-morning, Claudie makes tea in a saucepan on the gas stove top. She hands a large mug to Lien.

"Cute," Lien says, looking at the mug. "The Lone Ranger. Is this meant to be you?" She studies Claudie with wide eyes.

Claudie flushes to her hairline. "Yeah, I guess." She's not accustomed to people pursuing things with her. She's also annoyed with herself for blushing. Neither of those things means she needs to be short with Lien. She tries again. "My mum gave me the mug when I came up here."

"Was that long ago?"

"Three years."

"Oh yeah, you said. Right. So the wilderness is your thing. I have to admire that." She's not laughing. Her eyes are unblinking and interested.

Claudie tries to reflect that intensity. "I—yeah. I guess it is one of my things." Lien doesn't look away, so she goes on. "When I first moved up here, well, I was used to a big city so it was tricky at first. I had no idea how to avoid the mosquitoes, how much water I had, how to get the generator working. But I was committed to being here, and it didn't take long to learn things. I'm used to it now."

"I think—" Lien pauses; her gaze shifts away to the ceiling, then back. "I don't know. I think you must know yourself pretty well, to live out here."

Claudie's smile is half wince. "Sometimes." She tries to come up with something more. "Anyway, I know all about me. Let's talk about you instead."

"Of course. Sure. Lien Hong. Sydney. Fashion and music journalist." Lien smiles brightly, a party smile. It sounds as though she's said those exact words at a thousand events.

"Is that on your business card?"

"No one uses business cards any more. But it's my twitter bio."

Claudie has nothing to add to that. "Twitter, huh. Well, the journalism explains all those questions you've been asking."

"Sorry. I didn't—I asked because I'm interested."

"No worries. Okay. So, journalism I get. And music. Tell me about fashion."

"It's interesting too. The choices people make, the aesthetics and culture and fun of it," says Lien. She crunches up her face as though in apology. "But yeah. I see. Not your area."

"Are you saying my outfit isn't the height of style?" Claudie waves her hands over her clothing. She's glad she's wearing one of her better black T-shirts; this one fits well across her chest, and her jeans are decent.

Lien laughs. "I'd never say that." She frowns at Claudie and takes on a serious persona. "I have some insight into the industry, Claudia Ranger. Wilderness chic is the next big thing. We're going to see this aesthetic in New York and Milan." She looks Claudie up and down and says, "Gorgeous." She's laughing, but something underneath the laughter is not false. Her glance runs across Claudie's skin. Claudie tamps down on a shiver. Lien's eyes catch on hers, then swing away.

The silence stretches between them.

By mid-afternoon, the power hasn't miraculously re-connected itself. Lien uses some of their limited phone battery to call Beau.

"Yeah, I'm fine. No way, babe. No, I'm just glad you're okay," she says. She moves to the corner of the room. "Okay, I can't talk now. Love you."

When she hangs up, she laughs. "He's feeling guilty about having a good time in town and leaving me here all alone."

"Yeah," Claudie says. "I'll bet you wish you could be with them."

"No, I don't—I don't feel like that. It's not like I'm alone up here. I mean. I'm sorry for taking up your—"

Claudie interrupts. "Hey. You promised. No more apologies."

They smile at one another.

Claudie goes into the kitchen and opens the silent fridge. She doesn't keep too much food around. She knows herself too well; if she had food for a month she wouldn't see another human that whole time. But they need to eat, and what's here will go bad.

"Any chance you cook?" she asks Lien.

"Oh." Lien eyes the fridge as though it might attack her. "I guess, not really. No. Not usually. I used to, but I haven't done much since I was a kid helping my mother."

"You don't cook at home?"

"We've got really good take-out where I live." Lien blushes.

Claudie grins at her. "No worries. You want to try something for us now?" Lien's eyes widen. Claudie goes on. "Hey, I'll help. But I only cook a few different things. I'd love to try something new with what I've got here. I'm sure you can manage something."

"Okay," says Lien. "I mean, I really don't—Is the stove working?"

"Yeah, it's gas."

Lien doesn't answer for a long minute. "You're serious."

Claudie steps out of the kitchen. "Sure am. I have to put you to work somehow. I'm not expecting cordon bleu. You can use anything here. I'll help."

"Okay." Lien nods to herself and pushes to her feet. She hobbles into the kitchen. She hunts through the freezer, then opens the fridge. She chatters to herself. "You've got so many vegetables. Can I use them in a stir fry? And ginger. Frozen peas. Those'll do." She looks up. "Any chance you're hiding a lime somewhere?"

"There's a good chance," says Claudie. "I freeze lemons and limes when I get them."

"And what about some mint?"

"Not sure. I've been fighting the birds over my herb garden for the past few months. The bloody cockatoos keep chewing their way through the mesh. I'll see what I've got."

It's not raining heavily. It's a steady patter on Claudie's head and shoulders as she bends over the herb garden. The world outside smells drenched and warm. Claudie doesn't need to rush. The plants are mostly okay, overly wet but protected from the wind by the wall and eaves. She stands the cover supports up, empties water from the tray at the base, then drapes the mesh cover back to give the herbs room.

Lien takes the mint. "I... Hey. It's not like I really recall how to do this," she says. "My mother would marinate everything with lemongrass, but I think if I use the lemon zest and the mint, and you have soy sauce... I don't know. It might taste similar. This could work."

Lien's eyes are hopeful, as if she's offering something. It's instinctive to reassure her. "Sounds good to me. You'll be fine. What could go wrong?"

The first thing that goes wrong is that Lien turns, gasps in pain as her knee twists, and drops the knife she's using to zest the lemons. It misses her toes by an inch.

They freeze.

"Sorry," says Lien.

"Okay. You don't need to apologize. You need a seat," says Claudie. She pulls over a stool. Lien perches on it above the kitchen counter. She's graceful but it's going to prove difficult to cook if she can't move around the kitchen.

"And you need a sous chef," Claudie says.

It's a tiny kitchen, enough space for one person. Claudie is comfortable in it alone. But now she moves around Lien, trying not to touch her, sliding past her from behind when she asks for the chopping board.

"Do you have a larger knife?" Lien asks. Claudie moves past her again. "And maybe a metal wok or a thin fry pan?"

Claudie nods. "Yep." She bends to get into the drawer. Lien is close. Her hip brushes Lien's thigh. When Claudie straightens they look at one another. Claudie steps back out of Lien's space.

Lien moves her stool closer to the bench. She cuts the vegetables carefully, then marinates them in lemon and lime and ginger and mint. She might not cook much, but her hands are precise, beautiful to watch even when they're unsure. Claudie stands to one side, gets the oil, scoots behind Lien for peas, tries not to brush up against her. As she works, Lien seems more sure of herself. She lines everything up, then throws oil and vegetables into the hot wok. It's done.

Then well done. And suddenly everything seems to be on fire at once.

Lien gives every appearance of calm as she lifts the wok from the stove top and lets everything settle down. "Okay," she says. "You got a fire extinguisher here, Ranger?"

Claudie widens her eyes.

"I'm joking, I'm joking." Lien puts the wok on the burner and adds the herbs and some honey.

The night's still warm, but it's seven thirty. The light from outside is growing soft and pink. Claudie lights candles. Lien serves the food. They sit at the dining table.

"It's not great," says Lien. "I'm not really an improviser. Not with food. And I only partly remembered how to make it." She's beautiful in the flickering gold light.

Claudie looks away from her and down at her plate. "It looks amazing."

She takes a bite. The broccoli is overcooked but the flavor is good. Lien frowns. Her eyes seem worried, so Claudie smiles. "This is delicious."

"It's really not."

"It really is. You didn't have all the ingredients and you were stuck on a stool with equipment you'd never used before. I can only imagine how incredible it could be. But it's still good." Claudie rarely finds apologetic endearing, but on Lien it is. "You have hidden talents."

Lien grins then and huffs air through her nose in a soft laugh. "Deeply hidden talents, my housemate would say."

"Beau."

"That's him. He does most of the cooking at home. He's a wonder."

The table is small. They're close, sitting across from one another. Claudie avoids Lien's eyes; she looks out the window to the dark, then back. Lien toys with her fork as she chews and swallows.

Claudie scrambles for something to say. "Doesn't seem like the rain is going to let up anytime soon."

"Yeah?" Lien shifts in her chair. She stretches her leg past the table leg in front of her and winces.

Claudie says, "So the knee's an old injury?"

Lien nods. "An old injury that wasn't helped by falling down a cliff."

"I'll bet. But it could have been worse. Tell me about the injury?"

Lien's face is cloudy. "Yeah. I was—look you don't want to hear about this. It's late."

"I'd like to hear. Unless it bothers you. We've got plenty of time until this storm goes."

Lien's frown is dubious.

"The least you can do is make that time interesting." Claudie crooks a smile at Lien to soften her words.

Lien laughs, and her face clears. "Okay. It's not that exciting, but sure. When I was young I had dreams of a career in soccer. I was scouted by an agent when I was a kid. A lot of people supported me. I mean, it's tough for women to make a career of any sport, but I had plans. They were—going well. I'd gone to the best academies. I was playing for a good team; my coach was incredible. I was on my way.

"And then a dirty tackle killed that. I fought to get back, but I guess maybe I didn't fight hard enough. It was months before I could walk on it properly. It was never going to be the same and, well, the trouble is I had no savings. I needed a job."

"How old were you?"

"Nineteen."

Claudie considers her. Lien's compact, not slight but small. She could disappear into the wide open space out here. But Claudie's aware of the powerful muscles in her legs and arms, of the unexpected steel in her spine that got her here without whimper or complaint. "So you reinvented yourself."

"So I reinvented myself." Lien takes a breath. "That's a kind way to put it. Don't get me wrong. I love what I do. I get to talk about fashion and music. I'm fortunate; somehow I'm doing well in it. I work some magazines and I get to report on the festivals. The fashion there can be pretty amazing. I can't complain. This is a dream too. It was only—it was hard to give up that first dream. I let everyone down. I let myself down." She blinks and shakes her head. "But, hey. That was a long time ago."

"Do you play at all anymore?"

Lien shrugged. "No. I don't really have the time, and it's not like I'll ever be that good again." She blinked. "Huh. Sorry. I'm not usually so— I don't always blurt out everything to someone I just met."

"It's different here," Claudie says. "Out in the bush."

There's a strange, forced closeness, with all the noise and dark outside the cabin and just the two of them in the bubble of quiet lamplight inside.

Claudie continues. "It's not the same as meeting someone anywhere else. And you're stuck sitting down all day. We've got nothing else to do. We might as well talk."

Lien looks at the dark, rain-streaked window. "It feels as though you could say anything here."

"Exactly. That's 'cause you *can* say anything here."

The long silence is not really awkward. "Anything gives me a lot of options," Lien says. Her glance is warm. The heat runs up and down Claudie's back before she can get a hold of herself. She needs to get more accustomed to friendly and attractive company. She takes a bite of her stir-fry.

"So you live in Darlinghurst," Claudie says after she finishes her mouthful. "I saw Janie Edge play at Shady Pines. That's near you, right?"

"Yeah, that's a good bar. Bit of an outlier for Sydney. I always think I should be wearing one of those frilly gingham shirts and cowboy boots."

They talk about music and Sydney, then about places they've traveled and how much they love New York.

"Though when I think about it," Claudie says, "I've never heard anyone say, 'Eh. New York. Boring. It's not what I hoped.'" They've both finished eating, but neither of them stands.

"True." Lien laughs. "Okay. We're predictable. Tell me. Favorite city that's not New York."

"I'm still predictable. London," says Claudie. "Though I love Sydney and Melbourne. You?"

"Singapore." Her eyes are bright. "And Sydney. Of course."

"You've spent time in Singapore?" Claudie leans back on the wooden chair as Lien speaks. The chair's not comfortable but Claudie's loathe to move.

"I lived there. With my parents. That was ages ago."

Claudie laughs. "You're twenty-seven. There is no 'ages ago.' What was Singapore like?"

"I mean, it's like everywhere. Some good, some bad. I loved living there. I made use of my summer clothes. And met people from all over the world. It's majority Chinese so I had to brush up on my Mandarin. I studied fashion and journalism. Fashion Week there is amazing."

"What made you move to Sydney?"

"I—well you know I was young, and my parents are amazing, but they aren't exactly comfortable to be around. It's a busy society, and they're busy people, and sometimes that's hard to navigate. I wanted to be somewhere I felt safe."

Lien stops talking.

"Makes sense," Claudie says.

"I guess we should do the dishes," Lien says.

Claudie nods. "I'll wash."

"Have your parents visited you here?" Lien asks a bit later as they stand side by side over the soapy water in the sink.

"Sure. They're not far really. They live north of Sydney. Their place is pretty cool. It's almost in the bush. They grow their own vegetables and make bathtubs full of wine and drink herbal tea and walk everywhere. This place is more their style than mine, almost." She hands Lien a plate to dry.

"Do you miss them?"

"Yeah. Definitely. But we talk. My dad and I talk about the stars and *MasterChef* and whether people can be truly good. My mum and I talk about biology and anthropology mostly, and whether her chickens are being weird. They stopped worrying about me back when I was a teenager."

"Sounds idyllic," says Lien.

"How about your folks?" Claudie turns her head to Lien.

"I mean, we're not really like that. They're still worrying about me the same way they always have. But they live in either Hong Kong or Dubai, depending on the calendar, so I don't see much of them. They're good people. The work they support in Hong Kong is vital." She turns back to the dishes. Her profile is pinched.

"Is that… okay with you? Not seeing them?"

"Yep. It's not that we don't get along. But I don't think I'm quite what they hoped for. We're all better for one another in small doses."

"Got it." The dishes are in the drainer. The soft candlelight gleams on them and bounces from the windows. "You want a glass of wine?"

"Yes, please." Lien beams. "Especially if it was made in your parents' bathtub."

Claudie brings a candle when they take their glasses and sit on the deep chairs that face out over the bush. The rain's eased a little, or at least it's cycling through a quiet phase, but the sky hasn't cleared.

"First love?" she asks into the quiet.

"My first love?" Lien's cheeks are flushed in the shifting light. "Charles. Charlie. Nice guy. Snappy dresser."

"Snappy?" Claudie teases. She can't ignore the fact that she's disappointed it's a guy. Not that she assumed that if Lien were gay she'd want anything to do with Claudie. It's only that there is this connection—"Snappy dresser?"

"Hush," says Lien. "We were fourteen. We're Facebook friends now. The boy is hot." She thinks. "My second love lasted longer. Hansi. She was funny. Unbending and gorgeous. Sri Lankan. Her parents weren't too keen on me, though. I'm not Sri Lankan and not male either. They thought I was a bad influence. It was tough, especially for her."

Oh. So she's not only into guys then. Claudie keeps her voice light. "How old were you?"

Lien narrows her eyes. "When I fell for Hansi? Sixteen. We were in boarding school together."

Claudie chokes out a laugh.

"I know. But honestly it's not like it sounds." Lien's eyes are twinkling. "School uniforms are not that sexy."

Claudie's heartbeat flutters. She looks into her drink. "Okay then." Her cheeks are hot. She's not going to talk about it, but she also won't deny the attraction.

"So, what about you?" Lien asks.

"Me?"

Lien nods; her eyes are dark on Claudie's. "Tell me about your first love?"

"Oh." Claudie hesitates. "Dani. Danielle. Yeah." She falls silent. "She—There's not much to tell there." Claudie gropes for something else to discuss. She doesn't want to blurt out how much Lien's own vibrancy reminds her of Dani.

Lien's glance is searching but it's not unkind. "That's cool, Claudia Ranger. I'm not about to push you to talk about things if you don't want to," she says.

"You're not that kind of journalist?"

"Only if it's called for. Definitely not to a rescuer. Or my friends."

Claudie believes her. "Call me, Claudie," she says. "Everyone does." She taps Lien's almost empty glass. "More wine?"

Lien nods. "Yes, please."

On Claudie's way back to the chairs with the bottle, she lifts the six string guitar down from its place on the wall. She's not sure why she wants it. She doesn't play for people, ever. She leans the guitar against a chair and pours the wine. Then she sits and pushes her chair back a bit to give herself room to hold the guitar. It fits comfortably in her arms.

"Is it okay if I play?" she asks. Her insides twist with nerves.

"God, yes, please. I'd love that."

Claudie keeps her eyes lowered and starts with something simple. She's not rusty; she plays often, but she's uncomfortable. She doesn't sing. In the other chair, Lien is still. She holds on to her glass. Her eyes are warm; her chest lifts with her breath. Claudie keeps playing.

Three songs in, she stops.

"We've got ice-cream in the freezer," Claudie says.

"Oh. We can't let that go to waste."

"That's exactly what I was thinking."

"Thank you for playing for me." Lien's sincere. The candlelight shifts in her dark eyes.

They eat in their chairs, not talking, holding little white bowls of ice cream. For a time, they don't look at one another. Claudie stares out the window. The rain builds again. It batters the house as though it's never thought of slowing and never will.

Claudie's okay with that though. She can't imagine what would tempt her to go outside.

5

THE CANDLELIGHT HEATS LIEN'S CHEEKS. The isolation, Claudie's music—everything is intense. Lien would love to break the quiet, cabin-bound spell and head up the street to a bar, let the hum of people and fashion and chatter tone things down and distract her from thinking. Distractions are few and far between here. She grabs the empty bowls and glasses and stands to take them to the kitchen.

"Dinner was excellent," Claudie says. She hangs the guitar in its place. Her shoulder muscles shift under her soft T-shirt.

Lien's knee is stiff as she moves across the room. She's wearing Claudie's running shorts and knee-high sports socks, striped in navy and electric blue. The socks are quirky and cute. They're also suddenly soaking wet. Water is dripping from the ceiling. "Claudia. Claudie. I'm pretty sure we have a leak in the roof."

Claudie turns. "Damn." She studies the ceiling. "Fuck it. I'm going to have to get out there."

"Not now, though," Lien says quickly. She likes the image of Claudie fixing the roof with her sleeves rolled up, but it can't be done in a rain storm. Thunder rumbles over the bush. The walls shudder. "I'm serious. You can't go on the roof in this. You'd be struck by lightning or you'd slip and fall. Can we put out a bucket and collect the water?"

"I guess we need to for tonight." Claudie frowns. "But that's a pretty fast leak." She examines the ceiling. "Shit. There's a second one." She mutters, "It's an old roof. Tin. The fasteners have lifted. But it doesn't usually leak. I thought I had it all sealed off." Her face is red, as though she's embarrassed.

Lien's never sealed a roof in her life. "Hey. I'd guess not much is waterproof against this. We're basically underwater. Even a submarine would probably leak." At least they're both dry here. She has more reason to worry about Beau and the kids than the leak. "This'd be worse in a tent. Do you think they found somewhere else for my friends to sleep?"

"Yep. I checked in with my mate Shelley. They're sleeping at the visitors' center in town. I should have told you earlier."

"I'm glad they're okay."

Claudie crouches to grab a couple of buckets from under the sink. She stands easily and places them in position, finds a deep bowl in a cupboard, and lines it up under the dripping ceiling, too. Lien contemplates the water as the containers fill. This is the kind of thing that happens in old TV series or in books, not in Lien's life. And she's never had to skip a shower because the hot water's run out. She might need to be even nicer to their landlord.

The drips in the buckets ring loudly. The sound is a counterpoint to the rain outside that goes on and on; it punctuates the steady torrents pouring off the gutters and the wind battering the trees. Outside the cabin, there's no human noise at all. No cars, no strangers laughing, no thump of music up the road. The absence is overwhelming. It seems incredible that Claudie's been here for years.

Lien covers her mouth as she yawns. It's getting late. "I'll sleep out here in the chair tonight," she says. "I'm recovering fast. It's only fair."

Claudie shakes her head. "No. Don't worry. You can take the bed."

"Claudia," Lien pitches her voice low to sound firm. Claudie tips her head. Her eyes twinkle. Lien goes on. "I honestly can't steal your bed again. There's no way. And if you try and make me I'm afraid I'm going to insist on sharing."

Claudie considers her. Her eyes are careful, long-lashed and deep gray as the stormy sky. It's impossible to tell what Claudie will say. It twists Lien's stomach to think that something she has offered might be refused. No matter how many times she tells herself people are allowed to say no, refusal seems like rejection. She tries to laugh, but her laugh is trapped and nervous in her throat. "It's not like I'm going to seduce you in your bed." It's a stupid thing to say. Especially given that she hasn't showered for almost two days.

But when Claudie's gaze flicks away, her cheeks are pink. She speaks slowly. "Right. That's a pity, then." Lien's breath catches. But Claudie goes on as though she didn't say anything unusual. "Okay. Fine. We can share the bed. Why not?"

"Good." Lien's heart beats loud and fast.

"You take the bathroom first. I'm going to empty the buckets so they don't overflow in the night."

Lien strips off to wash herself. As she dresses again, she examines herself in the small mirror. Claudie's clothes are too large. They're faded black on faded black. They're not club gear or whimsical daywear or quirky street clothes that'll get you photographed. They're just clothes. But they're comfortable. Lien scoops her hair from her face. She looks good. Maybe. Kind of. Not like her usual self. And she likes her usual self. But she likes how she looks in the mirror too: relaxed and appropriate and easy.

When she exits the bathroom, Claudia is unbuttoning her shirt with her back to Lien. She shrugs it from her broad shoulders. Lien turns away. It's a new step, being trusted like this. From what she knows of Claudie, it's not a simple thing.

From the location of the lamp and the table beside the bed, it's clear that Claudia sleeps on the side closest to the door. Lien walks to the other side and lifts the netting to climb in. They don't say anything. The rain fills the silence.

In bed, Lien is careful to lie at the edge with her body straight up and down.

"You don't seem particularly comfortable," says Claudia. Her voice is amused.

"I am. It's fine. I'm good."

"I'll get some ice for you to put on your knee again."

"Oh. Thank you." Lien keeps still.

Minutes later Claudie hands over the ice, which is wrapped in a tea towel. Lien wraps her knee and lies down.

"I appreciate it," she says. "You've done so much for me."

When Claudie climbs into bed, she leaves a large space in between them as though it might hurt to brush up against Lien in the night. Lien tries not to be offended. She was doing the same thing.

"Thank you for sharing your bed with me," Lien says. Manners are doubly important when sharing a bed with the superhero ranger who rescued you.

"Not a problem."

Lien smiles into the dark. It's not as if she and Claudie bonded all day. They chatted; they worked side by side. They cooked. Claudie played music. They admired the view. It wasn't a remarkable day, really. But Lien is beginning to know Claudie. And knowing Claudie matters to Lien.

Lien lets her body relax, stretches out. The wind swoops through. It sounds like waves against the side of the house, rushing through the canopy over and over.

THE MORNING'S BIRDS ARE QUIETER than usual, but a few magpies and cockatoos call in the bush and let Claudie know the sun is up. She keeps her eyes closed. It's been years since she experienced the skin-certain presence of someone in her bed: the breath, the warmth, and the all-too-human heartbeat beside her. This girl, this almost stranger, has seen Claudie asleep and vulnerable. It's painful and humbling that a person's been so close to Claudie and has chosen not to hurt her.

There's another angle. It would be too easy to find the intimacy appealing.

She opens her eyes. Lien is still asleep. Her face is serene and sweet. When Lien opens her eyes, she'll chatter on about things that seem unimportant but shed light on everything; she'll move like a sportsperson, capable and balanced despite her injured knee; she'll smile and pad about on bare feet and light up the cabin.

But for now she's still.

Claudie walks into the main room. The ceiling's still dripping. She empties the buckets and bowl and lets the drips start to fill them again. After all the work she's put into the cabin, it's frustrating that the roof leaks the first time she has a visitor. She'll get up on the roof to fix the fastenings today.

In the kitchen, she lights the stove and puts on a pot of coffee. The day is steel gray, and the rain has set in, soaking the already-soaked deck and ground. The lightning died overnight, and the wind has shifted east. The easterlies will push the storm out to sea.

LIEN GETS UP. CLAUDIE HANDS her coffee.

"You're an angel among women," Lien says. The night's sleep has left her refreshed and buoyant. "You rescue me; you provide caffeine. What more can you do?"

Claudie frowns. Lien stops. She tones herself down. She can be overwhelming in full enthusiastic just-woke-up mode. "So. Are we getting up on the roof today?"

"I am," says Claudia. "Not you."

"Dude. Claudie. I'm not planning to clamber up on the roof and need another rescue. But you could definitely use my help."

Claudie's stubborn. "I'm fine by myself."

Lien persists. "I know. But think. I can hold the ladder and hand you things. One trashed knee doesn't make it impossible for me to do anything at all, Claudia."

"I'm not sure about that," says Claudie, but she's stopped arguing and she smiles with relative grace.

In a break in the weather, Claudia collects a ladder from the shed behind the rainwater tank. She slams her hand on the tank loudly enough that Lien can hear the boom. "Tank's full at least," Claudia says as she steps onto the deck with the ladder. "We might be stuck with cold water, but we have a lot of it."

"Oh, good. I should shower once the day's warmer. Be nice to clean up a bit." It's a small space, the weather is humid, and Lien's very aware that she hasn't washed properly since she drove north almost three days ago.

Claudie smiles. "You're fine. It's the bush. If I can reconnect the solar panels, I can even make it a hot shower for you."

Lien widens her eyes. "My hero." She puts her hands to her chest and sighs appreciatively.

"Don't swoon yet. Give me a chance to fuck it up first." Claudia's still smiling, though. As for swooning, Lien's not fooling herself. She's definitely past help on the swooning.

Claudie leans the ladder against the gutter so she can climb up. Lien takes hold at the foot. She tries to seem calm, strong, and certain with her hands.

"Hand me those metal flats," Claudie calls.

Lien steps onto the bottom rung and hands them up one at a time.

"And the drill. I'll put these in under the fasteners."

Lien doesn't talk while Claudie's on the roof. The drill whirrs against metal. Lien's attention is focused on the ladder. That's her job, and she's afraid Claudia might fall.

"I'm not going to topple off, Lien, if that's what's worrying you," comes Claudia's voice in a break in drilling.

Lien laughs. "Sorry," she says.

"No need," says Claudia. "You're not doing anything wrong. I just missed you talking."

Lien stares up at her. "Oh," she says. Her heart stutters. She holds tight to the ladder. She can't think what to talk about.

"Corrugated sheeting's best for this," Claudie says around the nails in her mouth. She hammers a sheet onto the roof. The drill's motor starts again. "It's not great up here. I should have noticed there was a problem before the storm."

"Well, how often do you get up there?" Lien asks. "You can't see everything."

"Apparently not."

"It's probably new damage. The storm brought a whole lot of stuff down. And the wind."

"It's the spaces around the fasteners," Claudia says. "Almost done." Lien stands on her toes to see from the ground. She's easy to impress with construction-related activity, and Claudie impresses her anyway.

"There," Claudia says. She slides down so Lien can see her boots. Almost immediately the rain starts again. Within a few seconds it's as heavy as ever. The wind picks up, sending the rain over the house in great sheets. Claudia can't hold her footing. Her eyes widen, and she gasps as her boot slips from the roof. It catches on the top rung. Lien holds the ladder firm as Claudie makes her way down.

"That was more excitement than I'd hoped," Claudia says. Her voice shakes.

Lien reaches out to touch her arm but draws her hand back. "You did great. Steady as a rock up there, like Superwoman against the storm."

Claudia gives her a crooked smile. "Um, thank you." She huffs out a soft laugh. "Really. Don't oversell me. It'll be disappointing in the end."

Lien's certain Claudia is wrong about that.

"It's tough going trying to get music made in Sydney," Lien says. They're in the living room chairs eating a late lunch of peanut butter sandwiches made with defrosted bread. "I bumped into one of the owners of that little record label Fish/Fish, and she was running kids' parties."

"The label sounds familiar." Claudie nods.

"I mean, I bet her kids' parties are the coolest but—"

"But it's not what she dreamed when she started the label."

"Yeah."

Claudie's phone rings. She leaves her plate on the arm of the chair to answer it.

"Hey, Shelley."

"Afternoon. How's it all going up there?"

"Place hasn't been hit by lightning yet." Claudie smiles. "But we still have no power."

"Right, I'll call on the radio next time."

Claudie steps toward the window. "You okay in town?"

"It's all good. I came into the office. Dylan was getting tired of me cleaning the house around him and listening to the emergency services on their radio frequency. The weather's clearing up. We should be back to our regularly scheduled summer heat soon. But it'll be longer before the water subsides."

"Okay. Good to know."

"The girl still okay there with you?"

"Yep. How're her friends?" Lien lifts her head.

"Last I saw them they were playing pool in Sheila's bar. Nice enough kids, but bloody intense when they get on the piano." Shelley laughs a belly laugh. "Hey, the reason I called. Iron Pot's burst its banks at Scalpel Gorge. Can you get in and take a gander at the flood protection down there?"

"No problem," says Claudie. The park's been working on a platypus habitat in that area; they need to make sure it's all okay.

"Thanks, sis."

"Talk soon."

Shelley hangs up.

"That was the station. I've got to work on something," Claudie says to Lien.

Lien shifts forward in her chair. "Do you want a hand?"

Claudie shakes her head. "Nope. It's a bit of a drive and then I have to hike in. And it's still raining. You'd be stuck with the truck for an hour or two. You're better off staying here."

Lien nods. "Okay."

"You'll be fine alone for a few hours." Claudie pats her arm then draws away. "You can play guitar. Or read some magazines."

"Yeah, no. It's not a problem." Lien's eyes are overly wide as she smiles.

Claudie takes it slow on the wet roadway, goes as far as she can on the unsealed roads, then steps down from the four-wheel drive and strides across the ground. Her boots squelch and stick in the wet mud. The creek's escaped its banks. It whirlpools between the rocks and the ferns. But the rain's mostly stopped. The insects have started up; their shrilling rises and falls. The lorikeets and magpies are screeching and calling to one another.

"You're right, Shell. It's close to bursting here."

The radio crackles in reply. Shelley's voice comes through. "You talking to yourself again?"

"Just keeping you up to the minute. I'm gonna signpost for anyone coming in from this side of the park." Claudie doesn't want to be fishing people out of the water downstream. She kicks at the inadequate barrier between the creek and the toilet block. "Plus I'd better get a few more sandbags down. The rain's stopped so it should be okay, but we've got more water coming down from the mountains so it could be wet around here tomorrow."

"Yeah, I believe it. You need help? I can get out there."

"Nope, stay put. I've got fresh sandbags in the truck. I'll be done in an hour or so. Then I'll head up to the Murray Scrub site and give it a once-over."

"Thanks, Claudie."

"How are the road warnings going?"

"It's a mess. This storm was a killer. And it's not over. But we're getting there."

It's going to be a long afternoon. Claudie opens the back of the four-wheel drive and hoists a sandbag over her shoulder. She's proud of the way her body handles this. She's balanced. Resilient. It's taken time and effort to get to the point where she can take on this kind of back-breaking work by herself.

Lien's back in the cabin. It's appealing to think of her there, glancing in the mirror, padding about in Claudie's socks, looking out the window at the sky.

Claudie has more to do than she thought. By the time she leaves the Murray Scrub site her muscles ache. The cicadas and frogs are out in force, their constant noise a familiar sign of nightfall. The sun settles down toward the mountains as she drives home.

Claudie climbs the stairs to the deck. Here she can watch the night fall. The red-gold sun hangs in place, briefly blazing at the edge of the world, pressed between the horizon and the undersides of the evening's heavy clouds. It lights the tops of the trees in bright rose and gold. Claudie pauses on the narrow deck. She lets her muscles unwind as the wind twists around her.

For three years, summer and winter, this view has been Claudie's alone. She's lived and worked under this span of the sky and hiked among the ferns and the scrub and the lush bush. She's watched for dangers from fire and flood, from human encroachment, from sunburn. It's beautiful, but it's not an obvious beauty; there's no sweeping coastline or mighty rock formations for tourists to ogle and photographers to capture. But there's an immutability to the place, a vastness and permanence that sits alongside the sharp beauty found in tiny things. It's only visible to those who wait. Claudie's had plenty of time to do that.

Although it's late, the air is still humid and warm against her skin. It's unsettling, like a stranger's heavy hand. Energy builds in Claudie's bones and tightens her lungs. The storm's broken for the time. The air is thick and electric.

The door swings open. "Hey," Lien says as she steps out.

"Beautiful, yeah?"

"I'm starting to agree."

They stand together without speaking. The clouds tumble across the sky, edged by the last rays of sunlight and heading east. A few distant stars brighten the gaps between the clouds. None of the stars are visible for long enough to point out to Lien and name, though Claudie can distinguish many of them now, more than she could before she moved here.

Claudie's watched this same sky on clear nights, during crisp winters, and through storms. From the deck of the cabin the world is huge; it seems to go on forever. She's always been tiny beneath it. Now, standing with Lien, the universe is less lonely. It's also less safe.

The rain starts again and quickly becomes heavy. They head inside.

"I MADE, UH, I MADE us some dinner," Lien says. She's annoyed that her voice cracks. But Claudie's intent and private. It was presumptuous, intrusive, to take over. Claudie's eyes shift to Lien's. Lien says, "I'm sorry. You were gone a while, and I couldn't get in contact but I wanted to be helpful."

Lien can almost see Claudie thinking. After a pause, Claudie says, "That was kind of you. Thank you." She steps into the kitchen and grabs a glass from the cupboard. "You need a drink?"

Lien shakes her head. "No, thanks." She's relieved. In the kitchen, Claudie fills the glass and lifts it to drink. Her throat bobs as she swallows. Her shirt is short-sleeved and the sleeves stretch around her muscular shoulders. A tuft of hair pokes out under her arm. Lien looks away, which is stupid. But the tuft of dark hair is intimate. The sight of it is more personal than the perfectly bare underarms Lien is used to seeing on other women.

Lien's mind flashes to other areas where Claudie might have hair. Claudie's lived here for years. She'd hardly be having regular waxes with smiling women in clean white coats. Lien chews on her lip. She hasn't touched a woman who's "au naturel." When Claudie glances up, Lien blushes as though Claudie might know what she's contemplating. She clamps down on her thoughts.

Lien lights candles, and Claudie sets the table. They eat dinner there, one on either side, their own little version of domesticity. The room's quiet around them as they talk.

"First CD I bought was Nirvana's *In Utero*. My dad looked at me for a long time, then shook his head as if everything was falling apart. But when he heard it he understood. I played 'Heart Shaped Box' about a thousand times that month."

Lien leans forward. "God, yes. 'Heart Shaped Box' was my favorite. My cousin burned it for me. I used to lie in bed when I was little and listen to it on my headphones over and over as though it had some deep meaning."

"It does!" Claudie's grin is amused and toothy.

Lien gasps and laughs at once. "Well, not that meaning. I was six."

Claudie's eyes are bright as her laughter joins Lien's. Lien thinks, *I could kiss you.*

THEY'VE FINISHED DINNER. CLAUDIE RINSES the plates; she's glad of the small space between her and Lien's bright sincerity.

"I'm having a glass of wine," Claudie says when she's finished. "Do you want one?"

"Definitely."

Claudia pours two tumblers full of her parents' slightly questionable Shiraz.

"Did your dad really make this in the bath?"

Claudie laughs. "He has a bath he's set aside in the cellar for the purpose. But I don't think he uses it any more. He has this friend with a vineyard and now and then they get together and make a new blend no one's ever wanted to try before."

She hands Lien a glass at the table but takes hers to sit in the deep chair near the window. It's a small room, though. She's not far away.

"I like this one," Lien says.

"My dad will be happy to hear that."

"You don't like it?"

"It's grown on me."

After a second glass, the wine goes down more easily.

"I'd love to hear you play again," says Lien. She sounds formal. "I listen to a lot of music. And yours is something special. Will you play for me?"

Claudie considers her. "Pick your poison," she says, gesturing at the instruments on the wall.

"Which one's your favorite?"

"I want you to choose," says Claudie.

It's not intended as a test. Not really. But Lien passes. "The acoustic six string please."

"Why that one?"

"It's obviously important to you. I love hearing people play an instrument that has a history in their hands."

Claudie picks it up. She plays something she's been working on first, a piece with some tricky countermelodies and a constant thwacking bassline. Lien's focused gaze thrums in Claudie's veins.

"Are there vocals?" Lien asks.

Claudie hesitates. This is too much. But Lien's face is bright and sweet. It's a joy to play for someone who wants to hear. A joy, too, that it's Lien rather than a koala or a passing snake. Claudie smiles to herself.

She starts playing again and sings along, keeping her voice soft below the thrum of the guitar.

Lien tips her head. Her face is intent. "I know your voice," she says, soft.

Claudie freezes.

"You were the lead singer of that band, that—Grand Echo." Claudie doesn't answer. Lien's frowning. "Weren't you?"

Claudie puts the guitar back in its place. "I was," she says.

When she sits, Lien's studying her through careful eyes.

"You don't have to stop playing," she says.

Claudie doesn't say anything.

"Sorry. Okay." Lien takes a breath. "Sorry." Her smile defuses the moment. "Guess I'm washing up then."

IT WAS STUPID TO PLAY, Claudie thinks. Stupid to try to impress this sunny, fashion-conscious girl the weather dumped in the cabin.

She goes to dry dishes.

After the washing up is finished, Lien says, "You don't want me to apologize. But I am sorry I made you uncomfortable. It wasn't intentional. I'd never seen you guys perform. And I didn't see you perform live. But you were on my playlists. So it just… when I heard your voice I had to say something."

"That's okay," says Claudie. "It makes sense." Claudie's discomfort is not Lien's fault.

Lien sits in one of the chairs.

"Thank you for playing for me. I enjoyed it."

Claudie sits. She might be exposed, but part of her is grateful. Part of her is amazed she could make it through a song. Part of her hates that this one girl can make everything different.

"I'll play for you again," she says. "Later. If you want. I just needed a break."

IT'S EASIER TO SHARE A bed now. They keep space between them but it's not awkward. It's easier to share a morning, too.

Late in the afternoon, Claudie steps out to check on her shed's waterproofing. Lien borrows her phone. It's black; heavy and old-school and not in a hipster way. It's also still three-quarters charged so there must be benefits to ancient technology. Lien sits cross-legged on one of the chairs in the living room as she calls Beau. The color fades from the sky, blue to creamy pink. The treetops shift from green to muted gold and gray. The scene is soft and achingly lovely, despite the vastness. White birds circle the treetops, squawking, then settle down.

She dials Beau's number. "Hey, babe," Lien says when he finally answers.

"Li! Hi! I was beginning to think you'd forgotten us altogether."

"No, no. Of course not. I don't want you to feel like that. Sorry. We don't have a lot of battery charge, and this isn't my phone."

"Li. I'm not mad. Just glad to hear from you."

"Is everything okay for you guys?" Country towns can be hostile to people like Beau and Kam and Megan.

"We're great. All good. Aside from having to shower in the Visitor Information building. How are you? Can you talk for a second?"

"For a second, yep. I'm good. I'm okay. Yeah." She's not quite sure how to explain how she is.

"Your knee's still messed up?" Beau sounds concerned. Lien wishes they were in the same room.

"It's fine. I mean, it's okay. But that's not the problem. The weather means I'm stuck here until the road's not flooded."

Beau hums. "Bummer. I'm sorry, Li. It must be awkward."

"It's not like that. Not at all. It's fine. There's… I don't know. There's stuff to do. I like it."

Beau's voice is high with surprise. "Oh. Good, then. Are you stuck in that creepy cabin we could see from the campsite?"

"That's the one. It's not creepy from the inside, though. I wish you could see."

"Me too."

"I miss having my phone."

"I'll bet."

"But enough about me, are you guys doing okay?" Lien tries to imagine what it's like. "Did the campsite get washed away? Is that why you're in town?"

"Not quite. The site's on pretty high ground. That first night some of us slept in our cars. But Raf and Matty managed to keep their tent up. So to speak."

"I don't want to know!" Lien laughs.

"And then we rebuilt tent city in the rain the next day. It was miserable. You should have seen us. We got everything up just in time for the rangers to come and get us. But it was a relief. We're staying in the community center here. There are beds and everything. It's weird. But it was good of them."

"What have you all been doing?"

"Playing a fucking lot of card games. Did you know your girl Annie's a secret poker shark? We had a drink at the local bar last night. They stared at us like we were from outer space for the whole first half hour. But they have some good vegetarian nachos. So there's that. And Megan and Matty got to dueling on the piano in the corner. It was mostly in tune, and some of the guys here love a sing-along. All these white cis men singing along with 'Working Class Man' and 'Downeaster Alexa,' you know. Annie made Matty promise not to play any hip-hop."

"Yeah, that would have been a nightmare. It all sounds, um, interesting."

"It kind of is. Plus, we've been getting to know one another better." Lien imagines his sly smile.

"A wild guess you're talking about you and Annie?"

"Yeah." His tone warms Lien to her toes.

"Lots to talk about?" she says.

"Yeah."

He sounds dreamy, and Lien laughs, but an image flashes in her head, the two of them together like that and learning one another's skin, finding one another's pleasure. It stings in a lonely way. "I'm happy for you," she says. And she means that, too.

"Thank you, love." Beau's voice is deep and warm. He moves on. "So. Tell me about this ranger woman. Thank fuck she found you. But what's it like? Is she cool? A bore? Some kind of hippie?"

"No. It's all good."

"Oh, wait a sec, has this woman kidnapped you?"

"No, Beau."

He pauses. She's not sure if he's joking as he goes on. "Okay, look. I know she's listening in. So if you want to tell me something that's going on then, um. Do something you'd never do. Like. I don't know. Call me something cute. Like baby or champ or something."

"I've probably called you champ. I went through a champ phase." She frowns. She's pretty sure she calls him baby all the time, too. But it's not important. She hasn't been kidnapped. "Beau. Honestly. It's

nothing like that. Anyway she's not listening in; she's out in the shed."
Lien blushes and she's not really sure why. She stops talking. Starts
again. "It's nice."

Beau's not easy to divert. "It's nice? What are you—Lien Hong. Do
I detect—Do you have a crush? I know, I know. She's could walk in at
any time. How about you knock once for yes and two for no?"

"Beau." Lien giggles. "What am I going to knock on, you fruitcake?"

That silences him for a second. "Well, okay. Hey, Annie's hanging
around looking like she has something to say."

"Hi, cutie," says Annie.

"You are," Lien replies.

"You have to tell me everything. What's Beau talking about? What's
she like, this mysterious ranger of yours?"

Lien draws breath. "She's fine. Normal. Nice. She's all park ranger
and competent."

"Oh. I see. Competent, hey?" Annie teases.

"No, that's *not* what I mean. It's been kind of fun. We've cooked and
fixed stuff and talked mostly. We talked about music a lot. Oh, hey,
guess what? She used to play for Grand Echo. You know. The indie
band. They were big in Sydney when we were in Uni."

Annie gasps. "Lien! You were rescued by Claudie Sokolov?"

"Yeah." She should have known Annie would remember Claudie's
name...

Annie sighs. "They were great. I remember that one video they did.
And I saw them live a couple of times, while you were over abandoning
me in Singapore. Claudie Sokolov... The girl is hot. Well, she was back
then."

"Annie," Lien protests.

"Well, she might be old now. Not that I have anything against that.
But please don't tell me that she got old and lost her sex appeal."

Lien pauses. "Nope," she says.

Annie chortles.

"I meant she's not old," says Lien. "And even if she were—" Annie's laughing. Lien imagines her with her head thrown back. Annie has a great laugh.

She hears Beau take the phone.

"Of course," he says. "Unbelievable. Our little Lien picked up a rock star."

Lien blushes. "I know. It's sort of… it's a bit. I wish you were here."

Beau's tone softens. "But you're okay. Yeah?"

"Apart from the knee I'm fine, Beau. Really."

"We'll see you soon. Love you."

CLAUDIE DIDN'T FIND A PROBLEM in the shed, which is a relief. She comes up the stairs and finds Lien in the main room. Lien turns away from the window. "Hey," she says.

"Hey." The day is brighter now. The clouds have lifted high; their undersides are curved and bright in the clear gray light. "Seems like the rain's clearing. But it'll still be a couple of days before the road opens."

Lien nods. She's obviously become used to the idea that she's stuck here with Claudie rather than having fun with her friends in town. At least she doesn't seem frustrated about being here anymore.

They have little they need to do. After breakfast Claudie heads out for an hour. She drives part way down the road then hikes in toward the upper section of the creek. The flow is still high; the green water twists and turns up the creek banks. She walks farther to check on what she can see of the upper estuary and the little natural dam that shapes the area. She buzzes Shelley.

"I'm at the upper section of Iron Pot. All okay here. Lucky as I can't bring any equipment in."

The radio crackles. "Great news. Thanks for checking it out."

"No worries. Pretty sure it's my job."

Back at the cabin, Lien's sitting on the deck with her back propped against the cabin wall and her muscular legs stretched out before her.

Claudie lets her gaze trace down Lien's bare legs. She lowers herself to sit beside Lien. It's sunny. The wood is warm under their bodies, steaming as it dries. Claudie leans on one bent knee; her attention is somewhere between the brightening sky and the girl.

"All your rangering done for the day?" Lien asks.

"Sure is."

"Good." Lien leans back. Her skin is warm gold in the sunlight. "It's incredible here. Though I guess you're used to it."

A few days ago Claudie would have agreed. Yes, she's used to being here. But everything is new now she's seeing it with another person. "Sometimes," she says. "Those clouds are altostratus." She points.

Lien repeats the name. "They're beautiful," Lien says.

Claudie smiles. It's true, the clouds are beautiful, scudding and rippling away mid-height in the sky. Watching them with Lien makes them fascinating. So many different things interest Lien.

"So tell me about your job," Claudie asks. "You write about music?"

Lien pulls her lower lip into her mouth. She's blushing. "Mostly I write about parties."

"Parties?"

"Parties and clubs. You know, where to go. Who's there among the crowd, what they're wearing. I write about the music too. And fashion. I mean, I'm not just a gossip reporter."

Claudie tamps down her disappointment that Lien isn't some prodigy *Rolling Stone* music reviewer. It's not as though Claudie needs a music reviewer these days. But she's impressed with Lien and wants her to be amazing. "You don't need to be embarrassed. It sounds cool. Not like anything I could do, really."

Lien considers her and grins. "Well, no, you have to like parties and people."

Claudie flushes. She's stung. "I like people. I used to like parties, too." It's mostly true.

Lien holds up her hands. "Sorry. That, no. That wasn't really what I meant. But—I guess. You're happy with your own company. I don't see that a lot back in Sydney. Most of my friends are out all the time; we're always busy at parties and surrounded by people. Everything's done fast or not at all. In Sydney it's strange to have time that's quiet. But here all your time is quiet. And somehow you don't seem lonely. You seem certain of yourself, here or wherever you are."

"It's lonely sometimes," Claudie admits.

"Do you have to stay here?"

"I guess not. I signed a contract for one year. That's been over for more than two. But I stayed." She thinks. "I could go if I wanted to."

Lien's direct. "Do you want to go?" She studies Claudie.

"There are good things. It's a good life. I'm still here so I guess I don't."

They watch one another. Claudie can't look away from Lien. Her eyes fix on Lien's throat, then her wide mouth, her dark and brilliant eyes.

Oh.

She swallows with difficulty. She can't kiss Lien; she rescued her. It'd be taking advantage of the fact that they're trapped here. It would be exploitative. She's not that woman.

Lien moves closer. The sky is bright blue and silver-gray behind her. Her tongue flicks out to touch her lip.

Claudie shifts away. "I need to go and um—take a look at the roof. From indoors." Her voice croaks.

Lien blinks. She freezes. "Of course. No, sorry. Of course." Her cheeks are red.

"It's not that I don't—Sorry." Claudie goes into the house.

AFTER A FEW MINUTES LIEN follows. This situation is not going to suddenly be less awkward. Even if she never goes back inside and stays standing here on the deck until she can get out of here, she'll still be embarrassed.

Inside, Claudie's putting away the plates and cups. Lien goes to help. The space in the cabin is cramped. It's always been small, but it hasn't been impossible. Now Lien tried to kiss Claudie; now Lien has to shrink into herself so she can move past Claudie without brushing against her.

But when Lien can look at Claudie again, Claudie's blushing too; her cheeks are pink under her tan as she turns away from Lien. However much Claudie rejected Lien, the electricity between them is not one-sided. At least Lien hasn't made a complete fool of herself over someone who hasn't even noticed her.

They don't have much to do in the cabin, definitely not enough to fill all the space they're keeping between them.

It's still daylight when Claudie steps into the kitchen to cook. She sighs, her head half in the pantry. "What can we make this time? We have a tin of beans and tomatoes—"

"Sounds like about half of a recipe for chili," Lien says.

"That'll work. That okay with you?"

"Of course. Hey, you know I'm gonna pay you back for all of this. Once I'm out of here."

Claudie nods slowly. "Okay. Thanks."

Claudie throws everything together in a big heavy pot and turns on the gas. "Best if it cooks for a while," she says. "Hey, I'm going out to check on the generator. If the water's gone, I can get it back on."

Lien watches from inside as Claudie stands on her toes to flick a switch at the power box thing above the door. Nothing happens. Claudie opens the door and grabs her tool kit. She pulls on her boots and heads out. After a few minutes, the light in the living room sputters and comes to life. The refrigerator clunks twice, then hums.

Claudie walks back in.

"You did it!" Lien says. She bounces across the room and grabs Claudie in a tight hug. "I can't believe it."

Claudie's eyes are bright. She's smiling. "I couldn't get to it before. There was too much standing water. It would have been really unhelpful to have electrocuted myself. But there was nothing much wrong. A circuit had blown. Stupid system. Do you want the first shower?" she asks. "It'll be hot in about half an hour."

"Oh, my god." Lien catches her breath. "Oh. No, you have it first. You fixed it, you deserve it."

"I think you're missing showers a lot more than I am," Claudie says. "Maybe more than any human." Her lips are pressed together, and her eyes twinkle. The certainty and fondness make Lien's heart pause.

"Thank you," Lien says.

Half an hour later she's standing under the flow with water rushing over her head. She's warm and soapy. The water pressure's not great, which makes sense. The plumbing probably trails from the tank up the hill. It hardly matters. Every second Lien spends under the warm flow makes her more herself.

She wraps herself in a towel. It's nerve-racking walking across the room, but Claudie keeps her eyes turned to the floor. "I got you some clean clothes if you want them," Claudie says.

Claudie's given her running shorts and another band T-shirt. As she walks into the bedroom to dress, she's pretty certain Claudie's eyes are on her back.

THE NIGHT'S CREPT UP. LIEN'S ready for bed. She brushes her teeth and beams at herself in the bathroom mirror. The room's tiny enough that she could touch both walls from the toilet. She spits and rinses her mouth. Her hair is a dark shining sheet. Finally it's clean. Claudie's Silverchair T-shirt is soft from wear. It hangs loose about Lien's body. Lien hitches up the neckline, but it's not much use. She is going to have to let go of the fact that she looks like a *Flashdance* backup dancer.

She walks into the empty living room. "Come out here," calls Claudie from the deck.

Claudie's leaning on the railing looking over the vast expanse of nothing. "Come and stand at the edge here," she says. "It's like the edge of the universe."

It's dark; there's nothing out there. The world smells rich and wet. Lien holds herself still and looks out with the cabin lights behind her.

"Wait a sec," says Claudie.

She steps back toward the house and reaches inside the cabin door. Everything goes dark.

"Hey—" Lien can't see a thing. They haven't had lights in days, and now Claudie's turning them off. The blackness seems complete.

"You're okay," says Claudie. "It'll take a moment for your eyes to adjust. I figured—It's been raining so much. You haven't had a clear night up here. I wanted to show you." She moves beside Lien against the railing.

And as Lien's eyes accustom themselves to the dark, the sky opens up above them. The Milky Way sweeps a path of light across the great black bowl. Around that the night extends from one clear horizon to the other, lit by a thousand layers of stars on stars, dazzling bright in the dark.

The universe goes on forever. It's huge, and Lien's tiny and breathless in front of it.

In that moment nothing is worth thinking about beyond that sky, nothing but the huge universe and Claudie's hand, steady and close beside Lien's on the railing, Claudie's warm body so near. Lien twines her pinkie around Claudie's. They stand under the stars, still and silent.

When Lien turns, Claudie's cheekbones are traced in blue-white and her eyes reflect a thousand pinprick lights. She's beautiful. She's from a whole other world.

Their kiss is inevitable. It's soft, on an exhale, careful lips against lips with nothing else touching but their fingers tangled on the railing. Claudie opens her mouth to Lien. Lien doesn't take a breath. She doesn't think to hold back. She turns to face Claudie, lifts herself to her toes and presses her tongue between Claudie's lips, catching Claudie's voiceless moan. She presses her body against Claudie's chest and breasts, needing more and closer. Claudie draws her in and wraps her arms around Lien's shoulders.

They break away. The whole world is stretched out around them.

"Oh," Lien says. She wants to laugh or cry or maybe stop breathing forever just to kiss Claudie like that.

"Okay." Claudie's voice shakes, but she meets Lien's gaze and smiles a private smile. Her eyes are asking a question. Lien nods and Claudie bends, still smiling, to kiss her again and again.

LIEN IS COMPACT AND BREATHLESS against Claudie. She's up on her toes and kissing back, so intently kissing back. Claudie didn't plan to kiss her. Honestly, using star gazing as an opening is a shameful cliché. But that shame that doesn't seem to matter to her body, which has entirely excised her brain.

Claudie holds on tight. She lets herself go. Her heart beats fast and hard in her chest.

When Claudie shifts back, Lien's brow is drawn into a tiny furrow. Her lips are pink and soft. She's too pretty to take in. But Lien grins brightly and comes after Claudie. They kiss again, slower. Claudie's mind is full. She slides her palm upward from Lien's hip and slips it under her own T-shirt to press her fingers in at Lien's waist.

"Can I take you to bed?" Claudie asks, speaking too quickly and keeping her voice low so it doesn't echo over the treetops.

"God, yes. Absolutely," breathes Lien almost before Claudie's finished speaking. Lien's voice holds a laugh, as though she's amazed there's any question.

Claudie presses Lien against the cabin wall before they go inside. They kiss again and again, open-mouthed and eager. They're rushed. Lien's injured knee is more obvious as they go through the door. Claudie narrowly avoids kicking her. She's clumsy, foggy with desire. Lien steadies her with a hand on her arm. They kiss again.

In the tiny bedroom, Claudie turns on the bedside light. Lien's eyes flick to Claudie. Her cheeks are flushed and her pupils are wide and black, confirming Claudie's welcome. Claudie moves the mosquito netting aside and lowers Lien across the foot of her bed. The bed is low to the floor, and Lien drops back hard onto it. Claudie helps to tug Lien up onto the pillows. They're not exactly graceful, but the netting drops around them as a veil and makes everything secret and enchanted, the two of them in all the world. Lien looks up from the bed covers; her gaze glints through her black lashes, both bright and dark.

Claudie holds still. "It's, uh, it's been a long time since I've—" She hesitates. Claudie's spent three years in the bush. She hasn't touched anyone except herself. And here's this gorgeous, polished girl, who's used to other polished people and so in control of her own self.

"I'm pretty sure you haven't forgotten anything. Please, Claudie. Come here," she says. Her soft voice breaks over the words. She reaches for Claudie, and that makes everything easier.

Claudie exhales as she moves forward. "Okay."

The rain has stopped. Even the birds and animals are quiet, save a tiny peep of a happy frog or the far off shrill of a cicada testing its wet wings. They can hear the sweeping wind in the treetops.

Claudie stretches her body out along Lien's and supports her head on one hand. Lien reaches out and cups Claudie's face, and Claudie bends toward her easily, kisses Lien again, and her tongue traces Lien's parted lips. She runs her hand from Lien's shoulder over Lien's chest. Lien's back arches, pushing her neat breast up into Claudie's hand. Her nipple is tight under the T-shirt. Claudie buries her fingers in the soft not-even-a-handful flesh of Lien's breast and kneads.

"Oh." Lien mewls at the back of her throat. Her hips roll upward against Claudie's.

Claudie moves closer, hovers over Lien, and supports her weight on her arms. Lien wraps one leg around Claudie's hip. Her heel smacks against Claudie's upper thigh. She tightens her grip and drags at Claudie, pulling her down so she lies heavily against Lien. They grind together through layers of clothing.

Lien's breath is tiny eager pants in Claudie's ear. It takes will power for Claudie to pause at all.

"Hold up," she says. She could come far too easily just rubbing herself against Lien's mobile body. Lien's moan is mostly a grumble, and Claudie smiles into it, but sits up.

Claudie runs a finger around Lien's waist, stretching the waist band of her own running shorts which have been dragged low on Lien's hips. Claudie's hand slips into the space between the pants and the warm skin of Lien's belly. When she looks back into Lien's face, Lien's lip is caught between her teeth, biting hard.

Claudie trails her fingertips over the soft strip of Lien's pubic hair, then lower. She presses gently, dips into warmth and wetness there. She doesn't breathe as Lien drops her head back, mouth open but noiseless, throat bared. Lien's hips rock upward against Claudie's hand.

Claudie buries her fingers deeper into Lien and runs circles into the softness, tracing over the nub under Lien's skin, then dipping farther into Lien's slit to wet her fingertips. Lien twists under her touch. Claudie runs her wet fingers in tight circles, rubbing harder. Lien arches up again. One of her hands drops to cover her eyes as her body writhes deliciously.

Claudie slides her free hand up Lien's body to cup and knead her breast. She rolls the nipple between her fingers, and Lien's head turns to and fro on the pillow with her hand fluttering to cover her eyes; she's lost in two sensations. Claudie's heart pounds. Her breath is rough to her own ears. She can't resist rolling her body to rub against Lien's thigh.

There's no one here, nothing to worry about. And they have all the time in the world. Claudie's groin coils with pleasure, but she holds back.

"Tell me what you want," Claudie says. She might not have done this in a long time, but she knows what to ask. She can read a body, she prides herself on that, but she doesn't know Lien well enough to read everything.

"Oh. I don't know. Keep going."

"Hey," Claudie cajoles. "Tell me."

"I don't, um—"

"More of this?" Claudie is direct in the face of Lien's shaky breathing and unexpected reticence. "Or do you want my fingers inside of you? Or my mouth on you. Or something different—"

She stops speaking as Lien holds still. It's awkward, asking, and maybe Claudie's got this wrong. Maybe women these days don't talk about the specifics of what they like in bed. Claudie shakes herself. She's not that old.

"What do you want?" Lien asks.

Claudie narrows her eyes. "I am *very* into all of that."

Lien releases a breath. "God. I mean. Me too. All of that."

"All that at once?"

"Hush."

Claudie lets it go. She sits up a little to pull her running shorts down from Lien's hips. The half-light from the stars traces Lien's belly.

"Please," says Lien.

Claudie settles on brushing her fingers over Lien's clit, then rubbing around and around. She doesn't slide down Lien's body. She can read Lien's response better through her fingertips and by watching Lien's face, even though Lien has a hand half covering her eyes. Lien's thighs tighten. Her breathing speeds.

Claudie kisses Lien again, then curls her body to take Lien's nipple in her mouth. Lien's exhale is shuddering and sweet. Claudie wraps her tongue around Lien's nipple and suckles, keeping her hand moving tightly between Lien's legs. Lien's hips buck upward; her body goes rigid. Claudie pulls off her nipple to watch her face. Lien's mouth is open. Her body thrusts up. She drops her hand from her face and meets Claudie's eyes. Lien's eyes are frozen on Claudie's face. She cries out, then bites her lip to choke off anything further.

Claudie holds Lien close as her breathing slows. She tries not to grind against Lien. Lien turns her head and kisses Claudie, deeply and with intent.

"Let me," she says. Her fingers fumble to unbutton Claudie's jeans. Lien sits up and grapples to pull them down. Claudie lifts her hips to help. Lien's so polished and lovely. Claudie's been up here in the rough for years. But as Claudie's pants slip over her hips, Lien devours Claudie with her eyes. Claudie's too brightly turned on to be shy.

THE NEXT AFTERNOON SHELLEY'S VOICE crackles through the radio. Claudie climbs out of bed to answer while Lien stretches out on the sheets.

"How you doing, sis?" says Shelley.

"Yeah." Claudie clears her throat. "Yeah, good."

"Hey, I'm sorry to do this to you when things are quiet, but the rain brought down a bunch of trees and some power lines. I've got the SES checking down this way but no one can get in to the upper roads unless I hire a Caterpillar."

"Right." Claudie glances back at Lien. "You want me to check on the power lines up here."

"Have you got something better to do?"

Claudie exhales. "No."

Claudie drives out alone. There's sweetness in leaving someone in her cabin—no, not just any someone. There's sweetness in leaving warm, dazzling Lien in her bed. Usually Claudie leaves her cabin locked and empty, with everything switched off. Now the place is filled with Lien.

Claudie focuses. The rain's stopped. As soon as the water subsides, Lien will be gone.

Claudie finds debris on a roadway. She clears it off and drives up the road, making similar stops several more times. When she's finished, she parks on the dirt driveway and walks to the cabin.

She smiles at Lien; she couldn't not smile. "I'm famished," she says.

Lien steps closer and kisses her. "As it happens, I've got an early dinner ready."

Claudie keeps smiling but her smile freezes. She might like the idea of Lien in the cabin and in her bed, but she's not so excited about Lien's habit of taking over the place, hunting through cupboards that aren't hers and cooking as though she owns the place. Claudie takes a breath and thinks. She doesn't mind Lien being in her space. Worse, she likes it. She doesn't want to consider how worrying she finds that. She could definitely eat dinner. "Okay. That's—you're too good."

They eat out on the deck. "It's quiet up here," Lien says.

A flock of sulfur-crested cockatoos wheels above the trees, screeching like frightened pterodactyls. Claudie laughs.

"You know what I mean, though," Lien says.

"You have time to think."

"Exactly. And today I realized I don't miss my phone. I mean, don't get me wrong." She holds up her hands. "There are a million places I want to post updates. And I'd love to show everyone pictures of this place, too. But I haven't missed all that contact as much as I thought I would."

"Maybe you're getting used to it up here."

"Maybe. Yeah. But it makes me wonder if—" She frowns for a second. "You know, I write a lot. I submit a couple of short pieces every day. Plus all the social media updates. It's a lot. It keeps me busy and working and pays the bills. And it's fun. But I don't know if it's long-term."

"And you don't know if it's everything you want," Claudie says. It's a question Claudie doesn't ask herself, most days. "What options do you have?"

"I'm not sure. All these people support me. They've been great. But sometimes—"

"It's hard to get a hold on what you want when everyone's waiting for something from you."

"I know I don't want to let them down." Lien meets Claudie's eyes.

"You wouldn't be letting them down if you found something better."

Lien nods slowly. "Maybe."

After dinner, Claudie grabs her guitar. They sit on the small sofa, close together in the fading warmth and with the last, late sunlight angled on the floor. Lien's thigh is pressed alongside hers.

After the second song she puts the guitar down. Lien's turned around and is sitting cross-legged facing Claudie. Claudie leans forward to kiss her. Lien stretches out beneath her, but the sofa is too small. They have nowhere to fit themselves.

"Do you think it might be bedtime?" Lien says on a giggle as they rearrange limbs.

"Definitely."

Lien slips out to stand, holds out a hand to Claudie, and leads her to bed.

THEY SPEND THE NEXT DAY between the bed and the deck: reading in the sun and talking over food and taking time to know one another's skin. Every touch sparks between them. The cabin is filled in a way it's never been in Claudie's years here.

In the afternoon, it's easy for Claudie to find the guitar in her hands again. They're outside on the deck. The sun's dropping behind the mountains, leaving the air gold and warm.

Lien leans back on the railing. She's silhouetted in yellow-gold as she contemplates Claudie.

"What's up?" Claudie keeps playing, but it's a simple strum pattern so she can keep her eyes on Lien and not mess up on the rhythm.

Lien speaks fast. "God, Claudie. You're *meant* to play."

"What?" Claudie slows the strum and stops.

"I watch you and—I can't not say it." Lien's voice is choked. "It's so clear that you're meant to perform, Claudie. You're meant to sing and play and be a huge rock star up on the stage." She stands upright and lifts her hands and keeps talking. "I can't understand why you'd lock yourself away up here. Loads of people can be a park ranger. But I've never heard anyone play the way you do. Or sing—" She trails off under Claudie's scrutiny.

Claudie's chest is tight, as if everything inside could turn to stone. "That is none of your business." Her voice is tight, too.

Lien opens her mouth as though she's going to speak. She closes it, then opens it again. "I know but—Claudie." Her eyes are pleading.

"You don't *know*, Lien. You don't know. You don't know what happened to take me away from it." Claudie takes a breath. "Your dream was soccer—"

"But this is different. It's different for—"

Claudie interrupts. "In what way?" The words are clipped. The blood whooshes in her ears.

Lien stumbles on the words. "You can still play. You can still sing. Your hands and your voice—they work. Beautifully. It's not like that for me." There are tears in her eyes, but her fists are clenched. "My knee is done. I *can't* play soccer any more. Ever."

"It's no different. My hands and voice might work but there are things I can't do. And you really don't know anything about it. Fuck, Lien."

They stare, silver gray eyes into sparking dark. Lien deflates. "You're right. I don't know. I'm sorry. I just—I'm sorry."

They have nowhere to go. They're caught in this small space under the big sky. Outside the world changes color as it shifts between day and night.

OVER DINNER THINGS RE-BALANCE. CLAUDIE's quiet at first, but Lien tells a story about a dress-up party at her place. Despite the tension between them, Claudie's laugh is loud as she throws her head back in the outback and the silence. After dinner, after dishes, the cabin is dark. They no longer need candles, but they keep the lights low, as though they're saving energy for something else.

"Are we okay?" Lien asks.

"Yeah. We're good." Claudie reaches to flick at Lien's braid.

Lien steps close to Claudie. She moves Claudie back against the bench and then she kneels on the wooden floor. She measures her words. Even looking up Claudie's body, it's harder to say than she anticipated. "Can I go down on you? Here."

Claudie's eyelids flutter. She swallows.

Lien reaches up and undoes Claudie's fly button by button. She tugs her jeans and her underwear down over her legs. She runs a hand up Claudie's inner thigh. Claudie shifts her legs apart and holds still. Her skin is soft; her leg is smooth up to her upper thigh. Lien strokes a thumb across her pubic hair. Claudie's shiver is thrilling. She spreads

Claudie's folds apart and buries her tongue in the salty tang of Claudie's slit. Claudie's hips buck forward, and Lien smiles against her, letting her teeth press against Claudie's skin. Claudie wriggles. Lien presses in farther with her tongue and buries her nose in Claudie's soft fur while lapping at her.

The room is silent, save for Claudie's breathing and her soft, nonsensical murmurs of encouragement. Claudie's knees buckle, and she shifts her bottom back against the bench. Lien moves closer, stretches her neck, and hums against Claudie's clit. She draws Claudie into her mouth and sucks.

"I need more, I need more," Claudie murmurs and drops down, lowering herself to the floor. Lien tugs her away from the bench and lets her lie down, then kneels between her legs and buries her face deep in Claudie. She holds Claudie's hips at an angle to the ground to get a better position and she thrusts her tongue deep inside, then returns to sucking her clit.

Soon Claudie is arching off the floor against Lien's face. She keens as she comes. She pants through a smile as she drops her hips to the floor. Lien crawls over her body to wrap her up in Lien's touch.

CLAUDIE WAKES TO ANOTHER CLEAR day. The weather's heating up. For a second she's disappointed. Clear days mean the floods will abate, the water will shrink away, and Lien will leave. Then all this surprising chatter and brightness and sex and sunshine will disappear.

Claudie shakes the thought away. This is fun, sure. It's a nice break. But things will go back to normal when Lien's gone. Claudie will have her silence and solitude back. She'll be able to look over the bushland without hearing someone making tea in the kitchen. She'll be able to play her guitar without anyone's intent focus on her.

She stretches in the bed. It's not as if she's suddenly accustomed to sharing it. But Lien's asleep beside her, asleep on her back like a kid; her face is restful and pretty and her breath is innately human and fragile. For a second Claudie is drawn toward her warmth. It's terrifying. It's also sweet; it's a welcome Claudie forgot she was missing.

Lien stretches and rolls to one side to face Claudie. "Hi," she says, and her smile across the sheets makes Claudie's heart stutter. She blinks. Lien's too pretty to look at directly for long.

Claudie reaches out to Lien's bare shoulder, watching to be sure of her welcome. Lien moves closer into her arms. However warm the weather, Claudie wants her there.

"How's your knee?" Claudie says.

Lien furrows her brow. "It's a bit better. I think. A good bit better."

"Okay." Lien won't be here long. There are things Claudie wants to show her. "Can you walk?"

"I can walk across the room pretty comfortably. Not sure I'm up to a marathon yet. Why?" Lien asks.

"I'd like to take you somewhere. If you can walk to the driveway I can drive you."

"We can drive out of here already?" Claudie can't quite read how Lien feels about the thought of getting out of the cabin.

"Well, not out of here. We can't get across to the campsite or the town yet. The road's still under water that way. But we can drive up the fire trail behind us. The place I want to take you isn't far."

Lien grins. "A mystery adventure. Of course I want to come."

Lien dresses in her little olive green all-in-one now it's clean and dry. It's adorable and it's ridiculous. That combination comes with the Lien territory. Claudie pulls on shorts and a T-shirt.

Even going down the staircase is tough on Lien's knee. Lien winces every second step. Her breath is tight.

"We don't have to go," Claudie says. "It was an idea, that's all."

"No way. We're going, Claudia. I've almost made it down. And I want to. It'll be nice to get out into the open. I was getting a little stir crazy."

Claudie nods. She shouldn't want Lien to be happy trapped in her tiny cabin; it's hard to be reasonable, though. Claudie shakes it off. They climb in the car. Lien puts a light, sure hand on Claudie's thigh as Claudie drives. Claudie sweats beneath it.

Higher up on Iron Pot Creek, the rocks have created a series of small swimming holes, breaking up the tumbling water. The surrounds are leafy; the sky is bright summer blue. Beneath it the pools are clear green; their pebbled floors are touched by the sunlight.

With the roads blocked, this place is more secluded than ever. The air is heavy with summer, and the cicadas are shrilling on and on.

"Let's go in." Claudie takes off her clothes and walks in to her waist. Lien hovers at the bank.

"You should join me. The water's gorgeous." Claudie smiles. "And some non-weight-bearing exercise is just what the doctor ordered for your knee."

"Yes. Definitely…" Lien shifts her weight. She's nervous. Claudie might have taken this too far. "Um. Are there crocodiles here?"

Claudie breaks into a grin. The pool is too small for even freshwater crocs. "One day I am going to teach you a little more about Australian wildlife." Lien's answering pout is endearing so she adds, "I'll let you teach me about haute couture, if you like."

"Deal," Lien says. But she hesitates. "So that's a no on the crocs."

"A big no on the crocs. Trust me." She won't tell Lien about the other animals that live around here. Almost all of them are too frightened of humans to make an appearance anyway. "I won't let anything eat you out here. Except me."

Lien coughs out a laugh, then nods as though she's convinced herself. "Okay." She strips off her clothes and lets them drop to the warm rock where she stands. She tests the water with one foot, then steps in.

She's gorgeous in the dappled light. She moves easily. The water shifts around her naked thighs. Claudie could watch her forever. Instead Claudie dives and lets the water wrap between her legs and support her breasts. When she surfaces, Lien is standing still with her eyes on Claudie.

"Come here," Lien says. Her voice is certain but her teeth press into her lower lip.

Claudie doesn't hesitate. She swims over to her, then stands. She can see the drops of water on Lien's skin. She steps close, almost skin to skin, and buries her toes in the pebbly floor. She licks water from Lien's collarbone. Her tongue traces a path to the tendons that run down Lien's neck. Lien lifts her arms and tangles them around Claudie's neck. She curls her fingers into Claudie's hair. She lifts Claudie's head so they can kiss.

Lien's body is wet. Her skin is alternately cool and hot. As Claudie presses against her, Lien begins to rub herself on Claudie's upper thigh. Her soft strip of pubic hair is rough against Claudie's skin.

"I could come just doing this," Lien says.

Claudie reaches around to cup her ass cheeks and urge her forward, faster and tighter against Claudie's thigh. "Do you want to come?" she asks. "Right here?"

"God, yes. Please." Lien arches her back as though she can't help it, then buries her tongue in Claudie's mouth. Their kisses are messy and primitive. Lien's hips thrust forward into Claudie, getting more frantic as she works herself, pressing a wet trail against Claudie. Her breath comes in harsh grunts.

"Come on, sweetheart," Claudie says.

Lien keens and thuds her head against Claudie's shoulder. She shudders as Claudie strokes her back.

"Let me," says Lien once she has breath. She reaches between them and rubs tight circles against Claudie's clit. Claudie is close already. She comes, gasping for air, with her head thrown back and her leg muscles shaking.

They hold one another, legs weak, caught in one another's gaze. They stand thigh deep in the green pool, surrounded by birds and trees with the wind and sky above them.

Lien blinks up at Claudie. Claudie kisses her softly and they half walk, half stumble to sit on the sun-warmed rocks. They dry in the heat, bare-skinned and easy. They take their time to dress.

"I'm glad you brought me here," says Lien. She waves a hand to encompass the bright sky, the clear pool, the rocks and the great trees around it. "It's unforgettable."

BACK AT THE CABIN, LIEN sits on the deck. The railings are lit burgundy-gold in the evening sunlight. She's plugged Claudie's phone into the amp. The first song is quirky folk, summery and rich with voices. Claudie brings two glasses of water and joins her outside; she dangles her long legs from the deck.

"Let's eat outside," Claudie says later. Lien's happy with that. They've cooked pasta and sauce again. But everything tastes good with a view. She'll have to remember that. She doesn't stop herself from thinking that everything tastes good with Claudie there, too.

The deck holds a bench and a lounge chair. They both sit in the lounge chair, sharing the space despite the vast expanse of world that's right there. Once their meals are finished, Lien places their plates on the deck and leans back against Claudie's broad chest. Claudie wraps her arm around Lien with her hand on Lien's ribs. Claudie runs her thumb across the underside of Lien's breast. Lien's skin is alight with nerve endings. They breathe together.

They both jump when Claudie's phone vibrates in her pocket.

Lien huffs out a giggly breath. "I'd no idea they had vibrate functions on phones that old."

Claudie glares at her, then tugs the phone from her pocket and frowns at the tiny screen. "It's your boy. Tell him to be quick." She holds out the phone.

Lien scoots to the edge of the lounge chair to take the call. "Beau. Hi."

"Hi, love, how's it going?" he asks. His voice is so familiar it warms Lien. She wants to tell him everything, of course, right now. But this is not the time, with Claudie so near they could touch. She mouths "sorry" to Claudie.

"Good. Really good. I mean, everything's good."

Beau laughs at her. She imagines his eyes squeezed tight with bemused entertainment. She's not usually inarticulate. "That good, hey? What, are things heating up with your ranger?"

Lien turns away from Claudie as the blush steals up her face. "Hush," she says. "We'll talk soon." She looks up at the clear sky. Soon it'll fade into night. "Hey, aren't the stars amazing out here?"

"Awesome," Beau agrees. "Unbelievable. I told you we should get in touch with our country."

"Claudie reckons the water's subsiding."

"Claudie reckons, does she?" Beau's teasing again. Lien stands and steps away from Claudie as he goes on. "Well good, lovely. I miss you." He pauses. "We all do."

"Me too." She's used to talking everything through with Beau. Of course, isolation has advantages, especially when it comes to skinny-dipping, but it leaves her untethered, too.

"So what's gonna happen next, then? Once it's all cleared, we'll drive over and pick you up and bring you into town?"

"I guess."

"Then we'll all head to Rivers Fest, as planned." He pauses. "And next week we'll go back to Sydney—"

"Dude."

"What?" She wants to thump him. He's being obtuse on purpose.

"Just... don't. I don't want to talk about that right now."

There's a pause, and then Beau exhales. "Okay. Sorry. It's like that, is it?"

Lien turns and props herself on the railing of the deck. She kicks a gumnut off the deck with her bare foot. Behind her the plates clatter as Claudie picks them up and walks into the kitchen. Lien sighs. "It's like that. Yeah. Moving on. How's Annie?"

She can almost see his cheeks flush and his eyes light. "Good. Yeah. We, uh... Yeah good."

It's Lien's turn to laugh at him. "Excellent, babe. Well, as things are going so smoothly, I'll leave you to it. I can't wait to see you, though. And really talk."

The lounge chair creaks as Claudie sits down.

"Me too. Oh. Also. Your girlfriend called."

"She's not my girlfriend," Lien says immediately. She frowns out at the one star in the evening sky.

"Whatever you reckon. But she called anyway. She hadn't heard from you and she was worried. Which is kind of fair, Li." Guilt sours her stomach. "I told her what happened, where you were. She was… horrified. And I think pretty hurt that she hadn't heard from you. I passed it off like you didn't have a phone."

"Which I don't. Not with her number."

"Yeah, okay. But, Lien, I know I don't have much in common with her, but she's a nice kid. Don't—"

"I know. Okay." Her irritation with him is unreasonable but sharp.

"She thinks she's your girlfriend."

Lien swallows. "Beau. I know. Stop."

Claudie's in the lounge chair, right where she was when Lien took the call. She's facing away as Lien hangs up and sits beside her. Lien bends toward her, but somehow Claudie puts a tiny space between them. Lien swallows.

"Who's not your girlfriend?" Claudia asks. Her voice has an edge.

Lien turns to face her directly. She keeps her voice light. "Oh. Back in Sydney. This girl—" She shrugs. "It's nothing."

Claudie's eyes are quick. "This girl—?"

"This girl I'm kind of seeing. But—"

Claudie draws back. "This girl you're seeing? This girl you *were* seeing?" All her emphasis is on the "were."

Lien blinks. "Like I said to Beau, she and I, we're not girlfriends. He knows that. I know that. Things are different in the city. It was just—It's a casual thing."

Claudie's back is straight. "Does the girl know it's so casual?"

"Well. Yeah." Lien must sound dubious because Claudia's eyes narrow.

"When did you last 'see' her?" Claudie shifts to the edge of the chair and swings her feet to the floor.

"There's *nothing* wrong here," Lien says. She feels guilty, sure, but Claudie's being weird about this. "You don't get how things are. This is—"

Claudie's voice presses in. "When did you last see this girl?"

"It was the night before I left to come here." Lien can't stop her voice from rising. "Hey. You can't be jealous. I hadn't even met you then, Claudie."

Claudie stands. She steps back, avoiding looming over Lien. Lien stands anyway and they face one another. Claudie's an annoying couple of inches taller.

"This isn't about jealousy. It's about honesty. Not just with me. Does this girl know you're casually not her girlfriend?"

Lien presses her lips together, caught between the unfairness of this conversation, the frustration of not being able to make it all clear to Claudie, and the way she wants to be blameless here and is pretty sure she's not, not completely. "No. I never said. But Claudie, she shouldn't expect—We've never talked about it. She's never said we *are* girlfriends either."

Claudie's eyes flash.

"This is not a problem," Lien says. "You're being unreasonable."

"How long have the two of you been 'not-girlfriends'?"

Lien sighs. "About two months. Almost three."

Claudie takes a breath. "Three months."

"Like I said, you need to believe me. We're not girlfriends," says Lien.

Claudie's silent, deflated now, but the air between them is still charged. Her voice is low and tight as she says, "Look, it's not my business."

Lien can't bring herself to answer.

They have the chili for dinner. It's been on the stovetop through the day, cooking beans and vegetables and spices. It smells good, but Lien's not really hungry. Claudie hands Lien a plate and a fork.

"Thank you," Lien says.

"Do you want lime?"

"Yes, please." Lien longs to break this all apart, get everything back the way it was. She'd love to reach out and touch Claudie, but Lien's angry too, under the surface. She can't work out what to say.

They don't sit at the table. Claudie stands in the kitchen to eat. Lien takes one of the chairs. The meal is separated, polite but mostly silent and uncomfortable. Lien's been looking forward to it all day as the smell of cooking filled the cabin. She can't enjoy it anymore.

"I'll wash up," Lien says as she finishes.

Claudie nods her thanks. "I appreciate it."

As they pass in the kitchen Claudie's arm brushes against Lien's. Lien holds still.

Doing the dishes is steadying: the repetition, the quiet of the world outside, and the regular clatter of the dishes in the sink. Afterward, Lien approaches Claudie, who's taken up a position at the window. Claudie's hair is pulled back. Her face is outlined in silver. Lien longs to trace her jawline.

"Hey," Lien says. "I'm sorry."

Claudie turns. Her smile is tight but it almost reaches her eyes. She holds up her hands. "It's not my business. I shouldn't have said what I did."

"No," says Lien. "But I could have dealt with it better. I should have told you before. It honestly didn't enter my head. But I guess it should have." She stands with Claudie, keeping space between them. "Claudie. I'll be out of here in the morning," she says. "Please. I'd hate to leave things the way they are now. It's our last night."

Claudie fixes her with a clear gray gaze.

"Damn it," breathes Claudie. She moves toward Lien, stumbles forward to kiss her. Lien almost moans with relief. She twines her arms around Claudie's neck and kisses her back.

They kiss in front of the window for a minute, another minute, with their mouths open and desperate. It's not glamorous. They butt noses; Lien's hot and sweaty and wearing something that was washed in a sink, and yet somehow Lien has everything she wants right now.

"Bed," says Claudie. Her voice is rough. "Please."

She pulls Lien across the room by one hand. They're still kissing as they open the netting and tumble onto the bed. Lien forgets how low the mattress is, it seems as though they both do, and they thud uncomfortably one after the other. Lien laughs a little, breathless. Claudie kisses her again. Lien moans. She's embarrassed and overwhelmed and brightly greedy for everything Claudie's offering.

Claudie rolls Lien onto her back. Her hands are sure as she unbuckles Lien's belt, then unbuttons the safari suit. The front falls open. Lien sits up a little to let Claudie tug it from her shoulders. She lifts her hips. Claudie slides the suit down Lien's body with impressive efficiency. Lien's ankles get caught up in it but she kicks one leg and pushes it off with her toes. Claudie moves up the bed on her hands and knees and looks down at Lien. Her eyes meet Lien's; her pupils are wide and black.

"Fuck." Claudie breathes. "Fuck. I want you—"

Lien wets her lips with her tongue. "You've got me. Anything," she says.

"Stay there." Claudie hops up. Lien listens to the water run in the bathroom. When Claudie returns, her hands are cool and just-washed on Lien's skin. She places a tube of lube on the bed, then kneels over Lien and kisses Lien's mouth as her fingers blindly press against Lien's mound, seeking. Her fingers push inside where Lien's body is warm and wet.

"I want to be inside you," Claudie says.

"You are." Lien half moans as she looks up. She wants everything. "Please, Claudie."

Claudie presses two fingers farther inside Lien, cool and blunt against Lien's heat. "God. I want to be so deep inside you."

Lien blinks, turned on as much by the thought of Claudie wanting her as the movement of her capable fingers against Lien's insides. Lien lets her legs drop apart and rocks up to draw Claudie's fingers deeper into her. Claudie curls her fingers around and stretches Lien open.

Lien drops one hand down to her own clit and rubs tight circles against it. Her body tightens in response.

"Hey. Gentle," says Claudie. "Not yet. I need you to relax for me. Unless you want to come first?"

Lien swallows. "No. I want this." She can't help but moan as she lifts her fingers away. She strokes her own mound comfortingly and lets the other hand fall to the bed.

"You're amazing," Claudie says. "Beautiful, beautiful." She presses a third finger inside. Her breath tightens as Lien rolls her hips up. "More?"

"Yes."

Claudie pulls her fingers out of Lien. They come free with a slick noise and Lien exhales. Claudie uncaps the lube, and pours a generous amount onto her fingers and over her knuckles.

Lien shudders, then shudders again as Claudie pushes her fingers inside. They go in easily this time, with Lien already wide open and the fingers cool and slippery with lube. When Claudie slips her pinkie in to the tip her knuckles press hard against Lien's opening.

Lien gasps. Claudie traces her thumb across Lien's clit, easing the ache. Lien's hips flutter up against her.

"Do you," Claudie pauses, swallows. "Do you want my fist inside you?"

Lien nods. She can't speak.

"Have you done this before?"

"No, but I've read about it."

Claudie half laughs, but the twinkle and the unconcealed lust in Claudie's eyes make it impossible for Lien to feel silly for long. "Okay. Okay. We're going to take this slow, sweetheart. Can you relax for me?"

"God, yes," Lien manages. She drops her legs farther apart to give Claudie more room.

It's almost not like sex, lying with her legs spread wide, so much time to think, breathing steadily as Claudie presses forward, pushes her whole hand farther and farther inside her. It smells like sex. Lien's body is coiled like sex, but the act is pre-planned. It's slow. It's a thinking kind of sex. Lien works out how her body opens up, works out whether she can take the whole of Claudie's hand, considers how to shift her hips.

"I'm going to fold my hand up a bit, make it long and thin," says Claudie. The muscles strain in her arm. "You'll be fine; you can take this. I promise."

Lien runs her right hand down to stroke at her clit again. She wants to be wetter. Claudie draws her hand out and adds more lube.

"Don't tighten up too much, baby. Let go and breathe in for me."

Lien breathes in.

"Then out. You'll open up for me." Claudie places her free hand on Lien's chest. Its weight is certain and steadying. Lien is owned, held fast, caught between the hand pressed on her chest and the hand stretching her open. Her body is at once powerful and longing for more.

Claudie presses her knuckles forward, making gentle controlled pushes against Lien's opening. Her arm muscles are taut. She twists her hand. Every measured movement creates a wave of motion through Lien's whole abdomen. Lien rocks up into it and takes another breath. She exhales. It seems impossible, there's no way this will work, but then Claudie's knuckles twist and there's a soft wet pop. Lien gasps, amazed. She's filled. It's unbearable and perfect. "God, stay still," Lien says. "Don't—"

"I won't. I won't move." Lien opens her eyes to Claudie. Lust and tenderness mesh in Claudie's eyes. "I've got you," Claudie says. "I've got you. Breathe, sweetheart."

Lien releases her breath. Claudie pushes a fraction farther in, the base of her hand moving right inside Lien. "Okay. My hand's curled into a fist," Claudie says, "All the way inside you." Lien only vaguely understands the words. Her body is focused fully on Claudie's hand stretching and filling her. Lien relaxes, takes a breath and lets her body fall into this feeling. She rolls her hips a fraction, just a tiny, testing movement. Claudie's fist sends waves of pressure through her belly and back toward her spine.

Claudie hums with pleasure. "God. You're so good. I'm so deep inside you, you incredible thing."

Lien keeps her eyes fixed on Claudie's and rolls her hips again. Claudie's breath shudders from her. Every movement either of them makes is enormous. It swells inside Lien. The slightest shift takes over her whole body. Her nerves are alight with Claudie's touch.

Claudie moves her free hand to cup Lien's breast and stroke it. Lien lets Claudie wash over her.

They stay like that, Claudie on her knees, for a long few minutes. "Are you ready for more?" Claudie asks. Her voice is rough.

Lien can only nod.

Claudie rocks her fist into Lien; her shoulders shift forward in tight, perfect thrusts. Lien spreads her legs farther and lets Claudie move impossibly deeper, filling Lien's lower body.

Lien moans, walking that thin line between mindless pleasure and focus. Her hips roll instinctively. "I'm going to come," she says on another low moan. "God. Fuck." She rolls her hips again and can't stop herself burbling meaningless words. Her voice is low but rising with her pleasure. When she comes, it tumbles over her; she keens into the room and her hips thrust upward onto Claudie's hand. Her mind breaks apart.

She settles down, her eyes on Claudie's as if she's anchored there. Claudie leans forward into a kiss. Her lips are soft on Lien's, her tongue laps inside Lien's mouth. Lien closes her eyes as Claudie shifts back.

"I'm going to pull out of you," Claudie says.

"Okay," Lien breathes.

Claudie turns her hand and slowly draws out, slowly, slowly. There's a soft sucking. Lien sobs at the loss of all that sensation deep inside her. Claudie keeps kissing her and murmuring against her skin as Lien sobs.

"You amazing girl, you did so well," says Claudie. "You're wonderful."

Lien settles against Claudie's chest. Claudie's still dressed, and Lien whimpers a protest as her cheek presses against rough cotton. "You should be naked," Lien murmurs.

"I'll take them off while you pee," Claudie says. "Go on."

When Lien's back, they curl close in the bed, tangled with one another.

Later, Lien wakes. Claudie's naked beside her. Lien reaches out to kiss her and Claudie blinks open her eyes. She's drowsy and desirable. Lien slides down to curl beside Claudie's hips and buries her nose in Claudie's thick curls. She traces a line with her tongue up Claudie's slit, tasting, then flattens her tongue and laps tiny pressing licks over and over Claudie's clit, while Claudie writhes beneath her.

LIEN OPENS HER EYES. THE early morning light slants through the narrow window. Its brightness is filtered by the netting around the bed and falls soft and golden across Claudie's shoulders. Lien closes her eyes. She can't welcome the morning, however pretty it is. Morning means she is going to leave this quiet bubble that's separate from any of the ordinary concerns of time and space and having more than one outfit.

"Hey," Claudie whispers.

Lien opens her eyes and turns to meet Claudie's gaze. She tamps down her nerves.

"Good morning," Lien says. She arches her back between Claudie's sheets. Her body is gloriously alive and aching. She's worried, sure. Nothing will be the same by the afternoon. But right now, next to this gorgeous woman and lit by a pale yellow dawn, she's going to enjoy this one moment.

Claudie stretches beside her. "Good morning." Her eyes are scrunchy with sleep. Her body is long, and her shoulders are wide, and her skin is lovely.

Lien doesn't resist. She rolls close to Claudie. She kisses Claudie's shoulder and sucks against it. Claudie lets out an undignified little squeak. Lien grins against her skin, then pulls her body up to kiss Claudie's jawline and the edge of her mouth. Her breasts are pressed against Claudie's bare skin.

Claudie rolls into Lien. Her body is soft and warm against the mattress. Lien runs her thumb around Claudie's nipple. It hardens to the touch, and Lien cups her breast with one hand, supporting the weight of it while sliding the other hand down Claudie's body to stroke between her legs. Claudie moans and arches her back. She murmurs, "Please, please, please." Lien never wanted anything as much as she wants Claudie's helpless "please." She kisses the words away and brings Claudie, begging, to orgasm. As Claudie's breathing slows, Lien rubs herself, sleepy and slick, against Claudie's thigh. The building pleasure explodes through her nerves and up and down her limbs. Lien doesn't want to ever leave.

Later in the morning, when she's a little more awake, Lien stares at the ceiling. Claudie holds her hand. She takes a tiny breath as though she has something to say, but stays silent.

Lien turns her head to Claudie. "I guess I'll be—I'll get someone to collect me?" she asks before Claudie can speak.

Claudie winces. She closes her eyes.

"I can take you." Her voice breaks from her.

"Claudie—" Lien says. She doesn't finish.

"I know. I know. But—"

"But?"

"It's not a good idea. This whole thing between us wouldn't make any sense in real life. We're at such different places. You're in Sydney; you're a big city girl. And I'm here. I'm staying here."

Lien says, "I'm not asking you to move, Claudie."

Claudie shakes her head. "You're the center of a scene that's all big nights out and this social media stuff I don't even understand. You have casual relationships. Your life works with that."

"But it's not as though I can't do serious." Lien doesn't mention that she's never tried. "I know you're worried about that. But Nic and I, we weren't exclusive. And then I met you, and that was it. This thing between us was never casual."

"We were trapped in a cabin after an intense situation."

Lien's words rush out. "It wasn't about being trapped. Or the rescue. I met you, and there was this instant connection. I've never had that before. Not like that. I want to tell you everything and hear everything you want to say. I want to touch you. Every time I look at you the whole world goes silent. It's different, and I just want a chance. I think we could be something to one another. I'd love to try."

Claudie's voice is tight as though her throat is closed. "It's not only that, though, is it? It's not about your life in Sydney. It's not about this girl, Nic. Not really. Obviously we have a connection. But we're never going to work. You've worked hard for the things you have. You're extraordinary. You're busy and gorgeous and fashionable, and your world is never still. I need something different. And—I don't want someone to interrupt my life. I've built something here. It's been hard but it's mine alone. It's a good life. I don't want a different one."

Lien's hopes crumble. She tried. She put her heart way out there and it was rejected. And how can she argue when Claudie doesn't want anything to change?

"Okay," Lien says. Her eyes sting. "Okay. I don't doubt you love your life. And yeah. My life is in the city. It's important to me. I have to go back to it."

Claudie closes her eyes, but her voice is steady as she says, "Exactly."

Lien has nothing more to say. Half her heart has gone.

Lien dresses quickly in her one outfit. She pulls on her muddy brown, ruined Volleys. When she walks into the living room, Claudie's standing near the door. Her face is closed off.

"I hope you can figure out how to clean those shoes." She half smiles, trying to make this okay.

"Honestly, that's not my biggest concern," says Lien. She hates that Claudie still thinks she's so superficial.

"I know. I'll drive you out of here," Claudie says. She holds the door for Lien, and Lien walks through. They don't touch.

9

LIEN CLIMBS INTO THE TRUCK. Claudie faces the steering wheel, but she hesitates, one strong hand on the wheel, the other on the ignition. Lien flashes to a hundred other things those hands can do. Claudie starts the car. Lien's stomach twists. She can't make this okay.

They drive in silence until Claudie turns on the radio.

The creek's up ahead. They pass a sign for the campsite. Lien is a whole different person from the one who arrived a few days ago. Well, maybe not a whole different person. She's still not sure she likes camping. But she made it through an actual storm and had time to think without people on every side. She can cope with silence now.

Lien turns the radio down. "Before we, um, go our separate ways, I do want to thank you. For the hospitality."

Claudie's eyes flick to her, faintly amused.

Lien blushes. "Hush. You know what I mean."

"I do know." Claudie's mouth lifts up at one corner. "I do know. No thanks needed. Honestly." For a second their gazes meet. Then Claudie turns back to the road.

When they cross the creek, the water goes halfway up the tires. Higher. They move forward slowly. For a moment it seems as if they'll need to turn around and head to the cabin. Maybe forever. But Claudie keeps the truck fording through, and too soon they're on the main road heading down into the town.

They find Lien's friends in the information center parking lot. They're standing about, eying the tents spread on the asphalt before them. The tents have obviously been laid out in the sun to dry, though they still look pretty wet.

The pleasure of seeing everyone waiting bubbles up inside Lien. As soon as the car stops, she reaches for her door and swings herself out of the truck. She limps across the parking lot.

"Li!" Beau beams at her, and Annie squeaks with pleasure and bounds over. They both hug her tightly.

"You survived," Annie says. "Not that we doubted it for a second." The others hug Lien too: Raf and Matty, Megan and Kam.

"With some help," says Lien. She looks back at the truck. Claudie's climbed out and is standing awkwardly beside it. She is beautiful and out of place next to Lien's friends.

"Hi. You must be Claudia," says Annie. She holds out a hand to Claudie. "I've seen you play. And Ranger Shelley told us heaps about you."

Claudie shakes her hand.

Annie goes on. "We're so glad you found Lien. No idea what she was doing wandering around in the bush at night." She frowns at Lien. "But we'd hate to have lost her. And this whole camping outdoors thing is new for us."

Claudie smiles. "Yes, it sounds like it. You're Annie?"

"I am." Annie's cheeks turn pink. She's clearly pleased to be recognized.

"And Beau," says Claudie turning to him. Beau shakes her offered hand.

Beau says, "It's good to meet you. Put a face to the person who rescued our girl."

"You too. I hear you've been tearing up the town." Claudie has relaxed. The others draw close, and she shakes hands all around.

Lien has no idea what to say. It's not as if there are any words that will make this moment right.

"Okay then," Claudie says. Her eyes are fixed on Lien but she addresses everyone. "Well, I'd better leave you all to packing out. Thanks for lending Lien to me. Are you going to be gone today?"

Kam nods. "We're off to Lismore this evening. The campground's near there. We'll set up before the festival tomorrow."

"Don't worry, we won't let anyone wander off in the dark," says Beau.

Claudie glances at him briefly. She gives a slightly forced laugh. "You sure your knee's okay?" she asks Lien. Her eyes glance down at Lien's leg then up.

"I'll be fine." Lien is warmed by the concern, even though it's unnecessary and won't make Claudie stay.

"Okay. Well—I really hope everything goes well for you in, you know, life."

"You too, Claudie." She pauses. "Take care."

Claudie shuts Lien's passenger door on the truck and strides around to climb into the driver's seat and pull the door closed behind her. She starts the truck. She winds down the window to stick an arm out and wave goodbye.

No one says anything.

Beau comes close behind Lien. "Hey—" She turns into his arms and buries her head on his shoulder.

IT'S THE SAME VIEW, THE same canopy stretching out to the horizon, the same great, wide sky. It's magnificent. Claudie looks out over it and is dissatisfied as she never was before. She's been up here three years. She's spent day after day after month by herself. She thought she was proof against loneliness.

She's not.

It's been two days. It's not all bad. The sun and stars rise at the horizon. Kookaburras laugh at her from the railing of the deck, their beaks deadly, their stocky cream and brown bodies puffed up in the wind. Lyrebirds hide in the wet green brush and sing. Silver-gray brushtail possums patrol from the gumtrees, their eyes round and black above pink noses. Chocolate micro bats form clouds of small brown bodies and translucent wings in the evening sky. Claudie's not really alone. Anyway, Shelley's right there at the other end of the radio. And Claudie likes the quiet. It's a relief to have no one taking up her space and inviting her attention. Her brain is easier, moving from bedroom to living room without the possibility of seeing another person.

But that's tempered by simply missing Lien. Claudie grew accustomed to the girl. The cabin seems emptier than Claudie thought possible, and she's always been alone in it. Lien's bubbling sweetness has infused the air.

Claudie's angry with herself, irritated that she let herself get used to something she was always going to lose. Everything was fine. This was her place, could have been hers for another ten years. But now it's as though her brain is waking up, prickling with pins and needles. It stings to make her empty bed, to sit in her empty living room. It hurts to see the instruments on the wall, and not only because she has no one to play to. She should have spent the last three years working on new music, but she's let herself stagnate.

She can work on that though. She lifts her autoharp down and sits, straddled, on the bench. She sets her feet firmly on the floor and raises the autoharp to her chest.

She bought it a few months ago, had it mailed to the local post office so she could pick it up there in the truck. The instrument's not familiar yet, not like her faithful six string or any of the six guitars she's got hanging on the walls or carefully stored beside her clothes in the cabin's few closets, but she's improving. She's got the rhythm part pretty well down. Now her fingers are slowly dragging new melodies from the strings. It doesn't matter that there's no one to listen except the wildlife. None of these tunes will set the world on fire.

It's not long before she sets the instrument aside. She's itchy with her own imperfections, the electricity in the air, the quiet, and playing an instrument she's unpracticed in isn't giving her any satisfaction. She grabs the six-string from its stand. Maybe one of her old songs will pick things up: a cover from the old days, an obvious love song she avoided playing while Lien was in her space.

But the six string is restless under her fingers, as though the instrument itself wants her to work on something new. The song pulls itself painfully slowly out of the air, out of her fingers and the strings and her voice. She has an idea for the lyrics; she scrawls them on a piece of paper and keeps going.

Time can drag out here. Before Lien, Claudie tried not to look at her watch unless she had a meeting or event to plan for. Watching a clock lets time seem as if it's all too real. But time hasn't dragged since Claudie saw Lien's phone far off in the dark. And now it's suddenly night; the stars are high in the sky.

Claudie's got plans in the morning. She's been constrained by the weather for too long now. She'll get in a quick run early, take the narrow trail that runs through the ferns and brush. It's about two miles round trip down the closest track and back to the cabin. She can escape her own head for a while.

She has a meeting with the North Coast Aboriginal Land Council at ten. As the Bundjalung Nation representative, Shelley will be there, of course, but the local elders want other park rangers along as often as possible. On the way to the meeting she'll check up on the bush regeneration at the western edge of the park and talk to the wildlife rescue staff about the release program. She might need to drop in at a couple of campsites and check everything's in order. An early night sounds good.

Claudie packs up the guitar and the harp, rinses her glass, and takes a quick last look to the horizon. The dark trees and sky stare back at her just as they did before Lien appeared. She's always been here alone. Everything's okay.

By early afternoon Claudie's finished all the things she had booked in for the day. The Land Council made some recommendations and decided how to proceed with protection of artifacts in the park. Claudie will be one of the people policing that protection. She admired the tiny baby bats Jemma and Dawn are parenting with the help of a heat pack and droppers of formula. The western bush regeneration is going well after last year's bush fires. Many of the tree trunks are blackened and striking among the green, but the new growth has come in. Shoots have grown directly from the trunks and branches, giving the trees a furred look.

Claudie has no food in the house, so she stops in town for groceries. She's lived here three years, but she's not a big part of the community, and everyone's a stranger in a tiny town. The old guys watch her out the window of the local pub. In the General Store, the owner, Jill, chatters away from her six-foot height.

"You should have seen the kids' faces. Santa Claus in the bush! And poor Ern in his suit. Forty-five degrees it was, or forty at least. He was sweating up a storm. But he had to give out all the presents. He's a good man, Ern. Poor Katrina for that matter, she's the one who'd've had to wash the suit."

Claudie smiles and nods and says, "I wish I'd been there." She should be more involved.

"Ah well, next time. You've got so much to do up in that huge backyard of yours."

Claudie heads into the Iron Pot Creek area, drives the main road, and then winds her way around the network of fire roads. She stops over and over to clear the road of branches and small trees and shovel dirt fill into some new potholes. It's hot work. The temperature is rising, and the air is still heavy with water. She's glad of the AC in the truck. The fire trails will be critical in a few days once everything has dried off. These summer days, bush fires are a constant threat to people and animals. When it's hottest and driest, Claudie will be posted on her balcony for long shifts as a lookout.

On her way back to the cabin, Claudie can't help but check the upper campsite where Lien's friends spent some of the past week. It's her job to keep an eye on the campsites. The kids left the place surprisingly clear, despite the rain. Good for them. Claudie finds a cigarette butt caught in a bush, which could be anyone's but at least affords her a moment of irritation that's directed at people who aren't herself.

She leaves the site without ceremony. It's not as though Lien spent a single night here. Claudie has no reason to waste her time pining over anything, especially not in this weather.

It's a quick trip home now the floods have subsided. She climbs the stairs to the deck. A green heat haze blankets the bush. Eucalyptus oil hangs in the air now the rain has gone. Claudie strips and showers, rids herself of dirt and sweat from the day's work. She spends her evening with the guitar again. A song's starting to take shape.

Shelley's been asking her to play at the local bar for two years. Claudie tries a few songs: a cover or two, an original. Maybe she can put a set list together. She plays until her fingertips hurt.

IT'S ALMOST TEN WHEN SHE calls Shelley.

"Was it okay, having that girl there through the storm?" Shelley says.

"Yeah. She was fine. Just a kid, really." Claudie's deflecting. Lien's twenty-seven and not really just a kid. "She got herself injured on the east slope of the creek, and I happened to hear her. Lucky, really. But you know how it is, I couldn't get her back to the campsite for a few days."

She can hear Shelley's grimace in her voice as she goes on. "Sounds annoying. I know how much you like sharing your space. Was she a pain in the ass?"

Claudie's glad that Shelley is on the phone and not here to see her flush.

"No. I mean, sure I didn't want a visitor. I'm not much of a hostess. But she was all right."

"Yeah?"

"So," says Claudie before Shelley can pry more about Lien. She steels herself to ask the question. "Is there still an open spot to play at Sheila's?"

"Sure thing, sis. I've been telling you it's there for about two years. I'll hook you up." Claudie imagines Shelley's face and her raised eyebrows. "When do you want a go? She's not having live music on Christmas Day or New Year's Day, too messy. But you can play in a couple of weeks. Or even grab this week if you want?"

"Okay. Yeah, I can do that." It's not as if she hasn't been practicing.

"Sure. Way to finish off the year." Shelley never gushes, but Claudie can hear the pleasure in her voice.

"You feeling smug?"

"You know it. So have you picked your songs?"

"Not—um. No."

"Nah, mate. That's all good. I was being nosy. You can decide on the day. A woman of your talents."

"You've never heard me play."

Shelley hesitates. "Just the one time, when I was coming up to the cabin you were playing your guitar. And then—Claudie, you do know the Internet exists, don't you?"

"Right, yeah."

Claudie never imagined Shelley would look her up. Her history wasn't as private as she thought. Shelley could have read a lot of stuff about the band.

"Don't get weird on me, Claudia. It was a good band. Though you know me, I'm more of a folk music girl."

CLAUDIE DRIVES DOWN THE MOUNTAIN. Every twist in the road brings her closer to her first performance in more than three years. She sits in her car in the parking lot near the pub and taps the steering wheel. She's spent days choosing her songs for the open mic but she's pretty sure she has them completely wrong. Maybe if she starts with the Beatles instead.

Claudie hoists her guitar out of the back. The pub's sandstone walls open to a pretty rough interior. The bar's corrugated iron and wood; the carpet is ugly swirls of brown. But the glassware is gleaming and there's more than one beer on tap. Claudie knows half the people here.

Across the room, Shelley waves. "Come plant your ass here!" She lifts her solid body to slide over. Her cheeks round out as she smiles.

Claudie sits between Shelley and tiny Arwen, who's a local school teacher. Up at the front, Nina from the post office is MC. The conversation whirls around Claudie.

"A bunch of kids got caught in the storm. I saw them as they left. They came into the shop to buy raincoats. Seemed a bit late for that," Jill from the General Store says.

"Yeah, one of them was stuck with Claudie in the cabin for a few days," says Shelley.

"Really?" Jill turns to Claudie. "They were nice enough, for soaking wet city kids."

"Yeah, she was okay. The one who stayed with me."

Shelley catches her eye, and Claudie turns away. The guy singing is pretty good: kind of a country sound with a harmonica attached to his guitar. He wails his way through "You Can't Always Get What You Want."

"You're up next, Claudia." MC Nina has stepped over to their group.

Claudie's stomach turns. She's been blocking out the nerves and pushing through, trying not to think about the last time she played. But now it all comes flooding in. The bar, the lights, her band. She closes her eyes. She thinks of the chords, of the chromatic passing chord that she wants to nail.

They applaud the guy.

"And next up we have our very own Claudia Sokolov. We've spent years hoping this girl would get up here. It only took the storm of the decade to get her on stage."

Claudie stares at her feet as she walks on stage. But once she's up there, the old muscle memories take over. She raises the microphone to the right height and smiles out over the hopeful faces. The pub holds thirty or forty people, all locals, all of them wanting some music.

Claudie starts to play.

When she finishes, the applause is loud and ringing. No more than for the last guy, maybe, no more than for the duo that'll come after, but it warms Claudie's heart.

She says into the microphone, "Now I'm going to play 'Throw Your Arms Around Me.' It's a bit of a sad song but it's Ranger Shelley's favorite, and I've been practicing for her."

Shelley whoops.

Claudie puts in some extra emotion as she strums. She lets the vocals sound mournful but keeps the rhythm mobile. The sound system's not great, but it gives her room to let the top notes break apart.

Shelley gets up with Nina and dances, a slow dance. Claudie grins. This is nothing like the old days with Grand Echo, when the crowds were an undulating mass in front of Claudie. It's less and it's more.

"For my last song I wanted to do a bit of Britney," says Claudie. The crowd laughs a little, not sure if she's serious. "But I think I'll save that for next time. If you'll have me?"

There are cheers, and not only from the people Claudie is sitting with. They want her here.

"So how about a song I wrote?" The chords come easily. She sings, and everyone listens. Their attention and applause is motivating.

Claudie sits as the next duo sets up. The girl opens the vocals. She has a sweet lilting voice. Shelley leans toward Claudie, "You okay, sis?"

"Yeah." She nods. "Hey, thanks for encouraging me to do this."

"Encouraging? I was ready to push you up there. I'm glad you got to it first." Shelley considers Claudie for a long time. "Was it having that girl stay with you, did that finally give you the kick you needed?"

"Something like that."

"Well, you'll need to thank her for me," says Shelley. Claudie's relieved Shelley doesn't go on.

A couple of songs later, Claudie's on edge. Too many people surround her; she's given too much of herself on the stage. "Early morning," she says apologetically. "I'll come back."

Now she's fed the beast of performing in public, she's not sure she could stop.

"I NEED TO BREAK UP with her," Lien says to Annie and Beau. They're near the festival main stage so, even though she has to shout, no one else can hear.

"With who?" asks Megan. *Okay. Well, apparently she can hear.*

Raf says, "You're breaking up with Nic?"

"No loss." Matty laughs and flicks his fair hair out of his eyes. "She always made me feel lazy."

Lien frowns. "Dudes. Stop. She's great. I like her. She's kind and funny."

It's irritating that they're so nonchalant. She starts to say something but Raf's back to dancing with some stranger while Matty whistles appreciatively.

"She really is a great girl, Nic," Lien says to Beau and Annie.

"And hot," adds Beau.

"And hot." Lien sighs. "But I do need to break up with her."

"I know," says Beau. He pats her shoulder.

"You can't do it over the phone, though," says Annie. "You need to wait till you're back in Sydney. It's not cool and it's not fair to her otherwise."

"Yeah."

"Plus we'd tease you for the rest of your life if you broke up with someone by phone," says Beau. Lien half-giggles. They've spent four years teasing Matty about breaking up with his last boyfriend by text message on New Year's Eve.

The band on the stage isn't bad: four white guys playing some interesting blues-meets-punk music. Lien takes notes and a photo to remind herself of what they're like in person. She can expand on it later.

"I'm heading to one of the smaller stages," Lien says. "There's this act I've heard about. Sacha Cossman. If you stay for the big finish, could you video a bit of it for me?"

Sacha Cossman is playing on the northeast stage. She's maybe twenty-five, blonde and broad-hipped. Her voice is strong and promises more than she's delivering right now.

"Bring out the accordion, Sacha!" calls a woman from the small crowd, and a bunch of other audience members erupt in cheers.

Sacha flushes. She glances offstage, then back to the crowd. "Well, if you're all asking for it," she says into the mic.

She rests her guitar against a stand, and a backstage guy hands her an oversized accordion. It's white with blue flowers etched on one side. It's beautiful and ugly at once. Claudie would love to see it. As Sacha plays, she sings over the top, something folksy and fluting, which sweeps up and down and makes use of her huge range.

Afterward Lien waves her press pass at the disinterested guy guarding the rope barrier and goes to meet the singer backstage, if a patch of grass to the side of the crowd can be called backstage.

Sacha beams as they shake hands. "Just a sec, Dani's around here somewhere. She handles my media stuff."

A slim woman with a dark, perfectly sculpted faux-hawk walks over and gives Sacha a congratulatory hug. Sacha's eyes give away the connection between them. "You were flawless, Sach," the woman says.

"Even the accordion?"

The woman laughs, showing even teeth. "I couldn't believe you even brought it along with you." She turns to Lien. "I'm Dani Alvarez, Sacha's manager."

"I was chatting with Sacha about an interview," says Lien. "I'm doing reviews and profiles for *Brag Magazine*."

"Cool. Any chance you can talk tomorrow? I don't like to put too much strain on her voice."

"No problem," says Lien. "Or else we can talk when we're all back in Sydney. I'm pulling together a Rivers Fest edition and I want to make space for a mini-feature on Sacha. Local girl making it to the big time."

Sacha points to her own face and grins a silent grin. She nods in enthusiastic thanks.

"That's fabulous," Dani says. She gives Sacha a gentle push. "Make sure you drink some warm water, babe. Don't want to wreck that gorgeous voice." Sacha grins and moves away. Dani shoves her hands in her pockets and sways. "So you're talking to festival people. Just the locals?"

Lien nods. "Locals for profile pieces anyway."

"Hey, you know who you should meet?" Dani's hands are out of her pockets again and moving to describe the person she's imagining. "Della Darcourt. She's—I've got her number right here."

She pulls out her phone.

"Okay that'd be great," Lien says. She leaves with two more phone numbers and a list of bands Dani's heard about. Dani shakes off Lien's thanks with confidence.

Back at the house they've rented, Lien types up her notes. The place is full and noisy; she's surrounded by her friends. Tonight Raf and Annie are cooking lasagna. Annie's dressed in a red-and-black belted dress, with her straight bangs and bobbed hair curled under at the ends.

Raf brings a glass of sauvignon blanc to Lien on the small porch. His beard is even thicker than when they were camping. "I'm coming in," Lien says. "Thanks."

Lien follows Raf into the kitchen. Everyone's there, drinking wine.

"So, babe, tell us everything," Matty says. He leans into his boyfriend. "Raf and I have been together too long. We need to live vicariously through your romantic life."

Lien shakes her head. "I don't know. There's no 'everything' to tell, really."

"Don't lie to us. We know you suddenly have a ranger rock star girlfriend."

Lien sighs. "She's not my girlfriend. Not even a tiny bit."

"Oh. But something happened. You're breaking up with the personal trainer."

Lien glares at Matty.

"Shut it, Matt," says Beau. "But we are interested, Li. We're your friends."

Lien sighs again. "It's kind of ridiculous. We were trapped in the cabin. She was—Well, yeah, she's a rock star and she's gorgeous. It was raining. You can imagine the rest."

"Romantic," says ever-pragmatic Kam. "If you're into that kind of thing." Megan kisses the top of Kam's dark head.

Lien looks around at her friends. "It was romantic. The electricity was out, so we had to use candles. And the storm was howling around us. She played guitar and showed me the stars. It was *really* romantic."

Matty heaves a dramatic sigh.

"Shut up, Matt," Lien says. "It was. But whatever. The woman's a hermit who lives in the mountains, and she made it super clear that she didn't want me to hang around."

"But she saved your life," says Beau.

"I don't know about my life," says Lien.

"We'd have found you eventually," says Megan.

"She at least saved your safari suit," says Beau.

"I think it's sweet," says Annie, who's standing by the oven.

"Of course you do," says Raf.

"Look at her. She can't stop thinking about this girl," Annie adds. Then, as Lien blushes, she says, "Dinner's ready."

11

TWO WEEKS AGO, LIEN HAD to resign herself to coming up north in the first place. Now she's resigning herself to going home to Sydney. Of course, not everything will be terrible. She's pretty sure a shower with no line outside the door will change her life. She can't wait for clean sheets and clean clothes and a full length mirror so she can feel like herself again. Also, there'll be way fewer flies.

But Sydney also means she has no chance to bump into a gorgeous park ranger while grabbing groceries or walking to the train. Somehow Claudie's had no last minute change of heart. Not that Lien was holding out hope but—damn it, Lien was completely holding out hope.

She could ask Beau for Claudie's number. He'd give it to her even if he made a face about it. She doesn't ask because she wouldn't call anyway. It would be stupid to demand that kind of attention from Claudie when it's clear that the demand would be unwelcome. Anyway, Claudie has Beau's phone number. And Beau's phone has remained stubbornly silent.

When they're ready to go, the others give Lien the front seat. "We're looking after your knee," says Annie.

Lien squints at her. "Really? This isn't 'cause you two want to play footsie in the back?"

Annie's blush deepens.

Beau swipes at Lien's head with a long arm. "What's the issue? Do you want to be crammed in the back with me?"

"Nope."

"Then let it go." It's sweet and odd to see him be so protective of Annie.

They're travelling home with more gear than they brought. They stack a wall of bedding and clothes in the middle of the back seat, separating Beau and Annie. Some of the extra gear might be Lien's fault. She's rarely met a band T-shirt she didn't like, and at the festival there were so many local bands, all of them meriting Lien's interest and most with eager volunteers manning the merchandise tables. Some of the T-shirts will need altering to get the neckline or sleeves right. Some she can rework with other T-shirts. She's going to have a band T-shirt renaissance.

The four of them don't sing on the way back. Late nights and long drinks and sunshine and cheering over sound systems have taken their toll. The car eats up the distance, mile after mile, farther and farther from the cabin in the bush. Lien rests her head against the window and watches the wilderness as it stretches out to the horizon. They cross bridges where a river curls away from the road, breaking up the gray-green mantle of trees. They pass farmland and herds of patient cows. In some places the road cuts through a hill and gray and orange sandstone cliffs tower above them. The wide bright bowl of the sky is changeless.

Eventually the road widens. More cars appear everywhere. The city rises in the distance: pale gray buildings jutting up in clusters against the distant horizon.

Megan deposits Beau and Lien and their bags on the street outside their place. There's no parking near their door, so it's a quick farewell.

"Bye, guys," says Annie. Her eyes land on Beau.

"I'll give you a call," Beau says before he closes the car door. "It was…" Annie blushes.

Lien drops her bags on the sidewalk. It's a comfort to be home, to their familiar terrace. It's also a return to reality.

She glances at Beau.

"Here we are," Lien says.

"Come on. Let's go home."

Upstairs, Lien closes her bedroom door. She leans against it and considers unpacking. It'd be good to get her clothes washed and hung out as soon as possible. They'll probably smell like dirt and moss and damp for all time. Instead, she deposits the bag on her bed and herself on a chair at the tiny desk in the corner. She turns on her computer. It's neighborly, the way it lights up with a welcome.

"I'm back!" she posts everywhere: Twitter and Instagram and Snapchat. She hops up to take a picture of her bathroom, filtered so it seems a bit less ugly 1960s tile and a bit more vintage and funky. She tags it: *The joy of a pee without an audience of spiders and frogs.*

She pauses and runs her fingers over the keys. Then she sighs. She types "Grand Echo" into a search engine. Song after song pops up. Lien selects the most popular one and pushes her chair back to listen. She selects another. They're good; Claudia's voice has gravel that would work for blues, but it's pitched perfectly over the top of some crunchy guitar with a strong electronic drive. The lyrics are simple and catchy and suit her emotive rasp; the guitars lift the whole thing.

Lien investigates further and pulls up a couple of articles. Grand Echo was moving up in the world. They were selling records and playing to sold-out crowds. They performed a triumph of a show at the Basement. Then the band stopped playing, putting an end to their runaway success. A month later their rep announced they had folded. Their frontwoman, Claudia Sokolov, walked away from the public eye. Lien studies the dates. If Claudie's been a ranger for three years, then she moved north a few months after the band stopped playing.

Lien finds plenty of information about the band—reviews of their music, profiles of their lead—but nothing about Claudie after they shut down. The drummer, Gretchen, played with the Rabbits for a while. The bass player, Tan, was a big part of Acacia. They've come together in a new band now. Mercy, on keys, started another band that didn't go far, then did some mystifying solo work. Claudia disappeared. Until Lien found her.

Lien goes back to the Grand Echo search and watches YouTube videos, some professional, others bootlegs made on people's phones from the backs of clubs, half blocked by people's heads and with drunken singing in the background. However they're filmed, the songs are great; the band has chemistry. The music has layers: the keys with the guitars, the bass, and the drums. Claudie was happy when she was playing. Her face showed it. Her body showed it. Every movement and key change and new song showed it. She was magnetic.

Beau's crisp knock startles Lien.

"Come in." Lien closes her laptop.

Beau narrows his eyes. "I have ears, Li. I'm pretty sure you're playing Claudie's band."

"Yeah. It was, yeah. Grand Echo. I was curious."

"Mmmhmm?" He wrinkles his forehead.

Lien moves quickly. "Here, watch this one." She opens the laptop to play him her favorite video. Beau looks over her shoulder. "See. They were good. She was fucking awesome."

"Yeah. I remember them on the scene."

"I don't know why she stopped. You don't just stop something you're good at without a reason. I want to find out that reason. I want to know why she's hiding by herself in that cabin. And why she won't come back." A new video starts.

When she spins her chair away from the screen, Beau's watching her. "Li." His voice is soft. "You can't investigate why she won't date you. It doesn't work like that."

"That's not what I mean. I wasn't—"

"No?"

She sighs. "Look, sure, we had this chemistry, and I think she's making a huge mistake. And it hurts. But that's not the point. At least, it's not the only point. It's not about dating. She was good, Beau. She loved performing and she was going places and she was awesome and she gave it all up. She could've stayed. We need more women in music, and she… she was made to be in music."

Beau relents. "She was good."

"She was better than good. She was fucking awesome. What would make someone that good and that in love with the music leave it all behind?"

Beau frowns. "Maybe we can't know."

"I'm going to find out."

He eyes her.

"Anyway, it'll make a great long-form article. I can send it to some of the web magazines. I've been saying for ages that I should write something outside the social columns. This is a good opportunity. For me."

He grins, then. "I'm not going to stop you, Li. I just like to watch you struggle to make up arguments for researching the girl you fucked last week. Tell me again that this isn't stalking?"

"It's not stalking!"

He kisses the top of her head. "I'm heading up to Thai Me Up for some food. Want anything?"

"Oh god, yes. I have missed their food like a limb." She pushes her chair across the floorboards and grabs her wallet. "Pad See Ew please." She's excited about dinner already. She hands him money.

"Vege?"

"Vege."

While he's gone, Lien tracks down the band Claudie's drummer Gretchen and bass player Tan are playing with. It's called Summer Fling, which is annoyingly appropriate. She ignores that and sends a message via the website, aiming for the right level of casual and professional.

"I met an old band member of yours recently and I wanted to ask you guys a couple of questions for an article I'm doing on the music industry."

She gets a reply back almost immediately. "Awesome. We're rehearsing tomorrow night at seven at Tan's place. You can come on over if you're free. Gretchen." She has a picture of a drum kit in her signature. Almost immediately another message comes. "You'll need this." It includes an address in Surry Hills.

"You're on," types Lien. She adds. "Do you guys have a favorite pizza?" She's never met a band that's not happier to talk over pizza.

She searches for the other band member, Mercy, but can't get a contact. She leaves her computer open and sits on her bed, flops back, and considers the ceiling until Beau hollers up the stairs.

The Thai food's excellent, as usual. Lien leans back on the sofa and soaks in the homey atmosphere. The house is narrow. Its living room runs between the front door and the kitchen that leads down a few stairs into the back courtyard. Lien and Beau spent months pulling the furnishings together. A chocolate retro wood-frame sofa aligns with one wall. Opposite, the TV is on a laminate table in faux wood and white. There's a lounge chair in caramel and cushions in teal and white. They've framed and hung some of Beau's photographs: a bicycle rack with multi-colored bikes in it, an A-frame house inclined into the sky, a group of guys drinking from tiny tea cups. There's a bookcase under the stairs. Everything fits.

Lien and Beau eat with the noise of the street and the thudding bass of their neighbors' stereo around them. After they've finished, Lien rinses the plates, then sits back down with Beau's long pale feet in her lap. She rests a hand on his leg. Her thumb traces his ankle bones. On the screen some Brits are trying to hunt down a bargain in a market.

"So things with Annie are good?" Lien asks in an ad break.

"Oh, girl." Beau's sigh is secret and happy. He brushes his feet against one another.

"Ah, you've gone squishy," she says. "I'm so happy. Except that you haven't told me everything. How did it happen?"

He leans against the arm of the sofa. As he starts, he's talking to the ceiling. "It was—It was that first night up there. I waited for you a while, but I got worried so I clambered out of the tent hunting for you. After a few minutes I called the others. Honestly, we were sort of panicking. I was completely freaking and Annie—I've never seen that face on Annie before. Everyone was hunting for you. No one knew which direction you'd gone, you fucker."

"Sorry."

"There was this tiny second when I was calling out into the bush. Everything was windy and hopeless, and Annie was next to me. I took a breath to yell for you again, and she reached out and she held my hand. It started raining then. And we both yelled at the top of our lungs."

"I'm so sorry."

"You don't need to be sorry. You fell. You got hurt. It was fucking scary, but it was an accident. Not long after that, you got us on the phone, and we could breathe again, we didn't need to worry. The relief made it easy to, um, make a move."

Lien laughs and pats his leg. "Beau Michaels. Are you telling me that you finally made a move?"

He blushes. "She was right there when I hung up; all of them were. Matty muttered about his soaking hair and Raf took him off to calm him down. Megan and Kam headed into their tent. Annie and I were alone. We were so relieved. Maybe she kissed me. Maybe I kissed her. Everything was easy after that."

She pats his legs, charmed and thrilled for them. The British people come back on TV, and they watch together.

"Now, what's going on for you?" he says in the next ad break. He shifts to face her. He's only like this, golden and sincere, when they're home alone. She hopes Annie sees this side of him.

"Some stuff." She considers him. "It was quiet in the cabin. Claudie's comfortable with silence, and sometimes she had to head out for rangering duties. So there was lots of thinking time. I'm pretty sure I've been avoiding thinking for, um—well for a while."

He nods. "I get that. You're busy. It's easy to do. And it's not always the right time to do work on yourself."

"Beau, it's been years!" she protests.

He shrugs and smiles. "It's not like you've been hibernating. You're surrounded by people who love you and think you're incredible. And some of us even know you."

She sniffs. "I could have made better choices. I feel like I've failed people."

"Never."

"Not you, bonehead." She flicks his knee. He shoves her with his feet. "But... My parents never understood soccer but they spent ten years getting me the best coaches in Asia and Australia. And then I gave up."

"You were injured," Beau mutters, but he doesn't stop her going on.

"And then I got a second chance to really love something and all I do is surround myself with parties and people and throw together clever tweets."

"You may be selling yourself short," Beau says.

"I don't want to disappoint people anymore."

"I still don't think you've disappointed anyone," Beau says. "I don't know your parents, really. But that one time I met them they seemed happy with you. I think they wanted you to call more often, maybe."

"They're not the kind of people who make disappointment obvious. You can't tell unless you grew up with them. But they do all that charity work and travel, while I toss up a story about the latest ankle boot fad in fifteen minutes."

"Well, I mean, we all need to know which ankle boots are in vogue." He swings around on the sofa and drops his feet to the floor. "But seriously, honey, this isn't a new thought for you. You've hated some of that stuff for ages."

Lien looks at him. "I have?"

"You whine at me every time you get five hundred thousand retweets on a post about flannel shirts or shoulder pads. I thought you knew."

"Huh." She nods. "Okay." She's quiet. "I want to write something that matters."

"Yeah, you do. And if I know you, you'll do it, too."

"Okay," she says again. "So I'll put time and groundwork into this piece I'm writing. And whether anyone takes it or not, I'll keep trying. But they'd be stupid not to take it. It'll be good."

"It will be good. All those thousands of followers can't be wrong."

She huffs at him. "I can get people talking. There's a lot more even in the fashion and music industries than what's on point one week."

"Though to be clear, you can't stop talking to me about fashion. You know I rely on you."

"Deal," she says. "I mean it's not as though I'm about to stop caring about clothes."

"Fuck no," he says. "And call your parents."

She spends the morning developing notes for her article, then helps Megan and Kam wash all the camping gear and tents to get them back to their various owners. She visits some vintage clothing places around the Eastern Suburbs to reaffirm her vintage clothing credentials. Annie's working at Clothes Were the Days, so she drops in and hugs her over the counter.

Annie waves her hands over a cardboard box and a stack of clothes on hangers. "Some lady brought in all these 1940s and 50s clothes from her mother's attic. It's killing me to wait for Laura to get in tomorrow so we can go through it."

Lien nods. "Call me as soon as you see anything. I'm feeling the 1970s punk thing this season, but you know I'd give my front teeth for a good housedress."

"You got it," Annie says. "Hey!" She reaches out to pop a jaunty hat on Lien's head. "Did Beau tell you he invited me over?"

"Oh. That's great. I haven't seen him so no, but great." Lien grabs the hat and turns it over in her hands. Lien has always invited Annie to things. She'll need to adapt to this shift.

"We're having dinner."

"Cool. Well, it's pretty late. I'll wait for you to finish up here, and we can go together," Lien says.

While she waits she sits on a step stool in the corner of the shop. She's hidden here, surrounded by racks of vests and dresses and dinner jackets. She calls her parents.

"Hello."

"Hi, Dad."

"Lien! Is something wrong?"

"No. Not at all. I just thought I'd give you a call. Where are you?"

"Hong Kong." She can see him in the penthouse, balding and rumpled but somehow at home in the glossy gold and white interior. Her mother has particular taste. There's a white baby grand piano.

"How's Maria Melissa?" she asks after her parents' long-term housekeeper.

"Fine. Her grandson turned four."

"And you and Mum?"

"We're well, thank you. Your mother is at the Newburys' planning this year's fundraiser. There's a dispute about tea."

"Some things don't change."

He laughs. "Well, this year they outsourced the music so at least we didn't need to go through that. How are you, Lien? Busy?"

She nods, though he can't see her. "Busy enough. I'm working on something new. A longer piece than I usually do. Oh and I went camping!" She tells him about the fall and the rescue.

Lien and Annie get to Lien's place right after six. At six thirty, Lien digs out skinny jeans and a band T-shirt from her wardrobe. She laces up her heavy black boots. She clomps on the stairs as she comes down to the kitchen, but still, Annie and Beau spring apart as though no one's supposed to see them.

Lien smiles to herself. She should tell them that it's okay for them to touch.

"We're cooking," says Annie unnecessarily, as they're standing in front of a wok and a saucepan steaming on the stovetop. "Dumplings and soup. We've got plenty, if you want to join us."

"Nah, I'm heading out. I want to talk to this band I heard about." She takes a teaspoonful of broth and blows on it before she drinks it. "This is amazing," she says, loving the sour and smooth saltiness of it. "Can you teach me?"

"Of course," says Annie. Her mother's an amazing cook.

"Should we save some?" Beau asks.

"No, I'm bringing pizza for the band. I have questions."

"Who are these people?" Beau asks.

"You don't know them." Lien swans out. "Don't worry, Beau. I've got this. Also, you guys are cute." Lien turns back. "Honestly, you don't need to pretend you're not all over one another. I love you both and I love you both being happy."

"We don't want you to feel left out," Annie says.

It'd be more isolating if they kept secrets from her. "I don't. Promise." She checks her hair in the mirror outside the kitchen.

She hops on a bus with two pizzas. They rumble down Oxford Street and over to Surry Hills. The band's rehearsal is in a freestanding house, which is unusual for the area, though the neighbors' walls are only a meter or two away. Its garden grows up the painted burgundy walls. A streetlight flickers on.

A bearded Asian guy opens the door. "Tan Quach," he says. "The bass player from Grand Echo." He's scruffy and hipster with a round face. He eyes her T-shirt, then nods her in. Lien shifts the pizza to one arm and follows.

On the way through the house, he says, "Like your shirt. So to give you a bit of background, Gretchen Tandy and I are working together. She's from the old band, too. I brought her in on percussion when our drummer quit. She's one of the best."

"Tell me about this band. Summer Fling?"

"It's awesome," he says. "Awesome. It really seems like we're going somewhere. This is my big chance. It's been a hard road to get here though." He opens the door to the garage behind the house.

Inside, a bass guitar leans against the wall. Tan picks it up.

"Hi, Lien," chirps a girl, presumably Gretchen, from behind the drums. "Ooh, pizza. Thanks!" She flashes a smile at Lien. She's white and cute, with crooked teeth and platinum blonde pigtails.

Another white guy with a turquoise coif mutters, "Hey," and turns over a piece of sheet music. "We'll start with Glass," he says to Gretchen and Tan and an older guy with an electric guitar. "You right to watch?"

Lien nods agreement. The band is good. Loud. The lead has charisma. Gretchen and Tan work together well. They've known one another's beats for a long time.

Afterward, Lien, Gretchen, and Tan sit around the coffee table with pizza. The lead singer and guitarist, still unnamed, strides out into the night.

"So," says Tan.

"So, I want to talk about Grand Echo," Lien says. "I'm putting together this article on Australian acts that were on their way and how they ended."

"You said in your email that you met Claudie?" Gretchen asks.

"Yeah, I bumped into her up north where she's a ranger."

"Right," says Tan. "Hermit Claudie."

Gretchen glances at him, then shrugs. "We'll tell you what we can."

Tan's jaw is tight. "All I know is, it was rough. We were on our way to the big stuff, and she abandoned ship."

"It was roughest on her," Gretchen says.

"Yeah. I guess it was."

Lien listens. Gretchen continues. "It was the end of a short tour. Just the East Coast and Adelaide. It'd been pretty awesome. We finished up with a show at the Basement. I guess Claudie had been back about a year." She turns to Tan, who nods. "You know Claudie went to the US in 2010 hoping for a solo career, but that fell through for her. They were assholes. It was a mistake. Anyway, she was back and, like, she was finally in control of her music again. We were playing to packed-out venues everywhere we went. Something huge was happening."

"And then?" Lien prompts.

"And then we'd been back a few days and there was this accident. An overdose. Lou—Louisa. She died. You knew about Louisa?"

Lien shakes her head.

"She was another musician. She toured with us. Great songwriter. Guitarist. Magic with the pedals and the reverb stuff. She opened for us. She played her own stuff and sometimes helped out with road stuff or backing vocals when we needed an extra voice. I'm no use; I sing like a cockatoo. Anyway, she was our friend, Claudie's mostly, but all of ours too, and she died. Prescription painkillers. It was awful."

Gretchen's face is clouded. Lien aches for this girl she just met.

"We barely saw Claudie after that. Not at all. She came in for a bit, but she was silent and shaken, and it was tough. We were set to record a new album, but everything fell apart."

"It was a big blow," says Tan.

"And you haven't seen her since?"

"No."

Lien's trying not to judge. But Claudie's friend died, and she walked away from her career, and her bandmates didn't try to keep in touch.

Gretchen says, "We tried. We called and we called, and when she moved up north we suggested we visit, but... look, she was upset and she pushed us away. Lou was our friend, too. I hate that I gave up but you need to get it."

"It was rough on everyone," Tan says. "We needed to move on." Lien tries to imagine.

"I could have tried to find her again, though," says Gretchen.

Tan shrugs. He turns to Lien. "You met up with her. She's doing okay?"

"She's doing fine. She's not doing much music up there and not... I mean she's a bit quiet but that might just be how she is."

"I'm glad she's okay," says Tan. "If you see her or talk with her, tell her hi from us."

"Okay," says Lien. "Sure I will."

It's Tan's house, so Gretchen leaves with Lien. As they turn onto the main road heading to the bus stop, the drummer says, "Claudie really fell apart. She'd struggled with the industry for years, but she loved it. This was it. The end for her."

"Yeah," says Lien.

"I sometimes wondered if there was more to it. It might be worth talking to Dani."

"Dani?"

"Dani Alvarez. She was our manager. She and Claudie were close. You'd need to talk to her about it. She's around still. Managing a few young up-and-comers and some bigger names. I've seen her on the scene."

Lien nods. "I'll give her a buzz. Thank you. I really appreciate you taking the time with me."

"No worries." Gretchen grins. She waves as she crosses the road to take the bus in the opposite direction from Lien.

The bus arrives quickly. Lien leans against the window as they trundle past streetlights and parked cars. She's flattened by the band's revelations. Claudie struggled through all of this before Lien knew her at all. All the life that Claudie's lived before has absolutely nothing to do with Lien. But she's a journalist. She has something more to look into.

THE LOCAL MUSIC INDUSTRY ISN'T large. Dani who managed Grand Echo is the same woman Lien met managing Sacha Cossman at Rivers Fest. Lien already has her contact details.

"Call me Dani," she says on the phone.

Dani lives out at Coogee Beach in a small apartment block. She meets Lien downstairs. "Let's go get a coffee," she says. She walks with energy. Her hair's carefully spiked. Her eyes are quick and sure. She's wearing a white button-up shirt and skinny mustard jeans.

They sit at a table on the street at long narrow cafe across the road from the beach. The air tastes of salt. Lien's tea and roast tomato on toast is excellent.

"You want to talk about Sacha," Dani says. She leans back in her chair.

"Yeah, I want to set something up. But first I want to talk to you about Claudia Sokolov."

Dani raises her eyebrows. She draws the words out. "Claudia Sokolov. Well, I haven't heard that name for a while." She tips her head and studies Lien.

"She was the lead singer of Grand Echo. You managed them three and four years back."

"I know who she was, babe. I know who she was." Dani's making a point.

"You two were more than professionally connected?"

"That's public knowledge, of course. There's nothing wrong with that."

"No, of course not," Lien says. She's a little out of balance though, which she covers by hunting through her bag for a notebook and pen, then lifting her head in a suitably professional way. The woman's pretty hot. Her dark hair is short and perfectly styled. Her eyelashes are dark, and her close-set eyes are clear pale green.

"So, I'm doing some research for a story about what makes musicians abandon a career in music. The Grand Echo guys pointed me to you."

Dani raises her brows. "Claudie sent you to me?"

"Gretchen did."

"Oh, the drummer. Okay. Cool. She's a great girl. So. Grand Echo." Her tone is nostalgic.

Lien opens the notebook. It's interesting how sometimes people tell you things because you have a notebook. "Where do you want to start?"

Dani looks at her watch. "I need to meet with some kids I just signed. So let's keep this quick."

"Sure. Can you tell me what you know about why Grand Echo split?"

Dani's silent, and Lien looks up. "First, can you tell me about your interest in the band?" Dani asks. "Is it professional or personal?" Dani's smile makes it light, though it's weird to be asked.

Lien tames her blush. "Like I said, I'm writing an article about musicians and bands who were on their way to the big time and then left it all behind."

"Sounds good. But how did you even come up with Grand Echo?"

"I was in the wilderness up north heading for Rivers Fest. I'm not much of a camper and I had a fall in a storm, and Claudie helped me out. She's a ranger up there."

"Really. How romantic." Dani's eyes are knowing.

Lien shakes her head. "No, it's not like that. I guess I owe her some of my time. I was interested in her story."

Dani raises her eyebrows. "Fair enough. I don't know much, though. The girl left suddenly."

"Left you or left the band?"

"Left both. Both."

"So tell me. From your point of view, what happened?"

Dani sips her coffee slowly. "Did she tell you about Lou? Louisa?"

"Gretchen told me about the tragedy." She's not imagining the relief on Dani's face.

"It's no secret. Louisa was a friend of the band. We'd all been close for years. She was our opening act, and we were small-scale enough that she was traveling with us." Dani pauses. "We all liked her. Great kid. I mean, I didn't know her that well. But she was close to Claudie. They just understood one another somehow. But the girl had a pretty bad pill habit. When Lou's parents called Claudie and gave her the news, she was distraught. She never really recovered."

"How did Lou die?"

"It was an accident. An overdose of painkillers and—it happens. It was just an accident. But it was terrible. Claudie was hit hard. She was a bit intense after that. She wasn't around. And then a month later she shut her phone off and disappeared. She told us where she was going. But she didn't tell us how to keep in touch. It killed Grand Echo."

It's a sad story. And it makes sense. Something is missing, though. But Lien doesn't know how to pin it down. Dani has tears in her eyes, and none of these people need to talk to her at all.

She asks some more questions about the band's prospects and about their plans for the future, but when she leaves she's dissatisfied.

LIEN'S BEEN HOME FOUR DAYS and somehow she hasn't called Nic. It's not as though she's avoiding her. Not really. It's just easier to do the things that don't make Lien the bad guy.

But she can't ignore a person and hope she'll disappear. Nic's not her girlfriend, was never her girlfriend. But Nic deserves better than being overlooked. Lien breathes deep and writes a text.

I'd like to meet.

Delete.

Let's get together

Delete.

Can we meet up tonight?

She hits send.

Nic replies almost immediately, even though Lien's pretty sure she's at work at the gym.

Sure. Sounds a bit ominous. Do I need to worry?

It's impossible to answer that. Everything Lien can say leads to them breaking up by text message. She's not going to do that.

No. I'll come to your place if Bea is at training?

Nic lives in Newtown. They'll get some quiet in her house. Anyway, Lien wants to talk to Nic at her place. That way if it doesn't go well, Nic is already home, where she'll want to be.

The text comes back.

Okay.

No smiley face, no kisses. Lien bites her lip. Nic knows something is up.

It's still light out, but Nic's house faces the wrong way to catch the late sun. Lien's pressed the doorbell many times before. Usually Nic opens it with a beaming smile and a kiss. Now her smile is tentative.

"I'll take your bag," she says. Lien hands it over awkwardly and follows Nic down the hall to the living room. "Let's—do you want to sit down?" Lien asks. She shifts on her feet.

Nic perches at the edge of the sofa. "Sure." Her lips are set.

Lien can see no point in delaying. She sits opposite Nic. "I'm so sorry. I need to break up with you."

"Fuck." Nic closes her eyes.

"Nic, it's just… We have such different interests and I—"

"You know we've always had different interests. That's part of the fun."

"I know. I loved what we had. It was fun, and you're a great girl."

"But you're breaking up with me." Nic meets her gaze. "It's not just 'different interests,' is it? You met someone. At that fucking festival."

"That's not why—"

"Did you meet someone?" Nic's focused.

"I did meet someone. But not—"

"I knew I should have come to the festival. Everyone hooks up."

"I didn't hook up with someone at the festival. It's not like that."

"What, camping?" Nic thinks for a moment. "Oh, fuck, you're talking about the park ranger."

Lien meets her gaze. "Yeah."

"And you're going to do some kind of long distance thing? I know you. That'd never work for you."

"No."

"She's moving here already? Fucking hell, Lien. That's fast."

"Nic. We're not. We're not doing anything."

"You're not even together?" Nic gives a little pained bark of laughter. "And you're still breaking up with me."

"That's not the point. It's not about her, it's about us."

"You slept with her." Nic's voice is dull. Lien hates that she's hurt her.

Lien inhales. "You and I weren't exclusive."

Nic doesn't look at her. She swallows. "You might not have been. I was. But yeah, I guess I was fooling myself." Lien can't think of anything to say. "Ah fuck, Li. This is fucked. And you know what? Mostly I'm embarrassed. Because you went off and chased after someone who was probably a lonely old lady wanting a bit on the side. Is she even going to come to Sydney to see you?

"Probably not. I haven't spoken to her again. So probably not. But Nic, the thing is, it just clarified things for me."

"What, that you were using me till you could find someone different? You're a fool if you think she's going to uproot her whole life and come down here to be with you."

"You and I both deserve something better, Nic. It's not about her."

Nic's clear eyes are both skeptical and hurt.

"It's not *just* about her," amends Lien. "I think I need to spend some time alone."

Nic looks away. "Whatever you want to tell yourself. I still think we could have had something real. I could have made you happy."

"I know. I know. I know. It's only that I have to believe a relationship can be more. I don't want something that's just good enough."

Nic takes a breath. "It was never just 'good enough.' That's the worst part. It was never just 'good enough' for me."

"I'm truly sorry," says Lien.

Nic slows down and takes a breath. "I don't want this break-up. Honestly. I don't want this."

"I know." Nic's hands shake, and Lien's not sure, for a second, if she wants this either. "I don't want to trap us both and not even look for something better."

"You found something better? With a girl you won't see again maybe ever." Nic sighs. "The thing is, Li. I thought this was it..."

"I'm sorry."

"Okay."

"I really am."

Nic sets her shoulders. "Okay. Can you go? Please."

"Of course."

"Go. I'm feeling pretty stupid right now. And used. I don't want to look at you."

Lien heads home. The thought of Nic in her house, crying in her living room, is painful. But there's nothing she can do. She's the last person to be able to help.

Beau's in his room. Lien stands in the doorway until he looks up. "I broke up with her, Beau." Her eyes sting.

"Oh, babe. You had to." He stands, and she wipes her eyes. "Want to talk about it?" he asks.

"Not really."

"Want to watch reality TV instead?"

"Yes, please," she manages. "Thank you." He follows her downstairs.

GRETCHEN AND TAN'S BAND IS playing at The Factory, opening for a rock duo from Melbourne. Lien hovers at the back of the dance floor. It's all good stuff, though not new.

Once they're finished she walks over to the band. Gretchen grins to see Lien. Her face is lit by the stage lights, which reflect from the drums. "Hey! You came!" she says. "Did you like it?"

"Absolutely. You and Tan were great."

"We were better in the old days with Echo," Gretchen says. Tan frowns at her from where he's putting away his bass. "Come on, you know it's true," she tells him.

Tan shrugs and heads to the bar with the others.

Lien helps Gretchen pack up the drums. They carry the kit out to the back lane and pack it into a station wagon there.

"We were going somewhere new with Grand Echo," Gretchen says as she slams the trunk closed. "We'd started something. Claudie was out from that awful US producer's net, and Dani had stopped trying to make us into a pop rock cookie-cutter band. Claudie was writing new originals. Top stuff. You should've heard it."

"Yeah? I can imagine."

"Yeah." Gretchen opens the back door of the venue. A wall of sound meets them. "You might not need to imagine it. We recorded some of it, a rough cut. But it was amazing. It was going to make a really awesome record. And then Lou. And everything was awful, and Claudie disappeared. I've no idea where that recorded stuff is. It was good." She thumps out the beat, one fist against her palm. They walk back onto the dance floor. "Have you heard these guys?" Gretchen asks, waving at the band on stage. "They do some amazing stuff."

LATE THE NEXT MORNING LIEN calls Dani.

"Gretchen thought there would be some old tracks from Grand Echo's last year together," she says. "I'm hoping you can point me in the right direction."

"Nope. Sorry kid, no idea," Dani says.

"Okay. Thanks for that. Do you remember who did the recording?"

"Yeah, not really. It was a long time ago."

"What about the studio? Sydney doesn't have that many," Lien persists.

"Yeah." Dani sounds irritated. "If I remember, we recorded at the studio on Fig Street. It's under the bridge in Ultimo. I can't help you more than that."

"Okay, thanks, Dani."

At the studio, the sound engineer is with another band. But he knows Lien, so he gives her access to the tapes from three years ago. It only takes five minutes to find Grand Echo's work. An hour later Lien is still writing notes. Claudie might not remember how good she is, but she needs to hear this.

CLAUDIE SMILES AT THE BARTENDER as she walks into the pub. He places a beer on the bar before she gets there.

"Thanks, Pete."

By the time she's finished her beer, the MC says, "Here's Claudie Sokolov back to play for us. I saw you walk in, Claudie. I'm pretty sure there are a few more people here this week. Is that down to you?"

A small cheer answers him.

Claudie smiles at the floor as she walks onto the stage.

"Evening all. I've got two covers and an original for you. First, some Billy Joel."

Loop cheers. He's the one guy at the bar who always wants Billy Joel.

After the third song, a woman shouts, "Let her play more, MC."

When the set is over, Claudie sits at their usual table next to Shelley.

"You're amazing, sis," Shelley says.

Claudie clears her throat. "It's your fault I'm here at all. But anyway, I didn't sit here to talk about me. Tell me what's going on in town."

It's been a long time, but Claudie's waking up again.

13

THE LOCAL STORE IS COOLED by a couple of large ceiling fans, but it's the middle of the day in the middle of summer, so it's still too hot. Claudie's there to find something inspirational to cook for her dinner. She walks out with tomatoes and lettuce and a tin of mixed beans. The cilantro is growing well up at the cabin, and she has onions and chili peppers. It could be worse.

"Hey!" The old guy who runs the post office hails her from across the road. She remembers his name. Neil. Claudie crosses the road.

"We've got a package for you," he says. "It's been there a couple of days. I'd've let you know but I still don't have a phone number for you. I was gonna send my kid to the park with it this weekend.

"A package?" The last things Claudie ordered were the guitar strings that arrived a week before Lien did.

"I've got it at the post office." His eyes, quick and eager, lift to her face, and Claudie suppresses her irritation. "I'll walk you back," he says. "I put it safely there under the front desk."

"Thanks."

"Been a while since you got anything in the mail now, hasn't it?" Of course he notices. It's a small town; it's been a small town the whole time she's lived here.

"It's not a big cabin up there. I think if I got another guitar I'd need to build an extension."

Neil laughs. "You got a few, that's for sure. Worth it though, the way you play. That's what I hear. Nina reckons you're the best guitar player the open mic night at Sheila's ever had. I been meaning to come and see you. I don't hear too well, though."

In the post office he goes behind the desk and pulls out the package. It's wrapped in brown paper. It's not large. He slides the package toward her as she signs for it.

"Thank you," she says. His eyes are glued to the package. She relents.

"Do you mind if I open it here? I've no idea what's in it." Inside, three layers of bubble wrap cover a small pile of CDs, along with a note. Claudie opens the note. It's signed "Lien." Claudie's heart stutters. Her smile pulls her face too tight as she folds the note and pockets it. The CDs are labeled with dates, that's all.

"CDs," the guy offers. "Photos maybe. Or some music. You got something you can play them on?"

"Yeah. I've got something in the cabin."

She packs the CDs up and drives back through the park. Cirrus clouds skim across the sky; the hills rise around the car. She's shaken. The whole way home her heart hammers out a prickling and hopeful beat.

CLAUDIE KEEPS LIEN'S NOTE IN her pocket until she's stepped onto the deck. The sky is still. The bush is tranquil below it. Whole hosts of birds are hidden there. They twitter and squawk as she unfolds the note.

"Dear Claudie," Lien's handwriting is neat and curvy.

"After I left I couldn't stop thinking about your music; the stuff you played for me and the Grand Echo tracks, too. I spoke with some people from your old band and they pointed me to the recording studio.

"And the studio guy played these recordings for me. Your original stuff. I don't know what these will mean to you, if anything. But I think they are remarkable. Unlike anything else. The way you use the electronic stuff to lift the guitars to a new level without overpowering your guitar work. And your vocals. I knew I enjoyed your music, but this is even more than I expected.

"So I wanted to send them. In case you want a reminder of your talent.

"And I wanted to say thank you. You rescued me and you woke me up to some things. My life's changing, and I will always appreciate that.

"Yours, Lien."

Claudie reads the note over again. Then she folds it into her pocket.

She rummages through the cupboard to pull out her old CD player. She wipes down the interior with a dry cloth. When she plugs it in, the CD player whirs to life. She selects a CD at random and positions it in the player.

The song that rolls over her is one she wrote the year before everything fell apart. It's quirky; the lyrics are overly wordy and complex maybe. But the guitars are sparse but interesting, and the echo in the electronics gives the lyrics space. Claudie's voice sounds fragile and growly at once, rich and mobile but perfectly in beat.

Claudie can't help imagining Lien listening. The girl always listened with so much of herself. Claudie touches the stack of CD cases on the table. Lien packed these up. It's kind of her to send them. It's a bit of a boost to hear this right now.

Claudie turns the music up and opens the windows to the treetops. She sits in the chair she slept in that first night Lien was there.

The lyrics aren't relevant; it's not a song about a crush on a faraway girl you can never have. Claudie thinks about Lien nevertheless.

When the first CD finishes she opens a second. Lien's put a note with this one, too:

"Track 4 is wonderful. I know you're happy where you are, but I am convinced that there is a market for your solo work. I'm not just saying that. I know the industry, and I have an ear for what's next. People would be excited about this stuff."

Claudie's not sure. But performing at the bar has become the best part of her week, and these recordings unlock a longing in her.

SHE'S BOOKED TO PLAY AT Sheila's open mic the next night. Everyone's there. She cheers for one guy who plays some pretty awesome folk. When she gets on the stage she plays some Rolling Stones. Then she plays an original, something she's played over and over again out in the bush for the past couple of years, something she played for Lien. It goes over well with everyone except Loop. But then, it's not Billy Joel.

"Sorry, Loop," she says. "Next time I'll play 'Downeaster Alexa' for you. But this one's something new."

When she's done, she sits with Shelley and some of the other locals.

"Did you hear they're moving the sand out of the park?" one of the guys asked.

"The mining-waste sand. That's good isn't it?" Claudie says. They don't mine coal in the park any more but there are reminders of that history.

"You won't be the one watching ten trucks a day go down your fucking unsealed road."

"You got a better idea to get it out of there, Graeme?" Shelley asks.

"Nah. Nah. Just wanted to make sure you all knew."

"That was a gorgeous set, Claudie," says one of the women.

"You're killing it," says Shelley and pats Claudie's thigh. "Thatta girl."

Claudie's only now ready to make these connections. She doesn't blame herself for that. Still, it seems pretty stupid to get to know these people right when she's realized it's time to go.

CLAUDIE CALLS SHELLEY BEFORE SHE does anything, before she even calls the National Parks and Wildlife Service. In Shelley's house, they sit on the soft red and cream striped sofa and drink herbal tea as though they're a couple of hippies.

"I'm thinking about moving back to Sydney, Shell."

Shelley nods and says, "I knew it. Ah, hell. I'm so happy for you."

"You knew?"

"Well, of course, sis. You've got the city in your veins, too. And your music. As soon as you called about the open mic I figured it was all over. I didn't know how long it'd take you to catch up."

"I could do music up here." Claudie's not sure whether she's trying to get Shelley to convince her to stay or to go.

"You could, but you haven't."

"Fair point."

Shelley sighs. "I only hope they find someone kind of decent to replace you. I'll make them let me do the interviews. I have an eye for that kind of thing."

The whole thing's going more easily than Claudie expected. She expected resistance, but only her pride minds that it's not there.

"You're not angry?" asks Claudie after a quiet moment.

"Of course not. It's your life. And I reckon it's the right decision for you. I liked you being here, but I'm not about to try and keep you." Shelley frowns. "I am a bit annoyed about one thing, though. I wanted you to be here when I, uh—No one except Dylan knows yet but I'm having a kid."

"Oh, my god."

Shelley turns back to Claudie and smiles as if she can't stop. "Yep. Watch out world, there's going to be a mini-Shelley running around."

"Maybe the kid'll take after Dylan."

"If we're lucky." Shelley laughs.

"I'm so happy for you. That's amazing."

"I know. Australia could do with another proud Bundjalung kid."

It's not only Claudie's life that's changing. Everything moves on. Shelley and Dylan will be teaching their kid about wildlife and camping and their language. Claudie gives her a hug. They don't hug often, but it's not awkward. Claudie wipes her eyes with the back of her hand. Shelley sniffs.

"Well, it's a long way off yet. Gives a mother time to get ready, I guess. More tea?"

As Claudie leaves, she says, "I'm nervous."

Shelley nods. "I'll bet you are. You haven't taken a risk like this in years. It's a good risk, though."

"I don't want to lose what I've found here, either. The wilderness, and you."

Shelley says, "You're not losing us. The park will always be here. Me too. Come up and stay with me and Dylan and the sprog any time."

"Thanks, Shelley."

A MORNING MIST HAS SETTLED on the mountain. Shelley drives with one hand as she takes a gulp of her coffee. She offered to bring Claudie down to Casino for the Sydney train despite the painfully early departure time. They drive past tangled trees covered in vines. As the car breaks free of the bushland, the sun dispels the mist and lifts over green and gold grasslands. The road scores sweeping curves through the fields as far as they can see.

Shelley says, "You reckon you'll see that Lien girl once you're back in Sydney?"

Claudie's heart compresses at Lien's name, even in Shelley's broad accent. "No," she says.

Shelley narrows her eyes.

"Hey, we had an interesting few days, but she's dating someone else. She's the kind of girl who's always dating someone else. She'll never stay still."

"I'm not sure that's a reason not to see her. She took the time to send you all that music. Maybe you should take a chance."

Claudie shakes her head. There are enough risks in going to Sydney. "She sent me music because she's into music. If she wanted to see me, she'd have sent her number. Anyway, I've got to rebuild a life in Sydney. I can't spend time hunting down people I've got no reason to see."

"You like her. That's a reason."

"I like a lot of people."

Shelley laughs. "You're a big old liar, Claudie Sokolov."

Claudie grins. "I like you."

Shelley laughs again. "I'll give you that one."

Casino station's quiet. The train is already here. Claudie and Shelley stand in the parking lot. The moment warrants a quick, fierce squeeze. Claudie lifts her head to the bright sky and blinks back tears.

"You were here the longest," Shelley says. She sniffs. "Of all the rangers. It's supposed to be a short-term role. Six months to one year, they say. You stayed."

"I stayed because I loved it."

Shelley shrugs. "I know. And also because you were hiding."

Claudie bites her lip and doesn't argue. "Not any more, I guess."

They stand together. Shelley shifts on her feet. "Right, well the train's due to leave. You'd better get on. I'll miss you, sis."

"I'll miss you, too."

Shelley squeezes Claudie's hand before she walks back to the parking lot. She turns back before she leaves the station. Claudie lifts a hand in farewell.

It's thirteen hours by train to Sydney, down the long coastline of New South Wales. Claudie has two seats to herself. The first part of the journey is mostly farmland. This summer's rains have kept the fields green. Cows watch the train pass. Toward Coffs Harbour, banana plantations press up against the train line. There's a brief point where the train crosses a sandy inlet and the ocean emerges between the trees, an endless dazzling blue. Claudie naps for some of the morning, scribbles some new songs in a notepad, eats a breakfast bar and later a sandwich. Towns slip past, then more bushland and hills rolling into the ocean.

Slowly, the city of Sydney spreads out before her. Shops and cars appear alongside the train tracks. The bushland thins. Claudie's in the suburbs of Sydney, surrounded by brick homes and backyards and suburban streets, long before she can see the city skyline.

She sent most of her gear into storage until she finds somewhere to live. She has two guitars, though, and a bag full of the clothes that will work in Sydney as the season turns from summer.

Her parents collect her from the station nearest their place. Her mother's waiting as she exits the platform.

"Sweetheart," Regina Sokolov says. Her hair is as long as it was when Claudie was a kid and tied in a thick, steel gray ponytail. She holds Claudie by the shoulders to inspect her. "Are you still growing?" she asks.

"Not since high school." Claudie smiles down at her.

"Your father's with the car," Regina says.

The car's the same make they had growing up, an ordinary white sedan. Her father helps lift her bags and guitar in. He's lost weight since she last saw him and his pants sit oddly around his hips, but his round face and gray eyes are bright with humor.

"Your room's ready," her mother says once they're in the car. She turns to pat Claudie's knee. Claudie feels young, here in the backseat again.

"I made your mother put some of her boxes of books in the attic," her dad adds.

"They weren't all mine, Vedran."

"They were fluid dynamics texts, Reggie. You're a physics professor. I'm a biochemist. They certainly weren't mine."

"Thanks for letting me stay, guys," Claudie interrupts before they start arguing about the relative value of the various sciences. Her sister's a hydraulic engineer. Claudie's out-of-left-field career in music had surprised them all, but the family's never been anything but supportive, if slightly confused.

"Of course we want you to stay with us," says her mother. "We're delighted. Your father wants someone who'll play Scrabble with him."

"'Eulerian' is not a Scrabble word, Regina."

"No, dear," her mother says.

Claudie's touched that they're willing to take her in with no fuss. They made no fuss about her leaving Sydney either.

"A cabin," her mother said. "I can imagine you there."

"Can you handle the loneliness?" her father asked.

"It's only a year-long contract," Claudie said. "And I've been unhappy for a while. I need some time to regroup, I think." But as soon as she got to the cabin she loved it and needed it and had stayed three years.

The house is at the edge of the bush, far from the train line to the city. Claudie will need to find herself an apartment soon, preferably one closer to public transport than her parents' place. She'll also need a job. She has a bit of a financial buffer; she's hardly used any money in the last three years. The cabin came with the job, and she barely left it. But she doesn't want to spend everything she has. Music's easier to make when you know you have money for food.

"You'll want a shower I expect," says her mother. "And we've saved your dinner."

"I'll set up a game of whist for later," says her father. "Or royal rummy."

Claudie's old room is bare-walled and mostly empty, aside from the floor-to-ceiling bookshelves that still seem to hold an impressive number of scientific texts. She sets her guitars in the corner, plops her bag on the floor, and sits on the single bed. Her posters used to hang here; she studied at the desk against the window. This was where she started dreaming of music and of women: the Lilith Fair and Tracey Chapman and Liz Phair.

She'll feel better after a shower. And a game of rummy might be fun, if she can recall the rules.

IT'S A TOUGH TIME TO be finding a place to rent in Sydney. At least, that's what it seems based on the legions of people who are at the first open house Claudie attends. The real estate agent is narrow-lipped and unwilling to answer questions. Claudie stalks out and doesn't bother to fill out an application. She's not going to get this place. She doesn't even have a regular job.

She's searching for an apartment in the Eastern Suburbs: Darlinghurst, Paddington, Rose Bay. She tries not to think about the fact that Lien lives near here. That's not what matters, it's certainly not why she's here. This might be Lien's neighborhood now, but long ago it was Claudie's too. She was one of the artists making the place. She doesn't know the bars and the locals by name any more but she knows the streets and the history.

The first nine hundred and seventy-five places she inspects are no good. Either there are a hundred applicants crowded into the living room and bedroom looking at the poorly built wardrobe or the wall has an actual hole in it or the place has no running water. Claudie's lived without running water in the bush, but this is Sydney. She needs to wash.

The nine hundred and seventy-sixth place is perfect. It has a nice neat kitchen and even a glimpse of Sydney Harbour if you stand on one foot and lean from the balcony. Claudie fills out an application form. But the agent's already shaking hands with a polished looking Indian couple, so no doubt they'll get that place.

Claudie stops at a bar on the corner. The bartender inspects Claudie as she pulls the beer.

"New to the neighborhood?" she asks as she hands over the cold glass.

"Not really," says Claudie.

It's early afternoon on a Wednesday, so the place is pretty empty. Two guys are gazing into one another's eyes in the corner. Claudie sits alone in a window that looks onto the sidewalk.

Across the street is a row of shops. A girl with a sheet of black hair, brown legs, and a short white dress looks into the window of one of them. Claudie recognizes Lien. She looks down at her beer, unable to breathe and unsure what she should say. When she looks up again the girl's closer and isn't Lien at all; she's white-skinned and blue-eyed and taller than Lien by approximately five feet.

Claudie shakes her head. She keeps expecting Lien around every corner and at every bus stop and in the queue for coffee, even though Lien doesn't drink coffee. Now Claudie's fucking seeing things.

The shop the girl was looking into is a guitar place. It has a "help wanted" sign in its window. Claudie finishes her beer in three mouthfuls and crosses over.

"Hi. You're looking for someone?" she asks, indicating the notice.

The woman behind the counter nods. She leans forward to shake Claudie's hand. "Yep. You got a CV?"

Claudie hands it over. The woman scans it, then she scans Claudie. The woman is not young, but she's wearing a kitten T-shirt, her skin is brown, her dark eyes are round, and her blue hair is in short pigtails that stick out from her head.

"I'm Dee Dobbins, the owner." She studies Claudie, looks back at the resume. "I remember your band around town a while back. You guys..." She trails off and frowns. "And you've spent the past few years—?"

"Working as a park ranger up north."

Dee raises her eyebrows. "What, a bit of a tree change?"

Claudie blushes and opens her mouth to answer.

"Nah, sorry, mate," Dee says. "Stupid question. I'm not laughing at you. It's a huge thing to work alone. I can't even imagine." She barely pauses. "You're gonna get back into music. Play Sydney?"

Claudie nods. "Yeah." It's the first time she's said it so clearly. "That's the plan."

Dee nods slowly. "And you want a day job. You ever worked retail?"

"No. Though I manned the band's merch table for the first couple of years."

"Can you restring a guitar?"

"Of course." Claudie's restrung a six string in the middle of a set while she kept right on singing.

"Okay." The woman looks at her with her head tipped to one side. "Right. The job's part time. Weekend days and Thursday nights are my busiest times so I'll need you then as much as possible. We'll be flexible other than that. When can you start?"

"As soon as you want me."

"I've got six guitars out back that need stringing. Want to start now?"

"Sure." Claudie's warmed to Dee.

Dee looks at the clock on the wall. "I make it one-thirty."

It takes a couple of hours to restring and then tune each guitar. Then Dee teaches her to handle payments and the phone. Claudie tries not to show how much she doesn't like having to answer the phone.

On the train home, Claudie stretches her legs out and leans against the window. She's tired. A train draws up beside them, heading the same way for this stretch of track. The carriages move in sync, making everything seem slow motion. A little kid is staring out the window. They travel side-by-side.

The commute home is not short. It's two trains, then a bus. But at least it's a commute now, not just a trip. She has a job she can put on the rental applications.

Through the window of the bus, the light's evening soft, and the streets wind around the bush. Claudie grew up here. It's not home, but nowhere really is. She gets off a stop early and walks.

CLAUDIE FINDS AN APARTMENT DOWN the road from the guitar shop. The place is tiny, but it's at the back of the building and it has a fire escape and an outlook over some trees. She'll have room for some potted plants and herbs on the tiny balcony. She can walk to the shop, the bus, and about seven hundred local bars.

The owner lives below and has taken over a room upstairs, leaving a living-dining-kitchen with a sink and stove top, a room about the size of a large wardrobe that will fit a bed, and a bathroom. The owner has a huge dog, an Irish wolfhound-Doberman mix with a bit of border collie. The dog takes to Claudie. Claudie takes to the tiny place.

She doesn't need a removal truck to move in. She barely owns anything. She buys a decent futon, a small sofa, and a new fridge, and has them all delivered. She hangs her guitars on the wall.

The bedroom and living room are divided by a large arch. At night, through the windows or standing on the fire escape, she can see the few stars that are visible in the city. Orion's there, of course. Even in the city it's huge and bright, the one constellation Lien recognized when they stood together on Claudie's deck.

It's early evening by the time she's all moved in. Claudie eats pizza perched on a stool at the tiny kitchen bench. The traffic noise isn't friendly the way the wind and burbling creek were up north, but there are voices from the back of the house next door, and someone's playing Kylie Minogue's early tracks. Humanity is close by, for better and for worse.

She hasn't told any of the band kids that she's back in town. She hasn't told anyone at all apart from her parents. Claudie eyes her phone where she left it on the sofa. It's time to call Mercy.

The phone rings and rings and goes to voicemail. Obviously Claudie should have called earlier. She should have called when she decided to move, on the trip down, in the weeks it's taken to arrange everything since she got here.

She stands to wash her plate and glass. Her phone rings. Mercy's name runs across the screen.

"Hello."

"Claudie?" Mercy's American accent is familiar. It's been too long since Claudie's heard it.

"Hi, Merce." She takes a long breath.

"How are you?"

"I'm good. I'm—" Claudie pauses. "How are you?"

"Are you back in Sydney?" Mercy asks. And it's like the old days—
she always knew. Lou and Claudie told one another everything—well,
almost everything—but Mercy knew what was going on without ever
asking.

"Yeah. I am. I know it's been a long time. I'm sorry."

Mercy says, "You still don't need to apologize, Claudia." Her voice
is soft with sympathy.

The phone line is silent. "Can we meet?" Claudie asks.

"Of course," says Mercy. She doesn't hesitate, but her tone is wary
as she goes on. "You want to meet up at a café? Or you could come to
mine? We could pull out some instruments if you want."

"I'd love that," Claudie says. Her stomach is tight with nerves.

It's afternoon and warm. Claudie's sweating. She holds her guitar
and bag in one hand and rings the bell at Mercy's house.

Mercy opens the door. "Hey."

Mercy never changes much. Her smile is soft; her eyes are large
behind her glasses and bright against her dark brown skin. Her curly
hair is tied in a topknot at the crown of her head. She's wearing olive
green. She probably wore the same shirt the last time Claudie saw her.

"Hey. God, it's good to see you."

"You too." Mercy's smile widens. "Come in. Mary's not here; she's
teaching a late class." It's good to hear Mary's still around. She and
Mercy have been dating since years before the band split up.

Mercy's place has a music room out the back. Claudie follows Mercy
down the narrow hall. A fat orange cat walks with them.

"It's damp so I don't keep much in here. But it's soundproof," Mercy
says. She uncovers a solid looking keyboard.

It's uncomfortable at first, sitting together after so long without really
knowing what to say. Mercy's never talked much about herself without

prompting and Claudie hates the thought of asking things she should know about one of her closest friends, things such as how everything has been in the past three years.

"Are you working on anything?" she asks instead.

Mercy turns on the keyboard. The cat leaps to the windowsill and stretches out there. "Sure. Just some stuff for me, really. I don't play out in the wild at the moment." She smiles crookedly.

"Can I hear it?"

Mercy hesitates. "You can play with me, if you like." She nods at the guitar in Claudie's hand. "You didn't bring that along to look at, did you?"

Claudie huffs out a laugh. "No. Of course not. But you should start."

It's been a long time since Claudie played with someone else, but this is Mercy. They were in a band together for years. Claudie will always know how she plays. Mercy warms up with a couple of arpeggios, then plays. Her music has more layers than it did before. Claudie can tell it's written for solo work.

"Okay," Mercy says, too soon for Claudie's liking. "You need to join in. I'm not suited to solos." She shifts her glasses.

"Okay." The trouble is, Claudie's stagnated. She's spent the past three years playing to herself and then the past two months playing covers in a tiny local pub.

"Go on," Mercy says.

"I haven't played much in a long while."

"You're not going to disappoint me, Claudie. Things are quiet for me too."

"Why?" Claudie asks the question she hopes people won't ask her.

Mercy looks at her directly. "I don't know. I never found a fit. Not a lot of bands are looking for the kind of loops and electronic work I do. And I never had confidence in my solo efforts. They don't quite work." She doesn't sound as though she's accusing Claudie, but Claudie feels as though she's wronged her anyway.

"I'm sorry."

"Hey. It's my job to find myself a creative outlet. And you're here now. It's time to hit me with something."

Claudie pulls over a sheet of music paper and scrawls some chords. She slides it to Mercy. "And you can put some Mercy loops and stuff in here. See?"

Mercy nods.

They start roughly but it comes together for a time, then dies as Mercy adds a new loop and misses the repeat. They try again. It comes together.

"I like this," Mercy says. She waves her hand at a section. "Do you have any lyrics?"

Claudie nods and adds a vocal.

Between songs they talk about where Claudie's living and Mercy's job in accounting. They don't talk about starting the band again.

"I miss her," Mercy says, out of the blue.

"Me too." She hasn't talked about Louisa in three years, but missing her is huge in Claudie's head and tangled with anger and about a million other things she can't say. "I didn't think I'd still miss her."

"Yeah. I doubt it'll ever go. Especially when we're playing."

"So," Mercy says as they pack up hours later. "Here's the thing. They've got an open mic at the Corner every Wednesday night. Usually you need to sign up weeks in advance, but one of the performers dropped out and suggested I could fill in. Next week. Maybe we could do it together."

After she drops the guitar at home, Claudie walks to the grocery store. It's open late. She buys too much to fit everything in her backpack, so has to take two carry bags. Outside, the sky is gray and the evening is cooling. The handles on the plastic bags dig into her hands as she walks.

She tends to walk through the curving backstreets rather than going the slightly shorter but infinitely more crowded distance along Oxford Street. The route is even longer carrying the groceries.

She opens the building door and lugs the bags upstairs. She unpacks in the kitchen. The room fills with the scent of ginger and lemongrass.

It was impossible to resist, even though it takes her straight back to that day with Lien.

It would be weird to call Beau now. It would be weirder to do nothing. She holds her breath as she sends a text.

Hi Beau, this is Claudie the park ranger from up north. I've moved back to Sydney and wanted to pass on my thanks to Lien for the CDs she sent up. Thanks.

Claudie's cooking when she receives a text from a different number.

Hey. I'm so glad you got the CDs and hope the move to Sydney went smoothly. Cheers! L

Then a second later her phone buzzes again.

Let me know if you want to meet up.

Claudie does want to meet up but she's not at all sure what to suggest.

I'm playing at an open mic next Wednesday.

Lien's response doesn't settle Claudie's nerves.

The one at the Corner? Sounds good. Might see you there.

CLAUDIE SQUARES HER SHOULDERS AS they head into the Corner Café. Her lungs feel tight. The place isn't a café at all. It looks like a hole-in-the-wall bar from the outside, but it opens up into a back room and performance space. It's designed for casual shows and is the kind of room where Claudie has always been at home. Claudie and Mercy find a table in a corner. They can't see much of the room except one corner's wallpapered walls and mismatched chairs. Claudie keeps an eye out for Lien but it doesn't look as if she's here.

It's almost eleven by the time Claudie and Mercy get up to play. While Mercy plugs in her array of pedals, Claudie scans the room from the tiny stage, which is set inches above the floor. The open mic is popular; the little room is full. People sit around tables, and others lean against the bar or the wall. Claudie's heart seizes. Lien.

This time it's an actual, real-life Lien. She's leaning into a conversation, there at a round table, among friends. Her shining hair swings forward and catches the low light. Lien lifts her gaze and sees Claudie. Her eyes open wide. Then she smiles, and Claudie forgets what she's about to play.

Mercy starts with a winding melody. Claudie shakes herself. She lets her fingers find the strings and press down, taking the weight of the chord. She plays by muscle memory alone. As soon as she hits the verse, the words will come. The songs go well. She only meets Lien's gaze between fifteen and three hundred times.

Afterwards the next band moves around Claudie, setting up their stuff and blocking her view of the tables.

"Great show!" says a kid with a scraggly beard.

"Thanks."

"You used to be with that band, yeah?"

He doesn't look old enough to remember. But sometimes she forgets it was only three -and-a-half years ago. It seems like a lifetime. "Grand Echo. I sure was."

"You were my sister's favorite local band ever. She's not here anymore."

"You mean?" Claudie frowns.

"London," says the kid. He gives a gloomy sigh as if his sister's lost to him forever.

"Damn. That's rough." It's nice he misses his sister.

Claudie glances past his head. Lien's friend, Beau, is standing. Annie too. Some of the others stand. The group is obviously leaving. Some women walk past. When they clear, Lien is still there. Claudie's heart stutters. She looks back at the tiny stage. The next performer's almost up.

"Least you have somewhere to stay," Claudie says to the kid. "There are some top venues in London."

"True," he says. Someone calls out to him. "Good talk," he says to Claudie and wanders off.

Claudie walks directly to Lien's table. "Hey."

Lien half stands. She's wearing a short dress in blocks of color: blue and teal and yellow. Her hair is shorter than it was and is streaked with a greener blue. She looks adorable. As she stands, her chair scrapes the floor. She sits back down. "Hi," she says. "Do you want to join me?"

Claudie does want to join her. She sits.

Lien says, "Hi. I can't believe you're here."

"Yeah. Nor can I, most days."

Lien takes her in. "So. You decided you'd move back."

"I did, yeah." Claudie's tongue won't move properly in her mouth. She toys with the seam of her jeans hen flattens her hands on the table top.

"Right." Lien takes a mouthful of her beer. "How's that working out?"

"Good. It's nice to play with Mercy again."

Lien goes on, mild and cheerful and infuriatingly unreadable. "You guys were fantastic up there. It was awesome when you started on 'Suddenly.'"

Claudie grins. "I know. It was the perfect choice for that spot." She pauses and Lien flicks her a glance. Claudie says, "I'm getting a beer. Can I get you one?"

Lien shakes her head. "I'm pretty sure I'm the one who owes you a beer. What are you drinking?" While Lien's at the bar Claudie tries to remember that she's nothing to Lien. She's the weird four-day-long cabin fling who took ages to get back in touch. Minus the cabin bit, Lien probably has heaps of those.

Lien slides the beer across the table. "Oh, hey, I have the best story for you," she says. Someone yells, "Bye, Claudie!" from across the room. Claudie holds up a hand and barely looks away from Lien's face. It's as easy as it ever was between them. They talk about Claudie's job and Lien's newly dyed hair, about Claudie's growing potted plant army on her fire escape and how Lien fixed a leaking tap in the kitchen.

Claudie only looks up to say goodbye to Mercy.

Once the pub's cleared out a little, Lien says, "I heard about your friend, Louisa. I'm so sorry. That must have been awful for you."

Claudie nods. She doesn't say anything. She's glad there's a band on stage to keep them both diverted.

166

Eventually Claudie fades. She scrunches up her nose. "I'm working tomorrow," she says. "And I'm tired. I'm so sorry, but I have to go."

Lien blinks, surprised as though she's just woken up. "It was good to see you." She looks at the time on her phone. "Oh, gosh. You're right, it's late."

"It was good to see you too," says Claudie. She reaches across the table, intending to squeeze Lien's hand. She stops herself.

Lien blurts, "I might get in touch now I've got your number. We could maybe hang out sometime. As… I mean, we could be friends." She gives a half shrug.

"Yeah." Claudie swallows. "I'd like that." She can imagine that. She can do friends. With Lien it's not simply that she's gorgeous. It's not simply chemistry. They always have so much to say.

"Can I help you get your gear out of here?" Lien asks.

Her tone is hopeful. Claudie wants to hug her. "It's only my guitar," she says. She smiles. "I can handle it."

They walk out together. The traffic has eased. The streets are washed greenish by the light from the streetlights and gold from the open doors and windows of bars. They walk half way home before they go their separate ways.

15

It's a few days before Lien gets up the nerve to contact Claudie, and even then it's not about getting together as friends. It's for a piece she's writing.

There are a hundred good reasons to write an article about the lost talents of the Australian music industry. Lien's not only writing because of Claudie, whatever Beau insinuates. It's an interesting subject; it's different from her usual material. If Lien takes her time with this, she's sure she can get one of the serious music mags interested.

She works hard on the groundwork. She arranges to talk with a couple of solo artists who threw in the towel and a couple of bands that collapsed; she sets up meetings with a psychologist and a music history expert. She researches and plans.

But the fact that she hasn't talked to Claudie, not even to tell her what she's working on, sits heavily in her chest.

She doesn't think too hard about the text to Claudie.

Can we meet up? I want to chat about something professionally.

The response comes ten minutes later.

Sure. I'm working today. Tomorrow?

They meet at a narrow cafe with stools and tall, dark wooden tables. The place serves excellent coffee and tea, but nothing much else. Claudie orders a long black. She's wearing a tight band T-shirt and acid-washed 80s jeans that she's somehow making work. She seems to belong in Sydney, more than Lien thought possible. Lien spent weeks after the cabin convincing herself that Claudie would never be able to live in the city. So seeing her here, and comfortable with herself, is confusing.

"How are you?" Lien asks once they're both sitting. She swings her legs back and forth under the stool.

Claudie manages a careful smile. "Good. Fine. Working, playing. I've been writing some music."

"That's good to hear."

Claudie exhales. "You know, you were right. I didn't like hearing it at the time, but I do need to be making music. I'm not myself without it. So I wanted to say thank you." Lien imagines the admission costs Claudie something.

"Honestly, you've got nothing to thank me for. I said what I felt in the moment. I could have been more careful. And I sent those CDs because I wanted to hear you play again."

Claudie's expression is warm. "Well, looks like you'll get your wish. You can't stop me appreciating it."

Lien shifts on her chair.

"So, is something up?" Claudie asks. "You seem on edge."

"I have to ask you about something."

"Yeah? What's that?"

Lien sits back under Claudie's cool gray scrutiny. "I hope you're not angry."

"I hope so too." She's not joking.

"So, I've been doing a bit of investigating and pulling together an article, something longer and hopefully more consequential than my usual work. I'm getting a sense of the music industry and how it kind of spits the most interesting people out sometimes. I want to write a long piece about musicians who left the big smoke or broke down and their bands folded."

Claudie narrows her eyes. "And?"

"And I want to put your story in there."

Claudie puts her coffee cup on the table. "You told me you wouldn't investigate me."

"Well, no. I mean, kind of, but this is different. This is about the music industry; this stuff is more public. I meant I wouldn't write about personal stuff."

"Music is 'personal stuff' for me."

"Yeah. But you know what I mean."

Claudie frowns. She doesn't look at Lien as she says, "I trusted you. You told me I could trust you. I had you in my house."

Lien's chest squeezes as Claudie's anger washes over her. When Claudie looks up again, Lien shrinks.

They sit in silence. But the article matters. Lien's not going to back down on this. She's trying not to be that girl. She says, "Claudie, the thing is, this story is bigger than any one artist. It's about how the music industry works, what it does to talent. It's about how tough it is to make a living in music even when you're the best, and how hard it is to be yourself and do well."

Claudie doesn't speak.

"I'm not writing about things that aren't already known. Not really. I'm bringing them all together. And it matters. It really does matter. Because you and I both love this industry, but it doesn't do its best by the finest people in it."

Claudie tips her head. "Who've you spoken with?"

Lien rattles off a couple of names. Claudie's interested. Lien's pretty sure she has her. "I'm serious about this," Lien says.

"Then you don't need me."

"I want you, though," Lien says. "Your story means something."

The cafe keeps moving around them. "Okay. Yeah, okay." Claudie relents.

"So I can interview you?" Lien almost bounces in her seat.

"You can." She half laughs. "Don't you know enough about me already?"

Lien flashes back to the ways she knows Claudie. "Um. Not the way I need to."

After a moment Claudie says, "The trouble is, the music industry isn't just my past, Lien. I'm hoping it's my future. So I can't say anything that'll damage my career."

Lien's ready for this. "I think this'll do the opposite for you. I think by talking about the industry we can make it better. People will listen. So your future will be better too."

Claudie finishes her coffee before speaking. "Okay. Fine. I'm in."

They set a date a week and a half away. Claudie's working extra shifts and the interval suits Lien. She has deadlines for a couple of local queer papers, and she wants to get all her groundwork finished before she starts interviewing musicians. She's not going to rush this one and disappoint herself or anyone else.

THEY WALK HOME DOWN OXFORD Street together. Lien's phone buzzes in her pocket. The phone buzzes again. When her pocket buzzes a third time, Lien slows down and pulls out her phone. The messages are all the same. The kids are going back to Gigi's for Thursday night drinks.

Lien doesn't think. "Hey. We're heading out tonight. Do you know Gigi's on the Square?"

"Yep."

"Looks like I'll be there at ten with some of the guys if you want to join us? They usually have a good DJ."

Claudie rubs at her wrist. She's considering it, at least. Lien's stomach flips annoyingly. It's not as if anything hangs on Claudie's answer. Claudie says, "Look I've got this idea stuck in my head. This song that

I need to get out. I'd love to go with you, but until I get this written I'm going to be no company at all."

Lien's disappointed. "Okay. Of course." She smiles. She wants to make it clear to Claudie that she's never going to pressure her to go anywhere. "Sure thing."

"Thank you, though."

Lien nods. They go separate ways at the corner of Lien's street. "See you later," Lien says.

Later that night Lien's phone buzzes with a text from Claudie.

Want to take a break and see the rock photography exhibit at the Powerhouse tomorrow?

Lien doesn't consider saying no.

The exhibit is mostly photojournalism—huge stage pictures of Madonna and Chrissy Amphlett among mainstays of the local indie scene. Lien and Claudie don't talk much. Now and then Claudie points out a particularly interesting fact or an instrument in one of the photos. It's a glimpse into the things that fascinate her.

A FEW DAYS LATER, THEY'RE on the phone. Lien's in her bedroom, lying back on the bed with her legs propped against the wall. She has the door to the balcony wide open. Claudie's at her place, up on the second floor with her potted plants and guitars. Lien hasn't seen it but it's a lot closer than the cabin in the bush.

Lien says, "So I'm thinking I can put a few profiles in to illustrate the broader story. Make it a bit eye-catching."

"Sounds good," Claudie says. A crash echoes down the phone line.

Lien raises her eyebrows though Claudie can't see her. "What was that?"

"The guys downstairs are redecorating or something. I'm trying to use it as musical inspiration rather than a distraction."

Another crash comes. It reverberates as if Claudie's in earthquake territory.

"That's what redecorating sounds like?" Lien asks.

Claudie snorts. "It seems to involve ripping out some walls or taking out the foundations or something. If you don't hear from me, the building's come down. Look after my potted plants for me?"

Lien laughs. "I'll love them like my own. Hey, did I tell you I have an interview with Lissy Anderson?"

"Nice."

"I wouldn't have got it if you hadn't recommended me—" Another crash comes down the line, this one bigger than those before it. "Oh, my god. It sounds like thunder."

"Yeah, the noise is not ideal."

"Soon your power will be out, and you'll be kicking your fridge." Lien wasn't planning to say that. They don't mention their time in the cabin much.

"Oh god, you remember that?" Claudie asks.

"Of course I do. I remember everything." Neither of them says anything. Lien waits for another crash. It doesn't come.

"What are you working on today?" she asks Claudie.

"Not much. Pulling together some new music. Mercy and I got some tracks down. I wanted to do a bit of editing on the laptop."

"With that noise going on? Are you writing thrash metal?"

Claudie half laughs. "I'll admit it's not going well. I mean, I'm only listening and pulling the sounds together. I'm not really playing anything. But the vibrations are intense. I might need to take it to the store."

"Do you want to come over here?" Lien asks before she thinks. "My room has a nook you could pop your laptop in. And I'm working, so I won't bother you. Promise. You might need to let Beau fanboy over you, though."

"Huh." Three crashes come in quick succession as though the gods have spoken—the renovation gods. "Okay," says Claudie. "Yes. That'd be great."

"You know where it is?"

"You pointed out the street the other night when we were walking home. What number are you?"

"We're in sixteen. It's got a red door, tomato red."

"I'll be right over." Claudie pauses. "Thank you, Lien."

Lien throws some of her clothes into the wardrobe. She straightens her desk and turns on the fairy lights. She runs her fingers through her hair. She considers changing. They're getting together to work; she's not supposed to be dressing up, but maybe a different T-shirt. Fifteen minutes later there's a knock at the door.

"I'll get it," Beau yells. He thumps down the stairs before Lien can call out.

"It's for you," he shouts a second later.

"Cheers," Lien says. She's already on her way down. At the bottom of the stairs, Claudie's framed in the doorway. She's gorgeous in tight jeans, a white shirt and black jacket. Her hair's tousled. She's the girl version of James Dean. Lien wishes she'd changed into something a bit more rock star.

"Hi," Lien says. "Come on upstairs." She looks at Beau swiftly. "We're working," she says. She's glad Beau's grown out of saying something embarrassing.

"Enjoy," Beau says, which is bad enough.

It's uncomfortable being in Lien's bedroom together. Lien scoots past Claudie to point out the window nook and the chair. "You can sit in the nook. Or, I don't know, on the bed?" She doesn't look at Claudie.

"The nook's great," Claudie says.

"We could go downstairs if you wanted. Only Beau's cooking and sometimes he sings and he's not really a singer."

"I'm happy here," says Claudie. "This is way better than what I had at my place. The whole floor was vibrating. He's been doing it for days. I tried a cafe one day, but the waitress wasn't too thrilled that I was taking up a table. I was almost glad to go to work yesterday. At least I got to escape."

"Your poor plants."

Claudie grins. "They don't have ears. They seem to be surviving all right."

"You're welcome to come and edit here whenever it suits you."

"Thank you."

Lien sits back at her desk. Open on her desktop is a half-written column about the timeless war between Melbourne's small bars and Sydney's club scene. Claudie settles into the nook. She pulls on her earphones. Her forehead furrows as she works.

It's tricky to write with Claudie there looking gorgeous and focused. Lien turns to editing a shorter article for the *Sydney Star Observer*. Now and then she looks at Claudie, but she doesn't interrupt, doesn't ask what Claudie's hearing. For now, the song is Claudie's.

An hour goes by. "Want a listen?" Claudie asks out of the silence. She doesn't look comfortable asking.

"Yes, please," says Lien. She tries to stop herself from bouncing across the room. "Absolutely."

Claudie stands to let Lien have the seat. She positions the headphones over Lien's ears. Lien holds her breath until she steps away.

The music's good, raw and interesting. It might be pioneering. The excitement builds in Lien's chest. She keeps her voice steady. "This is good stuff. Really strong." A third keyboard melody is looped in, and Claudie's vocals sit perfectly above it.

Claudie nods down at her. "Thank you. That's nice to hear. Especially coming from you."

Lien's heart buzzes with the praise. "So what's the plan for your music now you're here?" she asks when she's caught her breath.

Claudie hesitates. "Well, sometime I want to get up with Mercy to play at one of the bars in the neighborhood. Not just an open mic, an actual show. It'll take time but I'm working on it."

"Okay." Lien exhales. "Okay." This she can help with. There isn't a live music venue that doesn't know her. "I think I can get you into the Newcombe," she says. "Actually, kinda soon if you want. The booking manager will love you. He was whining about the lack of new sound the other night when I was there."

Claudie raises her eyebrows. "That would be... Really?"

"Really. It's a small venue but Sam has a good ear for breakout work."

"I'll need to check, but I'm pretty sure Mercy will be keen. Thank you. That would be perfect."

Lien grins. "Oh. It's not a favor. You know I want to hear you play a full set in public. You'll be amazing. And the guys at the Newcombe will be in my debt forever."

Claudie frowns. "Mercy and I are doing well, but do you think I should find a band, first?"

Lien's already thought about that. "Maybe. It'd be good to add the drum and bass. I can already hear the rhythm in the way you write the music. It's got an amazing beat behind it."

"Yeah. I'll get onto that."

Half an hour later Beau sticks his head through Lien's bedroom door.

"We're heading to the Arms," he says. "Annie and me and a couple of the others. You two want to join?"

Lien looks across at Claudie. "You interested?" She doesn't want to appear too eager. She breathes normally.

Claudie looks back and forth from Beau to Lien. "Okay. Sounds good."

THE PUB ISN'T FULL, WHICH is a relief to Claudie. Nine of them pile around a tall table with their drinks and a couple of packets of chips. Claudie scans the room.

The conversation is quick and mostly about people and places Claudie doesn't know. Claudie listens and puts together Lien's friends.

The tall Indian woman with a boyish cut, Kam, is dating the broad, no-nonsense white woman next to her, Megan.

Kam says, "We've decided to go visit my family at the end of the year."

"Big step," Beau says.

"I'm so impressed," says Annie from next to him.

"It'll be okay. Well, my sister will be okay," Kam says. "She's got past her constant protests that she just wants me to be happy. She's realized 'happy' doesn't mean 'exactly like her,' I guess. And my parents love me. I want to give it a go."

"That's great, guys. But don't feel like you owe them anything," Lien says.

Kam chews her lip. "No, I agree. But I'd like to give them a chance. For my sake, too. I hate that I'm lying to them."

Lien nods. "Yeah, I get that."

"Anyway, they can't afford to visit, and my dad's turning sixty, so Megan and I are going together."

"I'm confident. They are going to love me," Megan says. She squeezes Kam's hand.

The conversation turns to vintage clothing stores and how Annie was going to be first to a local estate sale but had an exam instead. Claudie drinks her beer and tries not to stare at Lien.

THE RENOVATIONS AT CLAUDIE'S PLACE haven't stopped, so Lien and Claudie are working in Lien's bedroom.

Out of a long silence, Lien asks, "Hey, are you serious about this music thing?"

Claudie frowns. "Yeah. Of course. What do you mean?" She's offended. She's always serious about band things.

"Then, my girl, it's time to get started on some social media. Twitter and Snapchat and Instagram. You have a name and a history, but you need buzz."

Claudie sighs.

Lien looks at her face and giggles. "I know, I know. You hate it. But it's honestly the only way to get people to come. Plus, you know me now, and I find that stuff fun. You're helping me with my article. The least I can do is help you lift your profile."

Claudie says, "We can leave it a few weeks. I don't even have a band yet."

"We can leave it as long as you like. But it's important, Claudia. The sooner the better. I'm not going to let this go."

Claudie nods. It's dangerous to agree to something larger and longer-term than whether they'll meet tomorrow. Claudie is pretty sure that, if she agreed to Lien writing two paragraphs on page eight of the newspaper, she'd come back to a headline article and a flier campaign. No, probably something more digital.

CLAUDIE HAS JUST ARRIVED HOME from work the next day when her phone rings. It takes a moment to recognize the number. She might have deleted it three years earlier, but she still knows it.

She stares at the phone. Part of being back in Sydney is banishing old ghosts. Dani is the oldest ghost of all.

"Hi," Claudie says.

"I heard rumors you were back in Sydney," comes Dani's voice. It's so familiar it sends Claudie right back thirteen years to when they first met. She'd been awed by Dani's confidence and impeccable style. "And now you're playing music around town. How's it working out?"

"Fine, thanks," Claudie says. She sits in the comfortable chair she got from a thrift shop she visited with Lien. "Why did you call?"

"Just being an old friend, Claudie. Catching up with you. Don't worry so much," Dani says. "It's worth having friends in the industry." She takes a breath. "So Lien Hong's managing you these days is she? Good for her. Good move from the social columns anyway. She's a cute kid."

"She's not my manager. We're friends."

"Those aren't mutually exclusive, Claudia."

"Depends on the person," Claudie says.

Dani sighs. "Okay. Anyway, I'm just saying I liked her."

"You met Lien?"

"You didn't know that?"

"I knew you'd talked, just not in person. It's no big deal."

"Yeah, she stopped by a while back. She said you'd rescued her. She's cute. I got the impression she had some plans for your career."

"I am working." She should probably stop there. "I'm doing it my own way. I'm not about to get caught up with someone making my decisions for me."

"Of course you're not. Is that what you think I did?" Dani says.

"Yep."

"Claudie. I was helping your career. You need to get over it. Hey, you know who you should meet?"

"No, Dani," Claudie says. "I should not meet anyone."

"It seems like a good fit." Dani's never been anything but persistent.

"Stop. I don't need your help. You're not my friend. You weren't then and you certainly aren't now."

Claudie hangs up. She wishes she hadn't answered. She doesn't need closure with Dani. She certainly doesn't need to be caught up in Dani's web of favors and contacts again. She pulls on her sneakers and goes for a run down to Rushcutter's Bay to clear her head.

IT'S LATE AFTERNOON ON A Monday when Lien interviews Claudie. The cafe they meet at is almost mid-way between their homes, and the barista is excellent. Claudie brings her coffee and Lien's tea to the golden brown chesterfield they usually occupy. The front window faces west, and Lien's lit from behind as the gold sun drops below the shop blinds. She's even beautiful in silhouette. It's infuriating.

Claudie takes a sip of her coffee. "I like the haircut," she says.

Lien runs her hand through her shorter, choppier hair. "Thank you."

"So this is it. Interview time," Claudie says.

Lien nods and draws a breath. She gets out a pen and paper.

"I need to ask, are you going to write about Lou?" Claudie says. Her stomach is heavy, as though it has rocks in it.

"I'm not planning to." Lien doesn't flinch. "Like, the article might include a sentence to say your close friend died. But I'm talking about the industry, not one tragedy."

Claudie looks at the steam swirling from her coffee. Up in the cabin the steam had been a friendly presence, had made her less alone in the bush. "You don't know everything about it," she says.

"No." Lien moves her chair around the table slightly. She's closer to Claudie now and half in shadow so Claudie no longer has to look into the sun to see her. "Just what I heard from Gretchen and Dani. Neither of them said much. But that's okay. If you don't want to talk about it, you don't have to. You're my friend first. I won't be using anything you don't approve."

For a time Claudie stays silent. "I trust you," she says at length.

Lien's eyes soften over the top of her giant mug of tea. She puts the mug carefully on the table. "You'd just come back from doing solo stuff in the US, I think."

Claudie nods.

"How was the band going? It would have been tough, I guess, getting back together after your time abroad."

Claudie looks at the posters on the wall beside the window. "It was fine. I'd taken a hiatus; we hadn't broken up. The US was awful to begin with. I'll tell you more about that, if it's relevant."

Lien nods.

"But right after I came back, I heard about Lou."

"And then you left the band."

Claudie looks out the coffee shop window. "I did leave. Again. Yeah."

Lien takes a mouthful of tea. "Because of Lou?" she prods.

Claudie hesitates. If she starts to talk, she knows all the words will rush out. "I'm going to tell you the whole story."

"Okay."

"Lou warned me, you know. Before I went to Los Angeles, Lou told me that Dani was in it for herself. I didn't listen. I was angry with Lou about it. Dani was my girlfriend, and, even though we didn't agree about everything, she'd brought me this great opportunity. I was getting a record deal. And one of my best friends couldn't be supportive when I was finally getting the things we all wanted. I thought she was jealous." She breathes. "But it was a fair warning, as it turned out."

Lien nods, her eyes focused.

Claudie says, "So, here's the story. I headed across to L.A. I had an understanding with a producer from over there. Dani went with me. She had all these suggestions. She wanted me to bleach my hair and change my name." Claudie smiles crookedly. "Sokolov is difficult to spell. The label had suggestions too. They had this image of what I was going to be for them. It seemed as though they wanted a new Pink—that pop-rock kick ass thing that really works for her. They had this idea of how I should talk, how I should dress, how they wanted me to sound."

"That would've been horrible," Lien says.

Claudie nods. "I mean, at first it was amazing, all the lights and a growing fan base and the opening gigs, the limo rides to the recording studios. I was making it."

"It's the dream."

"Yeah. Something like that. But it wasn't too long before I realized it wasn't working. I've got no problem with people earning money for what we do. I'd be pretty happy with that, actually." Lien nods her understanding. "But I felt like I was selling my*self* out. I was giving up who I was and giving up what music was too. I was getting something I wanted, sure, but I didn't want it like that.

"I didn't notice how much Dani was part of this until it was too late. I was old enough. I should've known what was going on but—I'd always been with her. I didn't see what she was doing. I've had to forgive myself for being an idiot."

"You weren't an idiot."

"Eh. I was. Anyway, the record tanked. And my LA dream was over. I came back home. Dani wasn't happy. She didn't want me to give it all up. We were barely seeing each other. She was traveling back and forth between new clients in L.A. and old clients in Sydney. "You're going to be huge, babe," she'd say. "Do it for us." But it felt like someone else was going to be huge. Not me."

"I get that. Absolutely."

"I mean, I can't complain. Honestly. They were giving me what they thought I wanted. They were definitely giving Dani what she wanted, and she was the one talking to them."

"But it wasn't what you wanted. So you came back—"

"So I came back, and, not long after that, Lou died." Claudie takes a mouthful of coffee. "She—she always had trouble sleeping, and anxiety sometimes hit her hard. She wasn't as careful about meds and that kind of stuff as she could have been. We were at the rehearsal space when I got a call from her mother. I walked home. It was a long way to Dani's and my place. I didn't cry, then. But I opened the door and climbed the stairs, and Dani wasn't there." Claudie swallows hard.

"Okay."

"She was in town, but I couldn't get her on the phone. I figured she couldn't help that. She didn't know what had happened. Later that day she came back, and everything seemed okay."

Lien nods. "Okay," she says again. She's watching Claudie closely.

Claudie shakes her head and keeps talking. "But it was weird, because *someone* had called the ambulance. And no one knew who it was. It was a part of the investigation into Lou's death. Because someone was there, at least afterward. *Someone* was at Lou's place."

"God," Lien says.

"Yeah."

"Dani." It's not a question. Lien already knows.

"Dani." Claudie doesn't cry about this stuff anymore. But she hates admitting it. "The police turned up to interview her. And they kept coming back. In the end she told me. She'd stopped by Lou's place and found… It made no sense for her to be at Lou's. So she panicked and ran off before she called the police. It's understandable. But it wasn't okay." Claudie doesn't know if Dani could have saved Lou. Probably not. But it will always be a question.

"They were having an affair?" Lien says.

"They were. Whatever, it's a common story, right? I just hate that it's my story. And Lou's. Lou was important to me. Dani too, I guess. And then they were both gone. I never told the others. It wasn't fair to hurt Lou's reputation. And honestly, I was ashamed as much as I was hurt. I couldn't look anyone in the eye."

"Hell, Claudie."

"Yeah. So Lou was gone. And it hurt to even think about Dani. And the band—I'd been seduced by L.A. and the lights over there and I'd fucked everything up."

"You didn't do anything wrong," Lien says. Her voice is shaky and her eyes are bright.

"I know that now. But there you go. That's what dragged me out of my dream life and up into a cabin."

Lien takes Claudie's hand.

"I'm fine, now. I miss Lou, but I'm getting the band back together. Not everyone gets a chance to do that. And you saw the cabin. That place was a dream too. In its way."

Lien meets Claudie's gaze with so much knowledge and warmth and memory that Claudie moves back. Lien releases her hand.

"Thank you for telling me," Lien says.

Claudie nods. "So, for the article you need to know more about my contract in L.A."

"That'd be great. I'll get us another cup?"

Lien walks over to the barista. The barista beams as though Lien's already a friend. Of course she is.

A DAY LATER, CLAUDIE CALLS Mercy. "Can I stop in? I've got some music thoughts."

"Sure. I'm home now if you're around."

They stand in the kitchen as Mercy makes tea.

"I talked with Lien yesterday, and she said she can get us a show at the Newcombe. We might want to leave it till we get a full band together. But it seems like a good prospect."

Mercy lifts her head from pouring steaming water into mugs. "Lien's your journalist friend?"

"Yep. I know we haven't talked about it, but, it'd be a great place to have a first show. Just an introduction. We could add some drums and bass to lift the energy for a live show."

Mercy doesn't move.

"Mercy?"

"I don't know if that's a good idea."

"Oh. Right." Claudie didn't expect that. She slows down. "Right. Because of last time?"

Mercy hands Claudie a mug and carries hers to the window. She props herself against the frame. "It's not that I blame you for going. It was hell. Lou held us together, and she was gone. But I don't know how I can trust this again."

Claudie sits at the table. "I'm sorry." She takes a breath. "It was tough, Merce."

Mercy pauses before saying, "It was tough for all of us."

Claudie swallows. She's never told Mercy what happened that day. She presses her knuckles against the hot mug.

"It was different for me."

"Yeah, I know that. But you never said anything, Claudie. I know, but I don't really know anything."

It's long past time to talk about it, but Claudie doesn't know how to start. "I'm sorry," she says.

"It's okay." Mercy turns and looks out the window.

Claudie can't let this go without a fight. She tries another angle. "The thing is, in every song that I've written I've imagined your keyboard work, Mercy. You make my music better. And I know I make you better, too. Will you give it a go, maybe talk to Gretchen? For old times' sake?"

Mercy raises an eyebrow.

"For the sake of the music."

Mercy presses her lips together. Then she holds out a hand to shake Claudie's. "Okay, okay. You win. But this is a trial."

"Of course."

Claudie keeps her face serious, but she's grinning inside.

With Mercy on board, convincing Gretchen to play will be easy. She and Mercy are close; they were old roommates until Mercy moved in with Mary. Gretchen might have another band, but she's flexible. All she wants is to play the drums.

THE NEXT DAY AT MERCY'S house, Gretchen sets up her kit. Claudie plugs her guitar into the amp. Mercy sits cross-legged in front of her keyboard.

"Tan's a no-show," Gretchen says. "I tried everything, but he's pretty committed to this other band and... Look, we're going to need another bass player."

"That's okay," Claudie says, though her heart sinks. It'll be hard to get the band together without him.

Gretchen's set up the pieces of her kit she brought along. "This is gonna be cool," she says.

At first it's not cool. Not even a tiny bit. Claudie seems to have lost the knack for explaining what she hears in the music. Mercy's tracks clash with what Claudie's imagining. Gretchen's beat is too much, too loud and showy in the small room.

For half an hour, for an hour, they tussle with it. Claudie tries to add vocals, but they seem to make it worse.

Claudie sighs. The lights are too bright. She says, "Maybe I'd better call it. This isn't exactly what I imagined."

"No," says Gretchen. "One more try, though?"

Mercy's silent. Claudie flicks at her pick.

"Look, to tell you the truth. I'm fighting with it," says Mercy. "I, I'm not over the way things ended. I know it's been a long time but I'm not over it."

"Maybe you don't need to be," says Gretchen.

Mercy continues. "But, Claudie, Gretch, full disclosure, the music hasn't been the same without you guys. And this stuff. This is good. It's different from what we used to do. The song's got more space in it."

Claudie half laughs. "Partly 'cause we need a bass."

"Partly 'cause we need a bass," Mercy agrees. "But I think... the lyrics are really something. This is good. It's new."

"Plus it's all love songs," says Gretchen. "You've never written those before. And they're good. I want to give it a shot." Claudie hadn't noticed she was writing love songs. She files that thought.

"So, one more time," says Mercy.

"One more time," says Claudie.

They do it two more times. It's not perfect, but it makes a difference. Mercy grins at Claudie from the keyboards. She flicks a pedal with her hand, and the loop echoes through the song exactly as Claudie imagined it. The drums lift it all, make it stronger, give Claudie's voice reason to be powerful.

"Okay," says Gretchen afterward.

"We still need a bass," says Mercy.

"We do," says Gretchen.

"But that was good," says Claudie.

"What shall we call ourselves?" Gretchen asks.

It hadn't occurred to Claudie that they'd need to ask. "Grand Echo," she says.

Gretchen frowns. "I just thought... I don't know. I thought we might want to start with something new."

"But we should stick with the name people already know us by. We spent years building that fan base. Some of it will still be there."

"It's not disrespectful to Lou and Tan?" Mercy asks.

Claudie looks at them. "I think it's more respectful. That's where the band came from. I want to celebrate our past, too."

"THAT SMELLS AMAZING." LIEN WALKS into the kitchen. Beau is standing over a wok, delicately turning tofu with a spoon.

"Kung Pao tofu with noodles," Annie says from the kitchen chair. "My mum's recipe. Well, she didn't use tofu."

"We're going to have way too much." Beau transfers the tofu to a paper towel with a slotted spoon. "Invite Claudie."

"Oh." Lien doesn't think too hard before she sends a text. Her phone buzzes. "She's walking over now."

Beau raises his eyebrows. "That was quick."

"If she's free, she's free. She's not a woman who messes around. It makes things easier."

"Admirable," Beau says.

Claudie arrives with a bottle of wine in brown paper.

The kitchen table's not really big enough, so they sit in the lounge room with their drinks on the floor and their food balanced on their laps. Annie and Beau take the sofa. Lien gives Claudie the caramel armchair. She pulls a kitchen chair in for herself.

"Did you finish that huge essay you were telling me about?" Claudie asks Annie.

Annie frowns while she finishes chewing. "Mmm. I submitted it on time. But it's not my best work."

"It was exceptional," says Beau.

"You only read the introduction," Annie protests.

"As if! I read the whole thing." Beau looks pleased with himself as he takes a mouthful of tofu. "This food is delicious, if I say so myself." He beams at them.

Annie rolls her eyes. "When?"

"When did I read it? While you were asleep, love. Ask me anything. I'm now an expert on free trade agreements and China."

"I imagine it would have cured your insomnia at least."

He smiles at her. "You made it interesting. So, Claudie, Li tells us your band's on its way. When can we watch you guys?"

"We're getting there," Claudie says. "Neither of you happens to play bass, do you?"

Annie laughs.

"Nope, not even for you," Beau says. "Everyone's better off if I stick to the dance floor."

Annie finishes her dinner first and places her bowl on the floor. She tucks her toes in under Beau's thigh on the sofa. Claudie looks away.

"We'll wash up," says Lien once everyone's eaten. Beau and Annie disappear into his room. Claudie follows Lien into the kitchen with Beau and Annie's bowls. Lien fills the sink with soapy water. Their faces are reflected side-by-side in the dark glass above the sink. It takes

Claudie back to the sink in her cabin, the lights reflected in the window and that vast outlook.

Once the dishes are finished, Claudie and Lien take over the living room.

Lien stretches out on the sofa. Claudie settles back in the armchair beside it. The windows are open, and the weather's cooling. She wraps her hoodie around her.

"So rehearsal was good?" Lien asks.

"It was so good. It didn't fall into place. It wasn't like some magical thing. We worked on it for an hour, and I honestly thought Mercy was going to kick us out. But then—"

Lien lifts her head. "Then?"

"Something happened. We got in sync, I guess."

"I'm so happy for you." Lien's sincerity warms Claudie.

"So all we need is a bass player. And some more songs; we've got about five or six together. Maybe later some gigs."

"So not much." Lien twinkles.

"Well, I wouldn't mind some recording time, too."

Lien sits up and drops her feet to the floor. She leans forward. "Right. I can't help with the songs. But I have an idea for a bass player you could use. His name's Boyd Burrows. He's sort of a friend of a friend. His band, Canley Reid, is on hiatus, and he's awesome. Soft-spoken guy and amazing on the bass. I'll give you his number if you like?"

"Sure," says Claudie. She'll check him out before she calls him.

Lien goes on. "Also there are other things I've been thinking."

Claudie raises her brows.

"Your posters from four years ago are still up at the Hopetoun Hotel and the Factory. You guys have a reputation there. I was at the Factory the other day. and the guy there was pretty excited when I started talking about you."

"Okay."

"It'd be a top place to have a show. You could do a warm-up at the Newcombe, iron out the kinks, and then get one of the bigger venues."

"I don't know. Would we have enough people to fill a room that size?"

"We won't if they don't know about it. But if I'm good at anything, it's letting people know about stuff."

Claudie looks at her carefully. It seems like a lot of work for Lien. "You'd do that?"

"I mean, it's not only good for you."

Lien crosses her bare legs. For a flash, Claudie recalls how those same legs felt, twined with Claudie's. She straightens in the chair and speaks more quickly than before. "That's a good thought. I'll look into it. But I won't let you work on it alone. Okay, I'm out of here. I've got work in the morning."

"Oh. Right, okay." Lien tugs her skirt down—it's tangled around her thighs—and hops off the sofa.

At the front door they stare awkwardly. Lien kisses Claudie's cheek; Claudie turns her face away. They manage a one-armed hug.

It's easy to be friends with Lien. She's interesting and generous and increasingly comfortable with silence. It's not easy to hug her, though.

It's raining heavily.

"Here." Lien reaches to the hooks beside the door and hands Claudie an umbrella. On the top step, Claudie opens a pearly white shade covered with tiny little cats or hamsters or something.

"It's so you," Lien says.

"Thank you."

Claudie walks home with rivulets running into her shoes. Her head stays dry.

"Can I bring someone to the next practice?" Claudie asks Mercy and Gretchen as they pack down in Mercy's studio. "He's a bass player."

Mercy looks up quickly.

"Okay," says Gretchen.

"I've been listening to his stuff, and he's good. You guys might know him. Boyd Burrows from Canley Reid.

"I've heard him," says Mercy. "That could work."

They're used to the three of them and no one else. But Boyd walks into the studio quietly. He's tall and thin with long red hair tied back from his pointed face. He doesn't take up too much space.

"Drink?" asks Mercy as he sets up.

"I'm good. Cheers." He waves the water bottle he's pulled from his backpack.

They try him out on the song that's kind of a sestina. It has a complicated rhythm that Boyd hooks onto quickly. He's good. He's really good. He's not Tan. Obviously. Though they both have beards. But Boyd is really good.

Gretchen throws a drumstick at him after the first run through. "This is great," she says. "I love the way you lean into it."

They take a break. Gretchen stays sitting on her drum 'throne.' Everyone else sits on the timber floor. Boyd takes a swig from his water bottle. The others drink tea. Claudie's amused. They used to rehearse with shots. How the mighty have fallen! But this might lead to a more effective rehearsal.

"You wrote the music?" Boyd asks Claudie when he puts his bottle down on the floor beside him.

"Yeah. Some of it recently, some of it's kind of been updated from work I did over the past few years."

"I like the songs. They're—I don't know. They're passionate," Boyd says.

Claudie's mind darts to Lien. Her cheeks heat up. Mercy leans against the keyboard stand and watches. When Lien looks at her she smiles.

Boyd goes on. "They're really good."

"Thank you," Claudie says. Boyd is a top bass player, and it's clear he wants in.

"Back to work, kids," says Gretchen.

Claudie nods. They unfold themselves and hop up from the floor. "We'll start on the next few songs. Bring us in, Merce, Gretchen."

Mercy plays a chord which reverberates in the walls.

"One, two, three, four!"

IT'S BEEN A LONG TIME since Lien had dinner alone with Beau. They eat at the small kitchen table.

"I miss this," Beau says. He waves his fork between them.

"Me too."

They talk about Lien's article. It's taking shape. She doesn't tell Beau that she sees Claudie in all her favorite sentences, not only the ones that are actually about Claudie. Beau talks about a photography exhibit he's been selected for. There are more stories to tell when they're not spending as much time together. Some guy at Beau's work has been stealing his pens. "I bought one of those label-making machine things. I'm labeling everything I own now."

Lien laughs. "And I thought only the good guys worked at non-profits."

Beau humphs. "You'd think."

"So, I hear you're seeing a great girl," Lien says. She's making light of it. But however happy Lien is that Beau and Annie are together, it creates a distance between them. She and Beau can't talk about everything any more.

"She's incredible," Beau says. "Sweet and smart and ridiculously gorgeous. And her body—"

"Stop right there."

Beau laughs. "Fair enough. But she really is incredible. It's almost scary how easy it is. I didn't think I'd get to have something like this. Really ever. I even met her parents."

"Oh. Excellent. They're good people. You deserve to be so happy," Lien says. "You and Annie both."

"We are. We so are. Okay, doll. Now tell Uncle Beau everything," he says. "Why on earth are you not sleeping with that gorgeous woman who spends fifty percent of her time in our house?"

"I'm not exactly sure," Lien says. "She thinks I'm too superficial."

"You are not!" Beau gasps.

"It's not that, exactly. She has this idea of me. Because I was dating Nic when we were in her cabin. And I told her I didn't like time alone. At the time I was used to writing a million tweets and attending a million parties and being busy all the time. She thinks we wouldn't fit."

Beau humphs. "What, and she hasn't noticed that she's with you most days? That's fitting."

Lien shrugs. "I guess she hasn't."

Beau eyes her. "Why don't you tell her then?"

Lien shakes her head. "I can't. I already asked her out once, basically. I threw all my cards on the table when we were at her cabin. She said no. Unequivocally no. It really sucked." She feels sick thinking about it.

"I remember." He leans back in his chair. "But Lien, this is kind of sucking anyway. You're already miserable. You might as well be miserable because you took a risk."

"I'm not miserable."

"You're a little bit miserable."

"And you're the expert on taking risk now?"

He takes a mouthful and chews slowly. "I just want you to be happy," he says eventually.

LIEN CALLS WHILE CLAUDIE'S WALKING to work. Claudie smiles as she answers.

"What's up?"

"So." Lien pauses for effect like a little drum roll. "I sold the article. The one with you in it. It's going to be the cover story for *Clash*." Her voice bounces with excitement.

It's great news that means Claudie's struggles will be public. Claudie's lungs tighten at the thought. But she's read the article. It's good: well-written and interesting. It looks at several artists, at managers and radio stations and psychology and history. It looks at gender and race and mental health and addiction. Claudie's lucky to have input at all into what people are reporting about her. Anyway, it's more about the music industry than it is about the individual musicians who left it.

She turns onto Queen Street. "Congratulations, Lien. I'm so proud."

"So, I'm calling to thank you. You were integral to it. I'd never have thought it up without you."

"You'd have thought of something else though."

"The thing is, I wanted to ask. I—it's my first cover piece, Claudie. Can I take you to dinner?"

"Sure," Claudie says. Her voice is higher than she'd like. She stops outside the guitar shop. Dee's changed the guitars in the window. The shiny aqua and baby blue bodies are cheerful.

"Good. Good. I'm feeling rich. They're paying by the word and they give me a supplement because it's a cover."

"Don't spend it all on dinner." Claudie opens the door to the shop and nods a greeting to Dee.

"Well, I'm an impoverished journalist. I'm just talking Thai or Indian at one of the local places. Being rich means I can order an appetizer."

"I can't wait," Claudie says.

IT'S DIFFERENT, GETTING READY TO go out, together and intentionally, for dinner. Claudie reminds herself that this is not a date. She doesn't want this to be a date. Still, she dresses carefully. She buttons her shirt and looks in the mirror. She puts a belt around the top of her low rise jeans. She knows what looks good on her long legs and broad shoulders.

The restaurant's a Thai place in Kings Cross. Claudie arrives first. The waiter seats her against the red wall under a recess with a lit up painting of Thai royalty. He brings two glasses of water. Lien enters while Claudie's smiling in thanks. Her smile freezes. Lien is in a creamy lace dress, something that's somehow old-fashioned and charming and also really, really short. She's wearing brown lace-up boots that are too heavy for the dress in a good way. She's given a nod to the cool weather by wearing a creamy knit scarf and striped yellow and gray gloves that go up over her elbow. She's adorable.

Claudie half stands as Lien follows the waiter toward her. Lien's smile is fond and sure.

"I bought champagne," Claudie says after Lien's seated. "To celebrate." She lifts the bottle from the ice bucket propped on the table and pours

Lien a glass. They clink glasses, meeting eyes above the glass rims as they drink. It's not bad. "I haven't eaten here before," Claudie says. "What's good?" She winces. She hates small talk.

Lien doesn't seem to mind. "Everything here is good. But we have to have the sung choi bao. It's sort of perfect."

You are sort of perfect, thinks Claudie. Her brain is impossible. Lien twitters on about whether they can share three plates. "Maybe we should have the ginger tofu and these little prawn and vegetable things. It's a celebration. What do you think?"

They've mostly finished dinner. The food is still on the table, but no one's eating. In the candlelight, Lien's face is mobile; her eyes sparkle. She's gorgeous and impossible to look away from. The whole night seems like a date. Lien leans closer. She touches her tongue to her lips. Claudie's thoughts must be broadcast on her face.

Lien says, "I signed the band up for some social media platforms."

"Oh." Claudie blinks. "Okay."

"I just thought it was a good idea to get things going. I know you're not quite ready, but I think it's time. I don't want you guys to miss out on the perfect handle."

It's laughable. Claudie was thinking about a date, and Lien's figuring out ways to boss Claudie's band around so it's more popular. Claudie should have known.

She closes her eyes. "I appreciate your help," she says, opening them again. "But—I've got my own plans. I'm not asking you to manage my second chance, Lien."

"I just want to help."

Claudie's jaw tightens as she speaks. "I know. But look, I've been in this place before. You're not supposed to build my dreams for me. I don't want to be anyone's little cause."

The bill arrives. Lien pays. She says nothing until the waiter has left.

As she stands she says, "Thank you for your help with the article."

On the street, the wind is cool and erratic. It stutters around buildings and trees. Lien wraps her arms around herself.

When they reach Oxford Street, Lien stops Claudie with a hand on her arm. Someone bumps into Lien and walks away muttering. They move closer to the street so they're out of the way. This neighborhood is busy. The rows of old buildings lined up along the sidewalk have been remodeled into shops and bars. Behind Lien, the street sweeps downhill toward the city where row after row of lit windows tint the night sky. The moon is huge and orange.

Lien's focus is on Claudie. "What you said before? It wasn't fair. I never thought of you as a cause." Her voice is choked.

"I only meant that you want to build my band for me. You can't. I need to do it for myself."

"I never wanted that. I wanted to help." Lien's eyes glitter in the streetlight. She lifts her chin. "But more than that, Claudie, I wanted to spend time with you. Tonight wasn't just about celebrating the article. I had this whole plan to um—to ask you to go on a date. With me." She swallows. "I wasn't looking for a cause. I was kind of looking for a girlfriend." Car headlights arc behind them. Lien goes on. "What I said up at the cabin? That I thought we could be something? This whole time nothing changed for me. I still think we could work." She squeezes her eyes closed before going on. "I know, I know. You don't. And that's okay. There's no rule that you need to be into me like that. But I kind of got my hopes up here." She shakes her head. "It hurts. So I'm not going to trail around after you trying to prove that I'm a different person from the one you created in your head. I can't make you believe this would work. You've already made up your mind that it won't."

She stands there with the city behind her and the streetlight in her hair. Claudie can't get her words together. Lien nods as though everything she's said has been affirmed. She turns and strides away. Her white dress reflects the green and red and white of the city lights. Her hair flies out behind her. She's across the road in a break in the traffic before Claudie has time to think.

Claudie can't breathe. The rest of the world keeps moving. Wind spirals in the trees that line the street. A few clouds tumble across the sky and block the moon. A siren wails in the distance. And Lien turns a corner and disappears.

Lien's the opposite of what Claudie needs. She's hectic. She's interfering. She's bossy. She'll move on. It's taken months for Claudie to realize that even though all of that matters, even though she'll have to learn about vintage clothes and be ordered around about social media, even though she's going to wake up every day to sunny conversation, she'd still choose life with Lien over life without.

LIEN CLOSES THE FRONT DOOR and leans against it. She blinks back tears. Beau and Annie look up from the sofa.

"How did it go?" Annie asks, though their faces show that they know the answer.

Lien shakes her head. Two tears slip down her cheeks.

"Oh, no," says Beau. "No, no. The woman is a fool. I am going to have to have words with her."

Lien tries to smile through the tears, but fails. She swallows. "I really wanted this," she says. "I really wanted it."

"We know. Come sit with us," Beau says. He moves over to make space between them.

"You can share the sorbet," Annie offers.

"Thank you," Lien says. "I'm okay. I'm going to go to my room."

Upstairs she turns on the fairy lights. She leaves her boots on, lies on the bed, and lets herself cry. The doorbell rings.

Beau's steps echo in the hall. The latch rattles, and the door swings open. His voice carries up the stairs to her. "I'm pretty sure this one's for you."

Lien wipes her face before she walks down. Claudie's outside on the front steps. She spreads her arms and lifts her shoulders sheepishly.

"Hi," Lien says.

"Hi."

They sit side-by-side on the concrete steps that lead down to the sidewalk. They're half lit by the streetlight, half shadowed by the shifting branches of the gum tree.

Claudie faces the street as she speaks. "I believed what I told you when you left the cabin. I didn't think we could work. I thought the time we had up there was just a make-believe. And then when I got to Sydney—well, you're still you. You're the kind of person everyone circles around. I figured that's the last thing I'd want. And the last thing you'd want." She faces Lien and swallows. "Truth is, I was scared. So I decided our connection couldn't be real."

Lien swipes at a tear. "I wish I could prove it to you," she says. Her eyes sting, and she blinks up at the streetlight.

"You don't need to prove anything. I was wrong."

"Oh."

Claudie nods. "I'd convinced myself I didn't want to be with you. But since I've been back—you've pretty much destroyed all my arguments. It took a while for me to notice."

Lien keeps her eyes on Claudie's profile.

Claudie frowns. "But I also convinced myself I wouldn't *get* to be with you. I thought—you said you wanted to be friends."

Lien sighs. She scrunches her face to look at Claudie. "I could *maybe* have asked you again instead of slotting myself into your life and hoping you'd work it out. Might've saved us some time."

"I don't know that I worked out my feelings until now, anyway."

Shadows from the tree shift across Claudie's face. The streetlight is reflected in her eyes. Lien kisses her. There's no rush; they suddenly have so much time. But Claudie's lips are soft and rough at once; her hands are strong on Lien's waist. Lien wants every part of her.

When they break apart, Claudie says, "I can't believe I didn't see it. Gretchen did, even Boyd. No doubt Mercy, too. They told me. All the songs I've written are about you."

Lien laughs, startled. "Oh no. I can imagine the lyrics. This girl took over my Instagram, and it's tearing me apart."

"Nothing like that," says Claudie. She kisses Lien again. "They're love songs."

Lien's heart skips three or four beats. "Well, that's a relief," she says. "Because I don't think I can stop myself taking over your social media now and then."

"I guess I can live with that." Claudie traces Lien's cheekbone with her thumb. They sit close together in the greenish light, as the wind twists down the street. "So Lien. Can I take you back to my place?"

Lien nods. "I'll grab a couple of things. Are you cold? You can wait inside with Beau and Annie."

"Oh, no." Claudie says, but she follows Lien inside.

Beau and Annie look up from the sofa. "Hi, girls," Beau says.

"Hi." Lien can't help but beam at him and Annie. "I'm going to run upstairs for a second," she says.

"I see," says Beau. Annie smiles at everyone.

Lien shakes her head and leaves Claudie to fend for herself with her best friends. In her room she grabs a change of clothes. She looks in the mirror and takes a shaky breath. The brightly colored light lands softly on her face. A murmur of voices travels up the stairs. She turns out the fairy lights and makes her way downstairs.

"I won't be home tonight," she tells Beau. She tries to sound cool, but Beau nods and grins, showing all his teeth, and Annie lets out a little squeak that ruins everything.

Lien and Claudie walk the back streets to Claudie's place. Traffic noise from Oxford Street blends with nearby voices and the general hum of humanity. A group of kids stands and smokes on a street corner. A cloud of fruit bats swoops above, catching the wind, wings translucent against the sky. A car revs its engine. It's an ordinary night in an ordinary city. But Claudie takes Lien's hand as they walk, and the city fades. They're the only inhabitants of a huge, secret world.

GRAND ECHO'S FIRST BIG SHOW since re-forming is at the Hopetoun Hotel. They could have gone elsewhere, but the Hopetoun is a classic place for local rock bands to cut their teeth. The building is an old house. The stage is in the former living room, with wood-framed windows and a flight of stairs curling up behind the bar. The room isn't huge, but the ceilings are high and the sound equipment is excellent.

The room is packed. People have been talking about this comeback. Lien made that happen.

On stage Claudie gets her guitar plugged in, then adjusts the microphone that was already pretty perfect. While Boyd and the sound guy mess with his setup, she glances around the room.

There are a couple hundred strangers here, some turned to talk, some bellied up to the bar, others already watching the stage. Lien's near the front, waving her hands and chatting to some people Claudie doesn't know. Claudie smiles. However much Claudie might be the one on stage, everyone in the room is drawn to Lien.

People cheer the moment Claudie speaks. "We're Grand Echo. Thank you so much for coming to our first show at the Hopetoun in way too long. We're gonna start you off with a new tune."

They open it up, perfectly in time. Claudie grins at Mercy and lifts her head to sing. She catches Lien's eye, then scans the room. She's always confident in front of a crowd like this with her guitar and her microphone. And this crowd is the most enthusiastic she's performed for. The music comes together. The crowd adds energy. Everything is alive. Claudie looks back at Gretchen, sings harmonies with Boyd, meets Mercy's focused look. And now and then Lien's eyes catch hers. Claudie buzzes to the soles of her feet.

Afterward, there are people everywhere: diehard fans and new enthusiasts. Claudie can't move until she talks with some of them. She waits for the crush to die down. As soon as it does, she makes her way to where Lien is propped against the bar.

"That was amazing." Lien's bouncing on her toes. "Even more than I already knew it would be. You're perfect. You guys sound incredible." She goes up on her toes and kisses Claudie.

Everything's better with Lien there.

CLAUDIE OPENS HER APARTMENT DOOR. Lien's sweaty and pink after an afternoon's soccer training with a local women's team.

"Shower," she says and leans in for a kiss.

Claudie grins. "How did you go?"

"Great. I'll only be a minute."

Lien strips off her kit as she walks to the bathroom. She leaves the door open and hums away to herself as the water flows. They're on their way to dinner at Mercy and Mary's place. It's not the time for Claudie to be distracted by the thought of Lien's skin under warm running water.

Claudie slides open the glass doors to the balcony and steps out. She looks up. This might not be the wilderness, but there's sky everywhere on the planet. Tonight it's turning gold at the edges. The streaks of cloud are outlined in light. Pigeons wheel in the air and ghost above the buildings.

Claudie's phone rings. She takes the call on the balcony. By the time she hangs up, Lien's beside her, her newly-washed skin wrapped in a towel.

"Who was that?" Lien asks.

Claudie stares at her phone. The news is still sinking in. "That… was the booking manager for Splendour in the Grass."

"Wait, what?"

"Yeah."

"Oh, my god. Oh. My god." Lien pauses. "What did they want?"

"They want Grand Echo. They want us to play Splendour in the Grass. It's not the main stage but—fuck, Lien. It's Splendour. The line-up is going to be huge."

"Oh my god, Claudie! That is massive." They beam at one another. Lien comes close and grabs Claudie's hand. She drops her towel. She picks it up and wraps it around herself. "Come inside," she says. "I'm naked out here."

Inside they jump around the room. Lien asks, "So what's your plan? What's your playlist?"

"Well, first I need to call the guys and let them know."

"Are you driving up? Will you camp there on the site?"

Claudie laughs. "Camping might be a bit rough for some of us. Not everyone's used to the outdoors."

Lien narrows her eyes. "I assume you're talking about Gretchen."

Claudie goes on. "Maybe we can rent a house up there. We can drive into Byron for our sets and hang around and see the other bands, but we can get away when we want some quiet."

"That sounds perfect."

"What's the chance someone will want you to cover the festival?"

Lien lifts her hands to shrug. "I'll talk to some of the local mags. But even if no one needs me to write anything, I am *so* coming with you." Her beam is pure joy. "Splendour, Claudie. You are on your way."

THEY BORROW CLAUDIE'S PARENTS' CAR and leave early, long before the winter sun is up. Lien wouldn't call herself a morning person, but they want to do the nine-hour drive in time to stop in to see Shelley and Dylan and brand new baby Ruby. Claudie takes the first driving shift. Outside the city, oncoming headlights light the cabin of the car then fade away behind them. The center lines of the road are bright in the black night.

"Tired?" Claudie asks.

"No way. I'm good." Lien covers a yawn.

"It's five in the morning, Li. You're allowed to be tired."

"Yeah. But I don't want you driving alone. You don't need to worry. I'm going to stay awake."

Claudie smiles. "Thank you."

There's scarcely any traffic. The city buildings rise up around the expressway. They're dark, just one or two strips of windows lit up by early workers. The sun won't be up for an hour or more, but above

Sydney Harbour the horizon catches the light. Lien says, "I found the greatest long-sleeved dress in this vintage place. It's as if it belongs to *Little House on the Prairie*. I had to bring it with me."

Claudie laughs. "It sounds about right for the festival."

The sun comes up before they swap drivers. Claudie sits in the passenger seat with her hand on Lien's thigh and munches on a granola bar. The wide open space expands in front of them.

"Music?" Claudie asks.

"Sure," says Lien. She's even amenable to Claudie choosing the playlist, especially if she sings along.

It's a long trip. The visit to Shelley's place takes more time than they expected. So the sun has already set when they arrive at the farmhouse they've rented. The house sprawls across a low hill and looks over the valley. Its lights welcome them as they pull in.

The rest of the band and a couple of friends will join them in a few days. But for now they have a house for eight with a view over the Byron Hinterlands and only the two of them to fill it.

Lien hops out of the car. She has the keys.

"I love that first time you open the door to a rental house," she says. "So many possibilities. So many rooms." She's giddy and tired after the long day.

"I don't care as long as one of them's a bedroom," says Claudie. She wraps her arms around Lien as they step onto the porch. Her thumb brushes against Lien's breast. Lien fumbles the key in the lock.

After dinner, Lien stands on the deck under the clear sky and lets the crisp white stars press down on her.

"Hey," says Claudie. Lien turns. Claudie's wiping her hands on her jeans.

"Hey."

They stand side by side.

"Do you miss your cabin?" Lien asks. She'll probably never stand looking from a deck without remembering the cabin.

"All the time. But, I guess, not as intensely as I expected. I have space in Sydney and I think I'd forgotten how much I love being around other people who are working creatively. There's more here than I expected." Even in the dark her gaze is clear.

"We could always holiday somewhere remote."

"We could. If we can ever afford a holiday again." Claudie laughs, but without bitterness.

"Cabins are cheap. Anyway, you guys are going to make it big time," says Lien. "We'll be holidaying on a yacht."

Claudie pulls her close.

They chose their room earlier, one with an en suite bathroom and a huge picture window looking over the grassy valley. Lien pulls on her pajamas and leaps onto the bed.

"Clean sheets are the best," she announces, wriggling her way under the covers. "Quick, get in!" She grins at Claudie.

The bedroom lights are out. Claudie's framed in the window, wearing her T-shirt and underwear and nothing else. Lien's no photographer but she would photograph that. "You know what, hold that thought," she says.

Claudie's lips quirk but she stays where she is. Lien closes her eyes to capture the image. When she opens them, Claudie is still watching her.

Lien draws a slow breath. "Take off your shirt," she says.

Claudie considers her. When she complies, she pulls her T-shirt over her head in a fluid movement. She holds Lien's gaze and slips off her underwear, reaches behind herself to unhook her bra. Her nipples tighten in the air. She's breathtaking. Her body is outlined in starry white. She stands with her arms by her sides, deeply comfortable in her skin. The great, bright sky is hollowed out behind her.

Lien aches to touch her. Her mouth is dry. Her eyes are heavy. Instead, she lies back. "Touch yourself for me."

"Okay," Claudie breathes. Her eyes are clear and dark on Lien's. As she slides her hand between her thighs, Lien mirrors her.

THERE'S A LIGHT FROST ON the ground in the morning. The sunlight reflects off it and lights their bedroom in gray and pale green. The whole world is hushed. Lien's tangled in the sheets and blankets. Her eyelids are heavy with lack of sleep as Claudie kisses her cheekbones and jaw and lips.

"Good morning," Claudie murmurs against her lips. Lien turns in her arms and presses herself against Claudie's sleep-warm skin.

There's nothing to do that day, no one they need to see. Lien brought some notes with her for an article she's working on; Claudie brought the autoharp and three guitars she'll use for the festival. But the house is secluded. The website promised a walking trail. The photos showed gum trees and moss green rocks with tiny, clear waterfalls tumbling between them. They have one another and a wilderness to explore, right outside the front door. Everything else can wait.

Epilogue

It's the height of summer in Sydney. At seven in the evening even the pavement is still hot. But once Lien, Beau, and Annie come close to Sydney Harbour they find a breeze.

They walk around Circular Quay, past the ferry terminal. Annie and Beau hold hands. Up ahead, the creamy sails of the Opera House curve upward; their tiled edges make bright lines against the rose gold sky.

There's a crowd of people outside the Concert Hall. "You couldn't get us into the VIP area, Lien?" Beau asks. Heat makes him cranky.

"You know I could, but I'm writing up this show. I want to walk in with the crowd and see it for real." She smiles at him. "Don't worry. You can meet the band afterward. I'll even get them to sign your merchandise."

Beau lets out a dramatic sigh.

The Concert Hall is shaped in honey-colored wood; the lighting is warm gold. They find their seats close to the stage, looking down from the front row of one of the steep balcony tiers. The room is full and humming with voices. This is no rock and roll show with fans calling out songs and the dance floor packed and moving as one. But it's the

Opera House. The acoustics are incredible. The walls and ceiling and seating were all designed for music. The place is an icon.

Lien scans the crowd. Some people are old fans, others are young enough that they have to be new. Her heart is full of bubbling pride in Claudie.

"Lien?" says a voice. Lien turns to the woman seated behind her. "Lien Hong, right? I recognize you from your byline."

Lien blushes. "Thank you."

"I had to interrupt you. I read your piece on race and designer branding last week. The conversation's important and suddenly it's everywhere."

Lien's probably glowing right now. "Thank you," she says again. "I'm proud of that one."

"So you're a fan of Grand Echo?" the woman asks.

Lien nods. "I love them."

The lights dim. Lien turns back to the stage as Claudie strides on, followed by the band. Mercy plays a winding melody on the keys. Claudie steps up to the microphone.

The show is extraordinary from the beginning. The whole room is there with the band. Gretchen and Boyd sound as if they've always played together. Mercy's keyboard work is intricate. Claudie's guitar is inspired. Her energy is tangible. Her voice surges over the room.

When she sings about love, which is honestly about half the time she sings, she looks up from the stage and catches Lien's eye. She's gorgeous. Lien's heart stops.

Fortunately it starts again.

END

Acknowledgments

MY THANKS

To my kids. You are exceptional. The world is way better than it was without you.

To Warner, wonderful early reader. You made Beau possible.

To Interlude Press. For your clear eyes and kind words, for your support, and for this glorious cover that reminds me what my book is about. And to Nicki. For your care and for the reminder that kookaburras aren't in everyone's backyard.

To Cameron, brightest and best reader. Your relish for real and kindly observed humans colours all my stories.

To Misha, companion in this universe from its earliest days.

To Jo, still my co-author whenever I make a joke.

To Charmaine, Christine, Rachel, Tania, Heidi. Finest of friends who've talked me down from the tree, shared glasses of wine, accepted uninvited mood boards, and kept me writing.

To Emily. There are thousands of things you should have seen. Here is one.

About the Author

PENE HENSON HAS GONE FROM British boarding schools to New York City law firms. She now lives in Sydney, Australia, where she is an intellectual property lawyer and published poet who is deeply immersed in the city's LGBTQIA community. She spends her spare time enjoying the outdoors and gazing at the ocean with her gorgeous wife and two unexpectedly exceptional sons. *Into the Blue,* her first novel, was published by Interlude Press in 2016.

One **story** can change **everything.**

@interlude**press**

Twitter | Facebook | Instagram | Pinterest | Tumblr

*For a reader's guide to **Storm Season** and book club prompts, please visit interludepress.com.*

interlude press
you may also like...

Into the Blue by Pene Henson

Tai Talagi and Ollie Birkstrom have been inseparable since they met as kids surfing the North Shore. Tai's spent years setting aside his feelings for Ollie, but when Ollie's pro surfing dreams come to life, their steady world shifts. Is the relationship worth risking everything for a chance at something terrifying and beautiful and altogether new?

[STARRED REVIEW] "... exceptional" —Publishers Weekly

ISBN (print) 978-1-941530-84-9 | (eBook) 978-1-941530-85-6

Burning Tracks by Lilah Suzanne

In the sequel to *Broken Records*, Gwen Pasternak has it all: a job she loves as a celebrity stylist and a beautiful wife, Flora. But as her excitement in working with country music superstar Clementine Campbell grows, Gwen second-guesses her quiet domestic bliss. Meanwhile, her business partner, Nico Takahashi and his partner, reformed bad-boy musician Grady Dawson, face uncertainties of their own.

ISBN (print) 978-1-941530-99-3 | (eBook) 978-1-945053-00-9

Certainly, Possibly, You by Lissa Reed

Sarita Sengupta is about to finish grad school when she realizes that she lacks a career plan, a girlfriend, or a clear outlook on life. She works as a pastry decorator, but is otherwise rudderless until a birthday party ends with her waking up next to Maritza Quiñones, a pretty ballroom dancer whose charm and laser focus sets Sarita on a path to making all of the choices she's been avoiding.

ISBN (print) 978-1-945053-05-4 | (eBook) 978-1-945053-06-1

CPSIA information can be obtained
at www.ICGtesting.com
Printed in the USA
LVOW08s0130250417
532058LV00001B/107/P